WHEN lightning STRIKES

RIVER HALE

This is a work of fiction. Names, characters, places, and incidents are either the product of the author's imagination or are used fictitiously. Any resemblance to actual persons, living or dead, events, or locales is entirely coincidental.

WHEN LIGHTNING STRIKES
Copyright © 2024 River Hale

All rights reserved. No part of this publication may be reproduced, distributed, or transmitted in any form or by any means, including photocopying, recording, or other electronic or mechanical methods, without the prior written permission of the publisher, except in the case of brief quotations embodied in critical reviews and certain other noncommercial uses permitted by copyright law.

Written by River Hale

ISBN 979-8-9911454-0-4 (paperback)
ISBN 979-8-9911454-1-1 (ebook)

PUBLISHED BY VICIOUS CITY PRESS

DEAR READER

Thank you so much for picking up this book and giving my first sapphic romance a chance! While this story is marketed as being on the lighter side of dark, I like to always say that darkness is subjective. There are some darker themes, such as bullying and homophobia, but if you're hoping for something super dark, this won't be it.

Also, please know that the chronic illness depicted in this story is one that affects everyone differently. If you or someone you know battles this same condition, chances are the experiences will differ than what you'll read about here. However, I still hope you'll find something to connect with.

For specific content warnings, playlists, and to sign up for my newsletter, please visit my website: www.riverhale.com

*To everyone battling a chronic illness.
I see you, warrior. Stay strong. Keep fighting.*

*And to my guardian angel in the yellow windbreaker.
I wish I could tell you how you saved my life that day.*

"The heart of man is very much like the sea, it has its storms, it has its tides and in its depths, it has its pearls too."

—VINCENT VAN GOGH

1

LOGAN

Shards of green glass rain like glittering emeralds onto the faded yellow tile of the kitchen floor. Water droplets cascade down the wall. Red rose petals from the flowers I bought my mother for her birthday yesterday flutter to the ground like crimson feathers. The shattering of the antique vase against the wall beside my head still rings in my ears.

The stench of stale alcohol hangs heavy in the air, mingling with the acrid scent of cigarette smoke. My mother's wide, bloodshot eyes search frantically for something else to throw at me while she screams, her voice even more shrill as it pierces through the ringing.

"If you're not happy here, then fucking leave, Logan!"

A deep rumbling of thunder shakes the house. A crack of lightning follows, a flash of light through the window illuminating the dimly lit room. Empty bottles and dirty dishes litter the counters. Smoke from the ashtray on the table drifts up and swirls in the air around my mother like a shroud. Her brown hair is a wild, tangled mess, an unkempt bird's nest on top of her head. Yesterday's mascara smudged beneath her eyes.

In the wake of the booming from the sky outside, something warm drips down my cheek. Judging by the sting, I don't think it's tears.

"I just want you to stop destroying yourself!"

"Fucking leave if you have a problem with it! Leave like they all did."

"They didn't *leave*, Mom." I desperately choke back a sob, refusing to be weak in the face of my mother's viciousness. "The only one who *chose* to leave was Dad. I think I understand why now!"

A terrible cry rips from her throat as she picks up a dirty plate off the dining table and hurls it across the kitchen.

I take a step and duck as it crashes against the wall above me. Pieces of broken ceramic rain down on top of me as glass crunches beneath my bare feet. Blood flows down my left arm like a scarlet river. I don't know if it was from the vase or the plate. I don't get much time to think about it before I look down and notice there's more blood smudged across the yellowed tile, turning it a sickly brown. My feet sting something fierce.

"You don't know what the fuck you're talking about!" Her savage shriek cracks with every other word.

"Right, Mom." The sarcasm drips from my tongue with a taste like venom as I roll my eyes to distract me from the pain coursing through my body. "Because I wasn't here. I couldn't possibly know what *you've* gone through. Make it all about yourself like you always do. How about you stick another fucking needle in your arm while you're at it?"

"You fucking bitch!"

She picks up an empty bottle from the table, but before she can raise it above her head, sirens wail outside. The bottle slips from her inebriated fingers and shatters on the floor.

Red and blue lights fill the kitchen along with my mother's indignant sigh.

"Not again."

My thoughts exactly, Mom.

Slumping into her chair as the old wood creaks, she plucks her cigarette from the ashtray with a shaky hand. She takes a long drag even though the cherry is down to the butt. She doesn't seem to notice.

I move before there's a rap at the front door. My feet are numb as I step through the graveyard of broken glass and ceramic, but I don't think that's a good thing. Exiting the kitchen, I walk gingerly across the small living room where there are more empty bottles and trash littering the coffee table. I pick up a thin, black sweater from the back of the couch and pull it on to cover the still-bleeding gash in my arm. At the door, I slip into a pair of slippers, grimacing when I realize there's remnants of glass in the soles of my feet.

There's another knock before I finally open the door. The lashing of rain grows louder, the wind trying to whip open the door wider than the few inches I've allowed.

Sheriff Ben Novak stands just on the other side as he's done several times before. The first time was almost a year ago.

It wasn't storming that night though.

The night he came bearing the news of my brother's death.

The tempest came after, bringing with it the first strike of lightning in the storm of my life.

His blond hair is damp, his jacket splattered with wet droplets. He looks younger than he actually is, tall and lean with kind, brown eyes. He stands beneath the cover of the porch roof with a deputy behind him.

"We got another call, Ms. Delaney."

"Everything's fine, Sheriff. I'm sorry for the disturbance."

He tilts his head, eyeing me shrewdly. "Everything doesn't look fine."

Shit.

I forgot about the cut on my face. The dried blood tugs cruelly at my skin as a peal of thunder rolls in the distance.

"I, um...I fell in the kitchen. Dropped a couple of dishes and cut my cheek on the counter. It's not a big deal."

He narrows his eyes, not believing a damn word that comes out of my mouth. He knows better. We've been through this before. Every time, I lie. I protect her. He wonders why.

Honestly, I do too.

His eyes rake over me. Not in a way that makes me uncomfortable, knowing he's just checking me for further injury. Again, like he's done several times before.

"And your feet?"

I peer down to see the tips of my mother's dirty white slippers stained crimson. Blood pools uncomfortably between my toes.

"Stepped on some glass." My voice comes out too raspy, my throat dry. I clear it away. "Couldn't avoid it."

He sighs heavily, and the look in his gaze shifts. I recognize it immediately, that infuriating expression making me tense, something in my chest coiling tight. I don't want his sympathy. I don't want *anyone's* sympathy.

"If you have glass in your feet and are bleeding that much, you should probably go to the hospital."

"No." I shake my head, my voice hoarse again. "No hospital."

"My wife is off work tonight. She could get you cleaned up."

He wants me out of the house, but neither the hospital nor his own house are appealing options.

"Or you could let me speak with your mother. See if she's in a state to help get that glass out of your feet."

That's even worse.

He takes a step forward, peering over my shoulder to see into the house. An exasperated noise comes huffing out of my mouth as I open the door wider, step out onto the porch, and slam the door behind me.

"Fine. Let's go."

Moving past the sheriff and his deputy, I pull the hood of my sweater over my head. It's not enough to keep the ends of my long hair from getting wet as I take the steps down from the porch, trying not to limp even while I can feel the glass digging deeper into the bottoms of my feet. Both cops follow me down to the street where their two cruisers are parked.

Sheriff Novak says something to the deputy that I can't hear past the fat raindrops that are pelting the top of my head and shoulders. I don't wait for them before yanking open the passenger door of the sheriff's cruiser and throwing myself inside. Ben slides into the driver's seat beside me. As we close our doors, the storm raging outside is muffled. Rain drums against the roof of the car, a steady beat soon joined by the hum of the engine.

Before the car pulls away from my house, I get a glimpse of curtains fluttering in the window of our neighbor's place. I'm sure it's the asshole who keeps calling the damn cops. He moved in several months ago, but I've never properly met him. I honestly don't care to.

The sheriff says nothing as he drives us out of the neighborhood, allowing a merciful silence to fill the car. I'm grateful for it.

It's not a bad neighborhood that I live in. It's quite nice actually. Maybe not as nice as the one he lives in with his doctor wife, but it's certainly not the worst. It's my mother and our fractured family who have made our home a hell.

Haunted.

By the ghosts of my brothers and father.

The demon that's possessed my mother.

I settle deeper into the seat as the warmth from the heater spreads through my cold and tired bones. Leaning my head back, I stare out the passenger side window, the world outside obscured by the veil of rain.

It doesn't even occur to me that I should've told the truth about what happened. I didn't consider it for a second. I never do. Before, there was always the chance of being taken away, but since I turned eighteen a few months ago, I don't have to worry about that anymore. I could leave if I had anywhere else to go.

There's a part of me that doesn't blame my mother. I *should*. I'm not making excuses for the way she treats me, but I don't blame her for what she's become.

It's been almost a year since my brother, Liam, died. He was only a year older than me. My other brother, Landon, went to prison for his death, and my father left a couple of months later.

I'm supposed to believe that Landon killed Liam.

I don't.

Even if it was ruled as involuntary manslaughter.

I don't know if my mother believes it, but it doesn't matter. It was enough to rip our family apart, for my father to give up on us, for my mother to fall so deep into her grief that she had to self-medicate just to keep herself alive.

So I don't blame her. I can't because I share the weight of their absence. It presses down on our home until it feels as though our roof will collapse. The ache of loss gnaws at my heart like a relentless tide eroding the shore.

As Ben parks his cruiser in the driveway outside his house, I peer ahead at the gray brick facade of the cozy two-story. The welcoming glow of the porch light casts a warm, inviting halo in the darkness.

And, yet, dread settles in my gut.

I shouldn't have agreed to come here. I've only been inside the Novaks' house once before—a dinner months before Liam died when our families were close.

It feels like eons ago.

The sheriff cuts the engine, and I fling my door open to brave both the storm outside and the one raging in the dark memories of my mind.

We walk up to the porch, hunched over against the rain. He unlocks the door and ushers me inside. The warmth and brightness of the house envelops me. I only wish it was a comforting embrace, something to help calm my squirming insides instead of making them writhe more fiercely.

The slippers on my feet make wet noises on the vinyl plank floor, whether from the rain or the blood, I can't be sure.

When I take another step, I know it's both.

At least it's not carpet I'm leaving trails of blood across.

While the sheriff locks the door and hangs up his jacket, I peer into the spacious living room directly to the left to see his wife sitting on the couch. Her eyes widen at the sight of me. Setting down her book beside a half empty glass of wine on the coffee table, she stands.

"Logan? What happened?"

Concern is etched all over her face as she comes to stand in front of me. It makes me itch, but I try not to let it show. Ben and Grace Novak have always been nothing but kind.

"She fell and dropped some dishes."

I cut my eyes at the sheriff.

Maybe I imagined the sarcasm because there's no deceit in his expression.

"She has some glass in her feet." He gives his wife a sweet, swift kiss before he heads past the stairs and down the hallway, stopping at the first door on the right. He opens it and pulls out a stack of towels.

"Oh dear," Grace says. "And your cheek?"

I sigh. "Hit it on the kitchen counter when I fell."

If she doesn't believe me, she hides it.

"Ben, will you help her to the couch while I get my kit?"

"You want me in your living room?" I ask while Ben lays down a towel over the expensive-looking area rug leading to the oversized couch. I shuffle my feet, a brief, white-hot pain shooting through them as I gaze down at the blood-stained edges of my mother's slippers.

Grace gives my right arm a gentle squeeze. "I'd rather you be comfortable."

She wants me to be comfortable even with the risk of me bleeding all over her nice furniture?

That itch returns, worse than before.

The doctor leaves, and the sheriff motions me over after laying down another towel in front of the couch. I walk gingerly, careful to only step on the towels, and take a seat in the middle of the soft, navy blue sofa.

Ben sets the rest of the towels down on the mahogany coffee table. "Would you like anything? Water? A hot tea?"

I shake my head, staring down at my lap as a wave of exhaustion washes over me. "No, thank you. I'm fine."

"I'll get you some tea," he says, and I can practically hear the easy smile in his voice.

When I'm left alone, I look up to peer around the room. It hasn't changed much since the last time I was here, which feels unfair. My own home transformed from a haven filled with love and happy chaos to a battleground warped by grief, ghosts, and demons. This house remained untouched. A pang of envy pierces deep in my chest.

Family photographs are displayed on damn near every wall, the faces of Ben, Grace, and their two children peering at me.

I scowl back.

I hate them both—Elise and Declan.

Elise is my age, Declan a year younger. We went to school together, but we never hung around in the same circles. Not that I even had a circle. I kept mostly to myself during high school, especially after rumors spread that I made out with Kady Satterfield in the locker room.

But are they rumors if they're true?

I didn't give a fuck. I've never apologized for who I am, and I wasn't about to start.

Elise may not have been one of the girls whose eyes followed me in the halls like I was a pariah, giving me a wide berth like I'd touch them inappropriately if given the chance, snickering behind my back like I was the biggest joke in school. She was, however, the one who received the most sympathy after Liam's death. The one who had the nerve to walk around with a haunted look in her eyes because her *boyfriend* was dead.

Not that I envied the sympathy. But it was still bullshit.

Because Elise had been with Liam the night he died.

Declan too.

"Let's take a look at those feet first."

Dr. Novak pulls me back to the present as she sits down on top of the coffee table in front of me. She sets her kit to the side, places a small trash can on the ground, and drapes a towel over her lap.

"We'll do one at a time," she says. "Do you need help taking the slippers off?"

I shake my head, sliding my right foot out of the slipper. Glass shifts. I manage not to wince as I leave the slipper on the towel on the floor and raise my foot, letting Grace situate it on her lap.

She winces.

"Ben," she calls out to her husband in the kitchen. "Bring some painkillers when you come back, please."

"I don't need any. I'm fine."

"You're going to want some before I'm finished," she says with a smile that somehow doesn't scream sympathy. Empathy, maybe. But not pity.

"Thank you."

And I don't mean for the painkillers.

Once the doctor has a bowl set out and tweezers in her hand, the sheriff comes back to the living room with a bottle of water, pills, and a mug with steam rising from it. He hands me the water first, then dumps two pills from the bottle into my hand. I usually hate taking medication of any kind and avoid it whenever possible—watching your own mother get hooked on pretty much every drug there is will do that to a person—but I know the doctor is right. This is going to hurt like a bitch.

I swallow the pills down with some water, then take the mug from him.

"I'll be upstairs," Ben says before leaning over and placing a tender kiss on his wife's forehead. "Let me know if you need anything."

As his footsteps fade up the steps, Grace asks me, "Are you ready?"

"Go for it."

She gets to work, carefully plucking out little bits of green glass from my feet with a steady, skilled hand. I sink deeper into the couch as the room blurs a little around the edges and fills with the sound of clinking glass as Grace drops the pieces into the bowl.

The last thing I want to do right now is pass out, so I bring the warm mug up to my lips and take a sip. The heat feels good between my hands. The hot liquid soothes my throat. I think it's chamomile, maybe with a hint of lavender.

I half expect the reason Ben left the room was so Grace could question me about my injuries, like I'd be more willing to talk to her. Fortunately, she doesn't. I would've stuck to my original story anyway.

While she works, brow furrowed in concentration, she hums a soft, gentle melody. I let it help distract me from the searing pain as each shard of glass is pulled free. It's always followed by a throbbing ache, a taste of what I have to look forward to over the next few days while my feet heal.

Soon, however, it's not enough, and I find myself glaring at Elise's graduation photo hanging beside the mounted flatscreen.

Elise claims to not remember what happened the night Liam died because they were all wasted—yeah, Landon was a dumbshit for buying them all alcohol. But I don't believe her. Or Declan when he said it was Landon's fault Liam fell off that bridge.

And took my entire world with him.

Now Elise fucking Novak is probably enjoying a nice summer before college while I'm stuck here because I've spent the last year just...*stuck*. Stranded in a storm. A year struggling to keep my head above the tumultuous waters when all I want to do is drown. A year mourning the fact I lost both my brothers in the span of one night, my father months later. And eventually my mother to her toxic coping mechanisms.

As the warmth from the tea starts to course through me, I push up the sleeves of my sweater. I decide not to tell Grace about the cut on my arm. She's already doing enough.

After she's gotten all the glass out of my right foot, cleaned it, and bandaged it, she starts on the left. When she's finished and is in the middle of wrapping it up, footsteps on the stairs reach my ears. They're softer than the sheriff's.

Elise stops at the bottom of the steps when her eyes find me.

"Oh. Hey, Logan."

I stare at her for a long beat, my mouth in a thin line. She wears baby blue pajama shorts and an oversized yellow T-shirt that hangs off one freckled shoulder. The long, blonde hair she got from her dad frames her heart-shaped face in loose, soft waves. Her hazel eyes she inherited from her mother narrow in on the side of my face. She frowns.

"Are you okay?"

"I'm fine."

Seems to be the catchphrase of the day.

She seems to take the hint that those are the only words I'm willing to speak as she nods and turns to head into the kitchen.

Grace finishes bandaging up my foot and helps me lower it onto the fresh towel on the floor. "How are you feeling?"

I open my mouth, then quickly close it again. I'm tired of saying *I'm fine*.

"Better now that the glass is out," I answer instead. "Thank you."

"Of course. Let me go wash my hands, and then we'll clean that cut on your cheek."

She takes the bowl of glass fragments with her as she leaves. I hear water running from down the hall when Elise walks back in from the kitchen. She stops again with a glass of water in her hand.

I can't stop myself from scowling at her now that we're alone.

As though cowering beneath my malicious stare, her gaze drops. This time, it lands on my left wrist, causing me to realize I've been absentmindedly rubbing circles over it with my thumb.

I follow her eyes down to the small lightning bolt tattooed there on my inner wrist—the one I gave myself the week after my dad left. It's not perfect, the lines a bit shaky. But it's not bad considering it was the first tattoo I ever did.

Snapping my gaze back to her, I glare even harder. "Can I help you?"

"You're the one in my house."

She looks like sunshine, but she's got teeth.

"And you killed my brother and ruined my life."

Other than the slight parting of her full, pink lips, she goes still. I can't help but smirk at the way my blunt words affect her, like they were ice barbs that froze the very blood in her veins.

Of course, I don't know if she did it. I don't know *who* did. What I do know is she was there that night. She was one of the last ones to see my brother alive—her *boyfriend*—and now he's just gone. It would've been all too easy for Elise and Declan to use Landon as a scapegoat, only wanting to protect each other.

When she finally speaks, her voice is so small and quiet I barely hear her. "Is that really what you think?"

Is she that surprised?

Sure, I've never outright accused her of anything, but, then again...I don't recall uttering a single word to her in the past year.

She opens her mouth to say something else when I haven't answered but stops short when her mother reenters the room.

"Everything all right?" Grace asks, looking between the both of us, probably easily sensing her daughter's distress.

"Yeah," Elise answers with an easy smile. "I'm going to bed. Night, Mom."

"Good night, sweetie."

I finally peel my eyes away as Elise climbs the stairs and Grace sits back down in front of me. She cleans the cut on my face, sounding confident when she says she doesn't think it'll scar. Not that it matters. I have enough scars on the inside that the outside doesn't matter.

After Grace has cleaned everything up—I offered to help, but she insisted I stay off my feet—she gets me a pillow and blanket from the linen closet.

I *really* don't want to sleep here, but I knew when I got into the sheriff's cruiser that I wasn't returning home tonight. Not that I want to go home either. I guess I kind of just don't want to be anywhere right now.

I politely thank Grace for everything. She tells me good night, then heads off to bed.

Settling into the couch on my back, I curl up beneath the silky-soft fleece blanket. I stare up at the ceiling, my expression eventually morphing into a scowl when I imagine Elise right above me on the second floor.

As much as I want to know the truth about what happened that night, I don't have any real hopes that I ever will.

The dim amber glow from a light left on in the kitchen spills into the room as I glance down at the lightning bolt inked into my wrist. The saying that lightning doesn't strike twice in the same place is a myth, and the tattoo is a reminder of that.

Thunder rumbles quietly in the distance as the storm outside is carried away by the heavy clouds.

The storm is over for now.

But it'll be back.

It always comes back.

2

ELISE

Eight years later.

It's been nearly two years since I was last home, since I last navigated these familiar streets of our small Colorado town. I still know them like the back of my hand.

I've only made the trip back home a handful of times in the last eight years I've been away at university. Now I'm here to stay.

I pull up outside the apartment building, parking my little blue car beside my mother's vehicle out front. My poor car is stuffed full, weighed down by what few belongings I had with me from my place back in Denver. There are even a couple of boxes beside me in the front seat.

Shutting off the engine, I step out and meet my mother on the sidewalk. She beams at me and immediately pulls me into a tight embrace. I hug her back just as hard. She and my dad were just in Denver a month ago for my graduation, but I've spent a lot of time missing them both over the years.

"I'm so glad you're home, sweetie."

"Me too," I say as we pull away.

I turn to look up at the historic building just at the edge of downtown. My mother said the inside apartments had recently been renovated, but I hope they still have that same timeless charm as the outside. With its weathered stone, intricate ironwork, and ivy climbing the aged walls.

My mom links her arm through mine as we walk up to the front door. "We've already paid the first three months of rent."

"You guys didn't have to do that."

"It's your graduation gift. Besides, your first year of residency won't be paying that much."

I've spent the last eight years between classes and exams, countless hours of study and rotations. It was starting to feel like I'd never receive my M.D. But I did. Now I finally get to be home and start my first year of residency at the hospital my mother works at. I don't mind that my salary won't be all that impressive.

My parents saved all their lives for mine and my brother's college education. They paid for my first four years, so I had a part-time job in Denver during undergrad and was able to put some money away in savings. I still have student loans, so I'm grateful for all the help I can get.

"I really appreciate it, Mom."

"We're so proud of you, Elise," she says, giving my arm a gentle squeeze.

We walk through the door of the building before I can

get emotional. I've been incredibly fortunate to have such loving, supportive parents, and I've never let myself take that for granted. Even when I felt like the weight of school and my future would crush me, maybe resented the high expectations placed on me, I've always found my way back to grateful. I can't afford anything less.

I know how quickly everything can be taken away.

On the second floor, my mother pulls out a key from her purse and hands it to me. I take it and unlock the door of my new home.

We step inside the small, cozy apartment, and I'm struck by even more gratitude that the heart and soul of the building has remained mostly intact. The interior still holds a testament to the architectural beauty of a past era.

The floors are a dark hardwood. While most of the walls have a fresh coat of white paint, the longer wall on the far side is exposed white brick. Wood beams run along the length of the ceiling, and expansive windows let in plenty of natural light. The kitchen is fully renovated with quartz countertops, white cabinets, and stainless steel appliances.

"What do you think?" my mom asks as she closes the door behind us.

"I love it," I answer honestly, a wide smile stretching across my face.

I go exploring the apartment. It's a one bedroom, but it's enough for just me. It's furnished with a small, dark green microfiber couch, a small entertainment center, and a queen-size bed in the bedroom. Other than that, it's pretty bare.

"It's perfect." I give my mom another hug. "Thank you."

"You're welcome, sweetie. It'll need a touch of your bright personality to make it feel like a home. How about we grab some lunch and then do a little shopping?"

I perk up. "The Village?"

She grins. "Where else?"

We leave the apartment, head downstairs, and decide to walk to my favorite café since we're not far. Plus, it's a beautiful day out. I've always loved summers in Colorado, especially in our small mountain town. It never gets too hot. Most days are near cloudless like today, the worst of the storms not usually hitting until the end of summer.

At the café, I order my usual—a turkey sandwich with avocado and a special raspberry chipotle mayo that I've tried hard to convince them to sell bottles of. I'm disappointed every time I come in and find they still don't.

"How are Dad and Dec doing?" I ask as we eat at a table outside.

"Your dad's great. Things have been pretty quiet around here, fortunately. Declan is…well, Declan. He's sorry he didn't make it to your graduation."

I wave the thought away. "He's busy at the shop. I know."

Declan went to the technical university in Colorado Springs to become a mechanic. Ever since he was little, he and our dad spent endless hours in the garage working on and restoring our grandfather's 1968 Plymouth GTX. It's his everyday car now.

"He'll be at dinner this weekend with his girlfriend," my mom says.

"Girlfriend?" I grin and raise a brow.

She laughs softly. "You know Dec. We'll see how long this one lasts. You're coming over for dinner, right?"

"Of course."

We finish up with our lunch and start strolling around downtown, mostly window shopping and catching up.

I'm thankful that my mother and I are close. After being away for so long at school, I've lost touch with most of my friends from high school. Many of them have moved away or have families and lives of their own. At least from what I've seen on social media. The only real friend I have lives several hours away in Grand Junction. Darcy and I went to med school together, and since she graduated a year earlier than me, we've only been able to keep in touch over the phone.

"Hey, wait," I tell my mom as we're passing by a small gift shop with gemstones and jewelry and clothing accessories in the windows.

We head inside, and I walk right past the display cases of crystals and shelves of books and incense to what caught my eye from outside. The back wall is full of artwork, most likely from local artists. Our town attracts a lot of tourists, so local art sells well.

One particular piece catches my attention.

It's painted on thick canvas. Heavy brush strokes form dark storm clouds above a silhouette of the mountains. But what truly drew me to it were the surprising bursts of colors within the dense, black and gray clouds, faintly glowing with blues, purples, pinks, and yellows. Like rainbow lightning.

"See something you like?" one of the women working the store asks as she stands beside me in front of the painting.

I nod my head at it. "This one."

"Really?" My mother stands on the other side of me, tilting her head and eyeing the artwork incredulously. "It's a bit…gloomy."

"No. It's beautiful."

Because it's not the darkness, the storm, that captivates me. It's the color. The light. That little bit of beauty that exists both despite and *because* of the storm.

"I'll take it."

The lady carefully removes it from the wall and takes it to the back to wrap it up for me. As I'm paying, I realize I didn't think to look for a signature.

"Could you tell me who the artist is?" I ask the clerk.

"That one's by Logan Delaney."

Oh.

My heart leaps into my throat where it kicks up at a galloping pace.

Of course it is.

I knew returning home meant having to eventually face the memories of a past that I left behind, but I didn't expect it to happen so soon.

I may never have known Logan all that well, despite having dated her brother in high school. They say you never forget your first love, and I've never forgotten Liam. Young love leaves an impression, deep grooves etched into your soul. We were close, sharing so much of our lives. He was my best friend.

Yet, when I hear Logan's name, all I can think about is that night she accused me of killing Liam. Of ruining her life. It opened those wounds wide open, cut them even deeper.

I've heard that beauty comes from pain, but I've never seen it as clearly as I do now, thinking about the painting in my hands.

"If you're interested, I could give you a call when she brings more in," the clerk says.

"Sure."

I don't even think about it as I write down my name and number on the slip of paper she passes me across the counter.

My mom and I leave the shop and head back to my apartment. She helps me bring up a few boxes from my car, and when we get upstairs, the first thing I do is unwrap the painting and hang it up on the bare wall of the living room.

After my mom leaves, reminding me about dinner that weekend before she goes, I crash onto the sofa. Tucked into the corner with my head resting on the arm of the couch, I stare at the painting, admiring the way the sunlight filtering in through the windows catches on the vivid bursts of color, making them pop.

The desire to fill the walls of my new home with more hits me with overwhelming intensity.

My mother only saw the storm, but I saw the unexpected beauty hidden within the depths of the dark clouds.

I can't help but want to search out more.

3

LOGAN

Vibrations shudder up my arm as I finish shading in the last bit of the fleur-de-lis with the needle. Once it's finished, I place the gun on my tray and wipe down the tattoo.

"What do you think?"

Alice lifts her arm and inspects the design inked into the skin just below the crease of her elbow. She smiles fondly. The tattoo is meant as a memorial to her grandmother, so my insides squirm a little while waiting for her reaction.

"I love it." She looks up at me with eyes glistening with unshed tears. "It's perfect. Thanks, Logan."

My nerves settle with relief, and I start cleaning up. As I cover her fresh tattoo, I go over aftercare with her.

"Thanks for coming in, Alice. You can pay up front with Tate."

She thanks me again and leaves the room.

I finish cleaning everything up, wiping down surfaces, disposing of the needles and used ink, and sterilizing everything else I used. Alice was my first client of the day, but I have a little time before the next.

After I'm done, I head up to the front, my feet tired in my heavy boots. Every wall through the hallway and into the lobby is painted black, decorated with photos of tattoos done here. Alice has already paid and gone, and the two red leather couches in the lobby are empty. Tate sits behind the counter with his feet propped up, doodling on a tablet. I plop down in the other chair, roll over to him, and peer over his shoulder.

"Rude," he mutters even though he doesn't stop drawing.

"You know, my boobs aren't *that* big."

He laughs. "Fuck off, Lo."

Tate hasn't tattooed any clients yet, but he's been working here nearly as long as I have and has recently decided to build a portfolio.

"Who's even getting pin-up tattoos anymore?"

He looks up just long enough to smirk at me. "Ask the *straight* guy I hooked up with last week."

My nose wrinkles. "I think you need to reevaluate your standards."

I roll my chair away to the computer, refusing to admit that I've thought about getting a pretty girl tattooed on me a time or two. Of course, by now, I'm quickly running out of room for anything like that.

"Do you know if Jacklyn is coming in today?" I ask as I check the schedule, clicking the metal bar in my tongue against my teeth.

"I don't think so. It's been pretty slow this week."

Jacklyn and her husband own the studio, A Touch of Ink, but they've been talking about moving away for a while now. Tate and I are here most often, along with another artist who only works on the weekends. I've been playing around with the idea of trying to buy the place off Jacklyn. It's the only thing I ever really see myself doing with my life, especially in a small town like this.

In another life, I probably would've moved a long time ago. There's not exactly much keeping me here.

My mom died five years ago. She did the one thing I begged her not to—destroyed herself. Drank and drugged herself to death. I didn't blame her back then, and I still don't blame her now. She did the only thing she could to cope with her grief, and when that stopped working, she gave up.

In yet another life, I might've been just like her.

Time doesn't heal all wounds like people say. There is no *healing*, just growing. Our pain doesn't lessen; it doesn't fade. It doesn't grow smaller. It stays the same, and we simply grow around it, giving it a little extra space to breathe.

My mother didn't do that. If anything, she shrank. Diminished to something so small that couldn't contain her grief, and it came spilling over until it drowned her.

Even after everything, I hope she found some peace.

My father never returned, not that I expected him to. He made it pretty clear when he left that his entire family died when Liam did. When he lost both his sons. I would've changed, made myself into another son for him, if it could have gotten him to stay. But I don't think it would have been enough anyway.

The only reason I'm still here is because I'm some person in between who my parents turned into after Liam's death. Like my mother, I can't let go. Like my father, I can't face it either.

I couldn't bring myself to get rid of the house. I still live there, under the same roof where we were all once a happy family.

It feels like a lifetime ago.

Even though I haven't been able to let go of it, I don't like it there. I crash at Tate's or Jacklyn's places more often than necessary. It's been years since I've stepped foot into any room other than my own, like I can forget anyone else ever lived there. I haven't touched anyone's things. Liam's and Landon's rooms are both still the way they left them.

That's the other reason I haven't left.

Maybe when Landon gets released, he'll want to come home. Maybe we'll be able to reinvent some semblance of a family, just the two of us.

Maybe. Maybe. Maybe.

Hope is a motherfucker. I've mostly avoided it whenever possible.

Landon doesn't call as much as he used to, and I've only visited him a handful of times because it's a long drive to make. And because it's difficult to see him in there when I know in my bones he doesn't deserve to be. He made me stop asking about that night a long time ago. I haven't brought it up since our mom died. That was a hard enough visit as it was, watching Landon realize that the only family he has left is me.

And maybe I won't be enough to bring him back home.

"Earth to Logan."

I look away from the computer screen, blinking a few times. "What's up?"

"Your eyes were starting to cross," Tate says with a chuckle.

"That's why they hurt then." I groan as I rub at them with my thumb and forefinger.

I've been having some mild eye pain for a few weeks now, but I've also been using my tablet to draw up designs more often. Maybe I should go back to a sketchpad for a while.

"Your next client won't be here for another hour. You could always go rest in the back for a bit."

"You sure?"

"Of course. I can hold down the fort."

The moment I stand to head back to our little break room with the comfy, worn couch that's calling my name, the front door of the studio opens.

I freeze.

It's not my next client arriving early to her appointment. I'm pretty sure it's not a potential client at all. It's…

Elise fucking Novak.

Well, that's not a face I was expecting to see anytime soon. I didn't even know she was back in town—not that I've been keeping up with her whereabouts. I see her fucking brother around enough as it is. Her mom. Her dad. The entire Novak clan is like a tether for the ghosts that still haunt me. If they're not plaguing my home, they're tormenting me everywhere else I go.

"Hey, Logan." Her voice is small, unsure. Cautious.

"What the fuck are you doing here?"

Out of the corner of my eye, I see Tate set down his tablet and lean back in his chair.

Elise's pale cheeks brighten a rosy shade of pink, clearly not expecting my level of hostility. That was stupid on her part. She may have spent the past eight years away at university, but surely she didn't cram so much into her brain that she forgot my parting words to her.

Nothing's changed.

"Well, I, uh…I saw your painting in that shop downtown."

I cross my arms over my chest. "Okay?"

"I bought it."

"If you want your money back, you'll have to talk to them."

"No, that's not…" She takes a step forward, acts like she wants to take another, but falters instead.

It gives me some kind of sick pleasure to see her so caught off guard, despite the fact she was the one who walked into *my* studio.

She hasn't changed much, just the normal kind of evolution that happens from teenage years to adulthood. Her body is curvier, her blonde hair shorter than the last time I saw her, flowing just past her shoulders. She's maybe two inches shorter than me and not as lean as I am. She's all soft curves in dark wash jeans and generous breasts beneath a light beige sweater.

So what if I can't help but notice? Doesn't mean I hate her any less.

Seeming to find a sliver of courage, she finally takes that next step forward and says, "I wanted to talk to you about getting some more."

My brows arch so high it hurts my eyes. "I'm sorry, *what?*"

"I just moved into an apartment, and, well…the wall's are kind of bare. And I love the painting. I thought maybe if I bought a few more directly from you, you could make more—"

"I'm going to stop you right there." I hold my hand up, my eyes narrowed. "I don't need any fucking handouts. Especially from you."

It's true that the stores I sell my paintings to make a nice little profit off me, but it's not like people are coming into a tattoo studio looking for artwork that's not meant to be painted on their bodies. It's mostly tourists that buy my paintings, souvenirs by a local artist. Besides, it's nothing more than a side gig.

At least, that's what I tell myself.

Elise juts out her chin a barely perceptible notch, a spark lighting up those previously apprehensive eyes. "I wasn't insinuating anything like that."

"No? Then what? Searching for some kind of penitence? Why don't you stick it in a sympathy card?"

Her lips part. There's a battle waging behind her almost mesmerizing gaze, a kind of sunburst made from the golden halo around her pupils that fades out into an autumn green. She should be leaving, giving up. But she's never struck me as the type to back down easily.

She glances over at Tate, who probably wishes he had some popcorn right about now.

"I don't know what you think, Logan," she says, her attention on me again. "I don't have anything to atone for."

"Well, then you can turn right around and leave. Because I have no interest in selling you anything."

There's another flash in her eyes, a flare in those sunbursts.

She can be angry all the fuck she wants.

Because whether she wants to admit it or not—whether she remembers anything about that night or not—she was still *there*. She could've kept Liam off that bridge. But she didn't. If she honestly carries no guilt with her whatsoever, then she's probably barely human.

When she still hasn't moved, I snap, "Was there anything else?"

Her jaw ticks, and now it's pissing me off a little that she feels like my treatment is unjustified. What the fuck was she expecting? That she could come back to town and we'd suddenly be besties?

Like the past has been erased instead of it growing with me all these years?

Eventually, she sighs. "No. But I'm sure you can find me if you change your mind."

I plaster on my best fake smile. "Like hell."

A faint, soft huff slips past her full, pale pink lips before she turns and walks out of the studio. The door, unfortunately, doesn't hit her nice ass on the way out.

As though the encounter took literally everything out of me, I collapse back into my seat. The chair rolls backward until I hit the wall, my shoulders hunched with the release of a threadbare breath.

When I feel eyes on me, I roll my head to the side to see Tate staring at me, a hook tugging at one corner of his mouth. He raises one hand in the air like a claw. The feral hiss he unleashes is actually pretty impressive.

I roll my eyes and drop my head back against the wall with a quiet thud.

"I'm just saying," Tate starts in a low voice, "she doesn't *look* like a killer."

My family isn't a topic I talk about often, even with Tate. He's been my best friend for years though, and after my mother died, I shared the story of our downfall with him.

"I never said she was." I reach up to pinch the bridge of my nose, eyes screwed shut. "It's just bullshit that she and Declan got away without a slap on the wrist while Landon went away for ten fucking years."

"You still don't believe Declan's testimony?"

"Fuck no. Landon provided alcohol to minors, sure. Reckless endangerment? *Maybe*. None of them should have been on that damn bridge while they were drinking. But involuntary manslaughter? Landon never would've risked Liam's life like that, getting into a fight with him right there on the bridge."

"And Landon never said what happened?"

I shake my head and sigh. "He said he doesn't remember."

"And that's what Elise says too?"

"It doesn't fucking matter. I'll never know what really happened that night."

Tate goes silent, and when he hasn't said anything for too long, I open my eyes to see him grinning like the damn Cheshire Cat.

His mischievous gaze finds me and he says, "You could try."

"What do you mean?"

He wiggles his brows. "Get into her pants."

"Ew! Gross!"

I lean over and slap him hard across his arm, but all he does is howl with laughter and rub at the spot my hit landed. It doesn't make me feel any better about his ridiculous suggestion.

"What the fuck would that even do?"

"You never know." He shrugs. "If she is lying about not remembering, maybe she'd be more inclined to tell you the truth. If not, you could at least have fun fucking with her."

Leaning back in my chair, I cross my arms and bite the inside of my lip in contemplation.

There was once a time when I would've done just about anything to find out the truth of what really happened on that bridge. I even craved revenge against the Novak siblings for letting my brother rot in prison.

Eight years has changed a lot.

It's not that I don't still want those things. It's just…is it worth it? Am I too jaded now?

Then again, seeing Elise has brought a lot of those past feelings surging to the surface. All the resentment and hatred. The desire to break something. *Someone*.

I look back at Tate, the corner of my lips twitching. "You, sir, are very bad."

The shit-eating grin he gives me takes up half his face. "You love it."

"Get back to work," I say as I stand. "I'm going to take that break."

More like plot Elise Novak's fucking demise.

4

ELISE

It's been two days since I walked into the tattoo studio Logan works at, and I'm still reeling from the encounter.

I knew how she felt about me after Liam's death. I never could forget the look of utter anguish and wrath on her face when she accused me of killing her brother. But I guess I thought it had more to do with grief than true animosity.

Turns out I was wrong.

And, unfortunately, she's even more intimidating than I used to find her back then too. The black tank top she wore showed off one sleeve of tattoos, her other arm nearly covered too. I wanted to study them more because they looked nearly as beautiful as her painting, but I wasn't about to stand there and stare at them while she spit venom at me.

It was about all I could do not to run out of there with my tail tucked between my legs.

Which I suppose is what I ended up doing anyway.

After that shit show, I'm happy to be in my parents' kitchen with my mom soaking up the aroma of vanilla and sugar as we bake my grandmother's recipe for madeleines.

I pitched the idea to my mom to do some baking before dinner this evening so that I could spend the majority of the day here instead of at my apartment. When I'm there, I can't stop staring at Logan's painting on my wall. Wondering if I imagined what I first saw in it.

How could someone so cold and vicious create such beauty within darkness when they have none in them themselves?

"Do you want to dip some of these in chocolate?" my mom asks.

I look up from where I'm removing a batch of the perfectly golden-brown cookies from their pan and laugh. "I can't believe you're even asking me that."

While my mom pipes chilled dough into the three pans for a second batch, I get out the dark chocolate and melt it down. After I dip the rounded edges of each cookie into the chocolate, I lay them on a wire rack to set. I do that with the entire first batch while my mom puts the next one in the oven and sets the timer.

She walks around the island counter and comes to stand on the other side to inspect my work. "I'm surprised you wanted to do all this baking today. I hope you're not expecting to get any sleep during your first year of residency."

"I just finished grad school, Mom." I set the last cookie on the rack and give her a cheeky grin. "I'm used to not sleeping."

"Good," she says with a soft laugh.

Moving to the sink, I place the empty bowl from the chocolate inside, filling it with water to soak.

I consider bringing up Logan to my mom, asking her if she knows how she's been, trying to figure out if she's been this hostile toward everyone all these years, if she treats everyone around town similar to how she's treated me. Or if her animosity is purely reserved for me alone. But the prospect of bringing up the one topic I came here to escape from stops me.

I wouldn't say I have an innate need to be liked, at least not any more than the next person. But the way Logan clearly hates me gets under my skin.

Okay, maybe I do have a tendency toward approval-seeking behavior.

The last time my mom and I spoke about Logan or any of her family was when her mother died. My mom called me to let me know.

I cried that night.

I cried for Ms. Delaney. I cried for Logan. For Liam.

I had considered coming home for the funeral, but I knew Logan wouldn't want me there. Sometimes I still wish I had gone for Liam.

Deciding not to mention anything, I help my mom clean up a bit. Once all the cookies are done, we get started on dinner. As we load two sheet pans with chicken and red potatoes and asparagus, we talk a bit more about the hospital and my residency. She works overnights in the ER, and that's where I'll be starting. I'm a little surprised that the hospital is allowing my mother to supervise me, but I'm also not considering it's a small town and she's one of the best doctors we have.

Dinner's about halfway done when my dad gets home from his shift. He comes into the kitchen, gives me a hug and my mom an affectionate kiss, then leaves us to change out of his uniform.

After almost thirty years of marriage, the love my parents have is still so sweet it makes my teeth ache.

We're just pulling the food out of the oven when the front door opens again and Declan walks into the kitchen with his girlfriend. His eyes immediately light up upon seeing me. He rounds the island and pulls me in for a crushing bear hug, lifting me off my feet.

I slap him on the back, wheezing with breathless laughter. "I can't breathe, you oaf!"

Chuckling, Declan drops me back to the ground. "That's what you get for not making time for me when you got back to town."

"I had a lot of unpacking to do."

And a lot of stalking Logan to do.

But I don't mention that.

It really was mostly the unpacking that had kept me busy. Figuring out where to find Logan only took a few minutes of looking through her social media. And then gathering the courage to go down to A Touch of Ink.

Turns out it was a wasted effort.

"Are you going to introduce us, Declan?" my mom asks, smiling warmly at the brunette standing in her kitchen.

"This is Sarah," he says, almost like he doesn't care what her name is.

He probably doesn't.

My brother isn't a bad guy, but…well, my mom has told me every time she's met a different girlfriend of his. Sure, he's handsome—boyish charm with golden hair and our dad's blue eyes. But this isn't a big town. I don't know where he finds them all.

"Nice to meet you, Sarah." It's my dad who says it as he walks back into the kitchen. Then he looks at my mom and me. "Why don't you ladies go take a seat? Dec and I will make the plates."

My mom, Sarah, and I sit at the large dining table, my mom wasting no time before diving into the routine interrogation.

"So where did you and Declan meet?"

Sarah blushes. "I had to take my car to the shop to get some work done."

According to my mother, that's the answer ninety percent of his girlfriends give.

A few minutes later, we're all sitting around the table with our plates. Conversation goes back and forth as we eat, my parents asking Sarah questions even though they're aware that trying to get to know her is most likely a waste of time. My mom brags about getting to work with me at the hospital, and Dad and Declan share stories about their jobs.

At some point, my gaze lingers on Declan across the table. With thoughts of Logan taking up so much real estate in my mind lately, I can't help but think about that night, trying to imagine it from her perspective.

Declan and I were both there the night Liam died. If my brother were accused of involuntary manslaughter, I probably wouldn't want to believe it either.

I guess I can't blame her for hating me.

But the truth is I really *don't* remember. Not exactly.

I had had a few drinks before, but that night was the first time I had ever gotten drunk. I had no self-control and drank until it left a gaping void in my memory. Declan testified that Liam and Landon were arguing on the bridge, and that resulted in Liam falling sixty feet over the edge into the river. They said it wasn't the fall that killed him, but that he drowned. He might've survived it if he hadn't been intoxicated.

As I watch Declan chatting animatedly with our dad, the only three things that managed to survive the black hole in my memory come back to haunt me like they often do.

One, shouting.

Two, a scream.

Three, a splash.

I didn't testify because those little things only came to me in nightmares in the months that followed. But when they did, how could I believe anything but Declan's story?

"You okay, El?" my brother asks.

I realize I'm still staring at him and quickly don what I hope is a relaxed smile. "Yeah, I'm good."

He nods, but his brow is furrowed like he's not entirely sure if he believes me or not.

Fortunately, my mom chooses that moment to announce there's dessert. She goes into the kitchen and returns with the pineapple upside down cake we made earlier that afternoon. After we're all completely stuffed, we talk for a bit longer before the four of us clean up the table and kitchen together. Declan and Sarah leave first, and I leave shortly after to return home.

Hopefully not to stay up all night staring at that damn painting.

My first night as an intern is over. My feet are killing me. I'm fucking exhausted.

I was at the hospital for over twelve hours, arriving an hour before my mom and leaving an hour after her. It wasn't a bad night, getting to work with my mom on a few cases. There was a lot of paperwork.

The sun has long since risen by the time I get home, washing the sky in shades of pink and gold behind the mountains like a halo. If I wasn't so tired, I might stop at one of the small cafés downtown to enjoy the nice weather with a coffee. Instead, I go straight up to my apartment, desperate to get out of these scrubs.

On my way to my bedroom, my gaze lingers on Logan's painting. My eyes always manage to find it when I'm near, and I stopped fighting it. I stopped wondering if I imagined things. I didn't. I still find it beautiful.

After stripping out of my scrubs and underwear and tossing them all in the hamper, I warm up the shower and step inside. It helps to wake me up a little so that by the time I get out and dress in soft, cotton shorts and an oversized T-shirt, I decide to read a little before getting some sleep.

Just as I sit down with a hot mug of herbal tea and my worn copy of *The Invisible Life of Addie LaRue*, there's a knock at the door.

I have no idea who I was expecting when I open it, but it sure wasn't Logan Delaney.

She stands in the hallway in similar attire she was wearing the other day—tight, black, ripped jeans; what looks like black biker boots; and a black shirt, this time with a black leather jacket over it. Her long hair that's so dark it's nearly black itself hangs down in loose waves past her breasts, a little wavier than mine. Her intense, gray eyes, surrounded by thick eyeliner and smokey shadows, are already settled right on me.

"Oh," I say dumbly before quickly clearing my throat. "Hi."

She doesn't say anything right away, blinking at me a couple of times before her gaze sweeps down my body. Moving slowly, leisurely. I'm nearly to the point of uncomfortable by the time her eyes find mine again, the corners of her mouth lifted in a grin.

"Cute PJs."

My wet hair drips onto my shoulders, making me shiver. I cross my arms over my chest. Not because I'm concerned with her checking me out, but because I'm not wearing a bra and I don't particularly like the idea of being in a state of vulnerability around her.

"What are you doing here?"

She shrugs. "I changed my mind."

When she speaks, I catch a hint of silver just behind her teeth. I thought I had noticed it when I saw her in the tattoo studio, but I hadn't been sure standing so far away. I'm still surprised she has all those tattoos but no other facial piercings besides the metal bar in her tongue.

My eyes narrow. "What happened to *like hell*?"

"I'm headed there anyway. Might as well take advantage of you and make some money on my way down."

"At least you're honest," I mutter with a roll of my eyes.

As though it's all settled, she says, "Let's see what we're working with." Then she's pushing her way past me into my apartment.

With a sigh, I close the door, leaving it cracked because she is definitely *not* staying. When I turn around, I find her standing in the middle of my living room, staring at the wide wall that's still bare except for her single painting.

"You have a lot of space." She places her hands on her slender hips, then looks at me with another wry grin and a tilt of her head. "You sure you can afford me?"

"Depends. Are you going to overcharge me because you hate me?"

"No," she says, doing that thing with her voice where she speaks sweetly even though she's anything but. "But I do have a condition."

I shake my head and let out a short, derisive laugh. "Of course you do."

Dropping her hands, she stalks toward me, moving so close that I nearly take a step back before she stops. So close that I can see blue flecks in her gray eyes. So close that I get a whiff of sage and something sweet. Apples maybe.

For several seconds, she stands there less than three feet in front of me, unmoving. Silent. Waiting.

Then that damn little grin is back. "Don't you want to know what it is?"

I'm not sure that I do.

But when I catch the painting in my periphery without moving my gaze off of her, I have to at least know.

"What do you want, Logan?"

The corner of her mouth lifts. "Let me give you a tattoo."

I nearly choke on air. Not because I would be apprehensive about getting a tattoo—I have one already and have thought about getting more—but because that was the last thing I was expecting to hear her say.

"Why?"

She takes one more step closer, and it's the first time I really comprehend the two inches she has on me. That small, annoying grin shifts into something more sinister, an almost malicious kind of smirk that has ice sliding down my spine.

"Because I want to hurt you."

I suck in a sharp breath.

So not only is she a bitch, but she's a sadistic bitch.

"Look, I'm sorry."

I sigh and finally drop my arms to my sides, ignoring how stiff they feel after keeping them folded across my chest for so long. If I'm going to apologize, then I need to be open and show her I mean it. If she's going to hate me, it's not going to be because of some stupid miscommunication on my part.

"I may not remember exactly what happened that night," I say, "but none of us should've been there in the first place. I'm sorry that Liam is gone. I miss him too."

Logan's jaw ticks. Her left eye twitches.

Somehow, my words only manage to fuel her enmity. I have a feeling that I could apologize until I'm blue in the face, and it wouldn't make a difference.

I open my mouth to mention Landon too, but she cuts me off. It's probably for the best.

"Do we have a deal or not?"

I swallow hard and tug my bottom lip between my teeth. "Can I think about it?"

"Fine. Call the studio if you decide you have the guts to go through with it."

As Logan walks away, I close my eyes to resist the temptation to retaliate with a retort I might regret.

While my eyes are still closed, the door to my apartment slams shut. I peer over at it, needing to confirm that she's really gone before I let my shoulders slump, not having realized just how much tension was coiled so tightly in my body.

Looking over at the coffee table, I frown at my cup, steam no longer billowing up from the mug, my tea cold.

So much for a relaxing morning.

5

LOGAN

She actually called. I almost didn't think she would.

When I walked into the studio two days later to Tate's mischievous smirk and a conspiratorial spark in his eyes, I knew what it was all for. I couldn't help but laugh at his maniacal cackling like he was some cheesy villain in a bad movie.

Elise had sent over the design she wanted—a delicate stargazer lily, including its stem, leaves, and a couple of buds. It's soft, like her. No black lines, only light shades of pinks and greens. It'll probably be one of the more elegant tattoos I've ever done.

I hate thinking how much it suits her.

As I'm getting the design ready for her appointment this evening, I wonder where she's going to want it. Where I'm going to be touching her. Hurting her.

That's about the time my thoughts spiral.

Her fresh shower scent with a hint of eucalyptus. Hair dripping, wet droplets dark on her oversized shirt. Full breasts, nipples damn near poking through the fabric when she shivered. Only the top few inches of those soft, creamy thighs covered by her shorts.

Fuck.

I wanted to dirty her up.

I fully blame Tate for putting those thoughts in my head. It's not that I was blind to her obvious beauty before. But…

This is Elise Novak.

I can't want her.

I *don't* want her.

Though, I suppose if I did, that would make the whole *destroying her* thing easier. And more fun.

Because the moment she opened her fucking mouth to *apologize*, that's all I wanted to do. It was an immediate one-eighty from wanting to dirty her up right back to wanting to ruin her instead.

She can apologize all she wants, but it doesn't change a damn thing. It doesn't bring Liam back. Or Landon. It doesn't make my family whole again. Nothing will ever make her understand just how much my world changed that night.

I blame them all.

Before Elise came back to town, at least I was doing somewhat of a decent job not letting the past completely rule my life. Sure, it's hard to go home sometimes. Sure, I still miss my brothers so much it aches. But it didn't consume me. Not like this intense desire for revenge does now that I've seen her again.

Seen how fucking *perfect* her life is.

She went off and earned her M.D. and returned home like ghosts don't live here. Her brother is here. Her family is whole.

Maybe my hatred is rooted in envy. Maybe everything she's said is the truth. Maybe she's the one least at fault.

I don't fucking care.

When she enters the studio that evening, I'm up front behind the counter with Tate. None of us say a word as I slide a tablet over to her. I lean against the back wall with my arms over my chest, watching as she silently fills out the necessary forms. She's wearing teal scrubs beneath a long, dark gray pea coat, so I assume she's going to work after this.

The thought of her having to suffer a twelve-hour shift at the hospital with a fresh tattoo has me sharing a wicked grin with Tate.

Once she's finished with the forms, I walk out from behind the counter and motion for her to follow. I lead her down the hallway and into the private room where all my things are set up.

Turning to her, I place my hands on my hips and ask, "Where's this going?"

She moves the bottom of her coat out of the way to lay her palm over the top part of her left thigh. "Right here."

A flash of heat flares down my spine as I stare at the spot. When my gaze finally meets hers again, I wonder if she knows exactly what she's doing to me. However, there's no sign of duplicitousness on her face, so maybe she really is as innocent as she seems.

I can change that.

"You'll have to take off your pants," I tell her with a small twitch of my lips.

To her credit, the only hint of discomfort is a slight purse of her pretty pink mouth as she takes off her coat first. As much as I'm tempted to push her as far to the edge as I can, I decide to give her some privacy as she strips off her pants, turning to my desk to retrieve the couple of stencils I have ready.

By the time I face her again, she's in nothing more than her scrub top, black socks, and black bikini panties with a bright pink hem.

That heat returns, hotter than before.

Why does she have to have this fucking affect on me?

I step closer and hold up the two pieces of tracing paper, trying like hell to keep my eyes on her face. I didn't know where she was going to want the design, so I made two different stencils.

"Which size? I can always do another one if you want it smaller or bigger."

"That one," she says, nodding toward the larger of the two.

I arch a brow. She barely blinks. I don't know if she's trying to challenge me or torture me because spending that much time tattooing her thigh is bound to do both.

"All right. Come stand over here."

At my desk, I set down the stencils then drop to my knees right in front of Elise. As I grab the razor and green soap, I peer up at her, deliberately slowing my movements as I start wiping down her skin and shaving the spot.

She shifts on her feet and averts her gaze, looking straight ahead. "I know what you're doing."

"And what's that?" I ask, not bothering to conceal my amusement.

"You're trying to make me uncomfortable."

After I finish shaving the area, I run my fingertips lightly over her soft skin, like I'm checking to make sure it's smooth enough. Really, it's just an excuse to touch her and draw out the goosebumps that rise from her flesh.

"Is it working?"

She doesn't respond, but when I peer up to look at her, I see her breasts are slightly heaving, moving with her rapid breaths.

I'll take that as a yes.

Laughing quietly, I get the soap to wipe down her leg. Once that's done and the stencil is applied, I stand and point at the large mirror taking up half the wall beside the desk.

"Take a look and let me know what you think."

She moves over to stand in front of the mirror, and I somehow manage to look away from the little bit of her ass I can see beneath her top to check out the placement of the stencil. I realize just how close my hand is going to be to her crotch the entire time I'm tattooing her. Hell, how close my *face* is going to be.

Shifting her leg around, jutting out her hip like she's trying to put on a show for me, she looks at the design from different angles before a satisfied smile slowly stretches her lips. "It's perfect."

"Great," I mutter, annoyed at the complete derailment of my train of thought every time I'm staring at her.

Taking a seat on my stool, I roll it over to the tattoo chair in the center of the room. I pat the cushion and tell her to sit. After putting on my gloves, I pour the ink and ready my gun, forcing myself to focus more than my brain wants to right now.

When I turn back to Elise, she looks perfectly at ease.

"Have you gotten a tattoo before?" I ask as I recline the chair to get her legs up.

"I have one."

There's a part of me that wants to ask to see it, but I decide to keep any personal curiosity I might have about her hidden away. Which is why I'm also not asking her why she chose the lily, even though I'm desperate to know. I'm not asking anything I wouldn't ask any other client.

"Afraid of needles?"

"No. I'll be fine."

Too bad.

I pick up my gun and wheel my stool closer. I place one hand on the side of her leg, the heat of her skin soaking through my glove into my palm, and meet her gaze. "Comfortable?"

The corner of her mouth quirks up. "Do you want me to say no?"

My eyes narrow, and I look away to turn on my gun.

Damn her for being able to read me so well. A moment ago, I thought I was rattling her just fine, and now *I'm* the one on the fucking edge.

Well played, bitch.

At least I get to have some real fun now.

I dip the needle in the green ink and bring it to her thigh to start on the stem of the flower first. The moment I pierce her skin, I feel the muscles in her leg tense slightly beneath my hands. Unfortunately, she doesn't make a sound like I might've been hoping she would.

After a few minutes of being a little too fixated on the soft body in my tattoo chair, I eventually become absorbed in my work. In the vibrations traveling up my arm, the whirring of the gun, the ink embedded into skin. Every so often, I wipe away the excess ink and the little bit of blood.

I've never been bothered by blood, and I certainly don't mind making Elise bleed. If only she would make a goddamn sound. I know the dry paper towel rubbing over open and raw flesh is one of the worst parts.

Once I've finished with the stem and leaves, I switch out the needle and color. It's only then as I'm wiping over the tattoo so I can start on one of the buds that she finally makes noise.

It's a low, breathy groan that has my insides doing flips. I feel it all the way down in my lower belly, whatever it is flicking a switch, lighting up a string of nerves. When I look up and pin my gaze on her, there's a shadow around the edges of my vision, narrowing in on her like a tunnel.

If she can tell what that sound just did to me, she doesn't let it show.

"Sorry," she mutters. "I might just need a short break."

"No problem."

I swivel on my stool to set the gun on my tray, shifting a bit on my seat to hide the fact that I'm rubbing my thighs together, trying to relieve the ache between them.

This plan is blowing up in my fucking face.

Giving her—and me—a couple of minutes, I clear a few things off my tray. And try to clear a few things out of my head.

"I'm good now," she says behind me, and I realize maybe more than a couple of minutes have passed.

As I get back to work, I quickly realize I shouldn't have started with the lower portion of the tattoo. Now that I'm on the flower at the highest part of her thigh, my hand is closer to her underwear. As I move onto the petal that opens up toward her core like a fucking neon arrow, the backs of my fingers brush against that bright pink hem.

It also doesn't help that she's making noise more regularly now. Little sighs and hisses and sucking of breath. Each one makes me grit my teeth harder.

Then something hits me. A new smell that lingers beneath the more potent scent of the soap. It's a little sweet, a little musky.

I pause my work, too curious to know if my suspicions are correct. Even with that smell clinging to my nose, I'm still surprised to see that the thin fabric over her pussy is damp, the darker area subtle against the black. If I hadn't been leaning over her so far, my face so close to the heat of her, I probably wouldn't have noticed.

And because I can't help myself, I look up at her. Her chest is heaving again, eyes closed, dark lashes fluttering against the tops of her cheeks.

"How are you doing? How's the pain?" I ask, once again unable to conceal the amusement in my tone. And maybe a little arrogant pride.

"It's fine. I'm fine."

I don't know if it's the pain that's turning her on, or me. I wanted to watch her hurt, but her arousal is an unexpected reward. As tortuous as this has been for me, the least she could do is suffer with me. Preferably suffer *more*.

After shifting on my stool again, I get back to work. It's even more difficult to focus than before as I finish up the flower and buds, shading them in and adding a little extra dimension.

By the time the tattoo is finished, the scent of her arousal is stronger, damn near competing with that of the soap. Her panties are practically soaked through, and I'd be lying if I said I haven't been tempted to find out just how wet she is beneath them. To dip my fingers under that pink hem to seek out the center of her. To run my tongue over the fabric just for a taste.

A couple of hours in my tattoo chair, and this woman is already fucking ruining me.

The smile on her face as she stands in front of the mirror to look at her new tattoo is a little shaky, her legs wobbly. She hasn't been able to meet my gaze since I turned off my gun. I wonder how badly she wants to get off right now.

But she doesn't acknowledge it, just pretends she didn't spend the last half hour in my chair soaking the leather.

"It's beautiful," she says in a small, sincere voice.

I watch her in front of the mirror a little longer than I probably should, captivated by the sight of her as she admires my art on her body.

My forever mark on her.

Something she'll never be able to look at without thinking about me.

Fuck, I hate how that affects me.

Desperate to get her out of here as quickly as I can, I cover the tattoo with a temporary bandage and go over aftercare. It's part of my job. I'm sure as an M.D., she doesn't need to be told how to take care of a tattoo.

As she gets dressed, still avoiding my eyes, she says, "Well, I hope you got that out of your system."

"Not even a little bit."

For some reason, those words cause her attention to finally snap to me. A blush blooms across her cheeks, bringing with it another desire to touch it, to feel the heat of that flush beneath my palms. As much as I'd like to solve the mystery of her reaction, I'd much rather her get the fuck out of here.

"But I suppose you kept your end of the deal." I turn away from her to start cleaning up my station. "You can pay Tate. I'll be in touch about the paintings."

Several seconds pass while I feel the weight of her gaze on me before her soft footsteps fade away as she leaves the room.

As soon as I've cleaned everything up, including the sad misfortune of having to wipe down the leather where Elise had been sitting, I slump into the tattoo chair. I prop my elbow on the armrest and rub at my tired eyes.

Now that she's gone, I can finally think clearly.

Now that I know I can get her wet, maybe Tate's idea isn't such a bad one.

Now all I can think about is getting Elise beneath me, taking her apart, breaking her until there's nothing left. And having a damn good time while doing it.

6

ELISE

Before heading to the hospital for my shift, I have to make a pitstop at home to change my damn underwear.

It was more than just a little surprising when I realized I was getting wet while she was tattooing me. I still don't know what was happening to me in that chair, but I try to tell myself it was just because it's been awhile since I've been intimate with anyone, since I've had anyone that close to that part of me.

With her hand on my leg, her fingers brushing my underwear, her warm breath occasionally ghosting over my skin, it was just some kind of biological reaction.

I know Logan is gay. I've never had any negative thoughts toward her for that like many kids at our high school did. I never even really felt uncomfortable around her because of it.

At least not until today.

Not until that look in her eyes when she told me to take off my pants. When she had to turn away from me after the first time I couldn't hold back a noise. The slight hitch in her breath when she stopped to ask how I was doing, probably around the time she noticed I was wet—because I doubt there was any way she couldn't tell.

I caught all of it even though I pretended I didn't. Whether it was all genuine or simply an act to fluster me, I don't know.

What was most shocking to me was my own reaction.

My sexual experiences may be limited, but they were all with men. Liam and I never went much further than kissing, and when I look back, I think that's because it was difficult for us to move past just being friends. I had a boyfriend for less than a year in undergrad, and then there was that regrettable one night stand. Once I started grad school, men and dating were never a priority.

Okay, so there might have been one drunk incident featuring a blurry blonde with breasts bigger than mine and a name I can't remember.

But that doesn't make me gay. Or bi. It was one time, and I was *very* intoxicated.

I never drank much after that.

Plenty of people are guilty of doing things that are completely unlike them, and, despite what some may believe, I'm not the exception to that rule.

Admittedly, Logan is…well, stunning, for lack of a better word. Her lean, tall frame. Her pale complexion that tells me she probably doesn't get much sun. Her unwavering confidence that makes her even more intimidating.

But none of it means *she's* the reason I got so turned on.

I'm straight.

Today was simply a one-off, a fluke, a freak accident. One I'll forget and never think about again.

With that decided, I swiftly change out of my underwear, being careful with the fresh tattoo. I consider throwing the panties in the garbage so I never again have to see the evidence of my awkward depravity, but I toss them in the hamper instead.

I spend the drive to the hospital with my music turned low, clearing my mind, centering myself. I can't afford to be distracted.

I don't always feel like myself when I'm around Logan. She brings out some stubborn part of me, a desire to rise to her challenges. I'm not a confrontational person, not very assertive even when I should be. Not that I'm a pushover. But when I'm with her, I don't mind the battle of wills so much.

By the time I park my car, I feel at least a little more like myself. I didn't spend eight years only learning how to be a doctor. I also learned how to leave my shit at the door of the classroom or the hospital. I've spent a lot of time perfecting that version of me, the one that feels in control of her life.

Damn Logan Delaney for throwing me off balance.

Five days have passed since I last saw Logan, since I sat in her chair while she hurt me like she wanted. I kept my end of the agreement, but I haven't heard from her since.

If I've sensed one thing about Logan, it's that no one can make her do anything she doesn't want to do. If she doesn't want to keep her side of the bargain, then there's nothing I can do about it. She probably really did get it all out of her system—with the extra cherry on top of humiliating me by making me have to change my underwear before work—and now has no plans of ever seeing me again.

That's fine. I'd rather have a quiet life than letting her flip my world upside down.

About the time I make the decision to simply give up and find another way of decorating my apartment, there's a knock on my door.

I swear to…

I open it.

It's Logan.

Of course it's Logan.

Without waiting for an invitation, she barges inside as soon as the door is open wide enough for her to carry in the large canvas wrapped in parchment paper that's in her hands.

"Come on in," I mutter, shutting the door without even thinking about it.

She's already unwrapping the artwork when I turn around. It's about the same time in the morning as the last time she showed up here, and it has me wondering what kind of schedule she's on. It looks like she might be wearing yesterday's makeup and clothes, the same leather jacket, hints of paint on her ripped jeans. While I'm already showered and in my pajamas again. I don't bother covering my chest this time though. She's already seen me in my panties.

In my wet panties…

I shake that thought from my mind and clear my throat. "Do you ever sleep?"

"Not usually at night."

So my theory about her not getting much sun is probably correct.

"So what are you? A vampire?"

Peering up at me, she gives me a toothy grin, showing her canines. "Think about all the fun we could have if I was."

I quickly look away as a heat rises up my neck.

Okay, so she's playing that game again. Unfortunately, with her in my home and me in my little cotton shorts, I have a feeling her tricks to crawl under my skin will be more difficult to fend off.

However, I forget all about that once she has the painting unwrapped and leans it up against the back of the couch.

I forget just about everything.

I'm stunned into absolute silence, a deadly stillness. In the blink of an eye, I've been transported out of my apartment and into this world that Logan's brought alive. I can feel the breeze of the coming storm on my face. I can smell the petrichor in the air.

This time, the swirls of color aren't hidden within the dark storm clouds that hang heavy in the background over silhouetted mountains. They're in the foreground, within the field of lilies that sway in a violent wind of the oncoming tempest. Pinks of stargazer lilies. Oranges of tiger lilies. Yellows of meadow lilies. The colors are a little muted by the gray sky overhead, but they're no less beautiful, standing in stark contrast to the storm.

"Why lilies?"

Logan's question pulls me back out. When I meet her gaze, I realize how similar her eyes are to the images she paints. Flecks of blue within the gray.

Color within the shadows.

Beauty hidden in a storm.

I shrug as I answer, "There's no super deep meaning." Peering back down at the painting, I consider it more. "Every time my dad has brought my mom flowers, it's always been lilies. I remember once when I was really young, I walked into the kitchen to see a vase of stargazer lilies on the counter. I guess I just decided then that they were my favorite flowers. Over the years, with how often my dad brought them home, they just…became a symbol of love."

There's a stretch of silence after that, long and tense. I'm almost afraid of what I'll see when I look at her. But I make myself do it anyway.

Breath gets trapped in my throat when I see the darkness in her stare, the tick in her jaw. It doesn't take me long to realize the reason.

"It's also a reminder to never take anything for granted. To remember how lucky I am."

"Yeah," she says, voice tight. "Lucky you."

"Logan…"

"Do you want it or not?"

A frown tugs down the corners of my mouth, and I sigh. "Of course I do."

After she tells me the price, I wire her the money from my phone. I consider giving her a little extra because she's not charging much more than what I bought the first painting for, and I really did half expect her to price gouge just because it's me. But I don't want to risk doing anything to set her off further.

I'm surprised when she offers to help me get the painting hung up on the same wall as the other one. Fortunately, by that time, she seems a little cooled down from earlier.

Taking a step back, she places her hands on her hips and stares at the wall. "You still have plenty of space for more." She tilts her head, giving my whole body a slow, sweeping perusal, lingering on the bottom stem of the lily visible beneath my shorts. "Paintings *and* tattoos."

"I'm not trading my skin for art."

That was clearly the wrong thing to say judging by the way her eyes darken again. It's different this time. It's not hostile, at least not *only* hostile. It's a little feral. Full of sinful promises.

"Are you certain?" Her voice comes out deeper, almost husky. "You sure did like the first time."

"I don't know what you're talking about."

Why the hell does she have to bring that up? Why couldn't she just let me keep pretending that it didn't happen?

Oh, right. Because she's a sadistic bitch.

"Don't lie to me, Elise."

There's something about the way my name flows past her lips that catches me off guard, making me unprepared for when she stalks toward me. I don't start retreating until she's already in my space, not realizing how close I was to the wall until my back hits it. Her hands come up on either side of me, splayed against the wall as her hot breath fans across my face.

"Admit it." Her voice is a purr that vibrates through me. "You got so wet sitting in my chair while I was hurting you."

"Maybe I just like pain."

I'm surprised that my voice comes out as steady as it does, especially because I have no idea what I'm saying. *Do* I like pain? My limited sexual experience never included any kind of kink exploration.

I lose all ability to breathe as her body presses against me. Her smaller chest crushes mine, the friction against my nipples causing them to harden. I tell myself it's just my body's natural response, but that excuse is more difficult to apply to the rapidly pooling heat in my lower belly.

"Really?" She leans forward, her voice a low whisper in my ear. "It had nothing to do with me because you're not gay, right?"

"Right," I answer, jaw clenched. "Now get off me."

"You don't want to test it? Find out which one it really is?"

My lips part with the intention of telling her no. Before I can, she rolls her hips against mine. I'm forced to tug my bottom lip between my teeth, biting it hard, because I swear a moan was just attempting to claw its way up my throat.

What the hell is happening to me?

I've never been into women before. At least not sober. And *nothing* like this.

Something warm and wet brushes against my jaw, just the lightest feathering of Logan's tongue. Soft flesh mixed with hard steel.

I shiver.

"So if I dipped my hand into your panties, you wouldn't soak my fingers?"

I can't stop it this time. I try. I really do. But the moan finds its way up and spills from my lips without my permission.

Again, I try to make excuses. It's just those filthy words. It's not her or the voice that says them. It's not her breasts pressed firmly against mine or the rolling of her hips. It's not the heat of her breath against my neck. It's not everything that belongs to *her*.

But when her hips leave mine and her fingers tease the waistband of my shorts with the softest of touches, eliciting goosebumps that spread up my arms, it all feels like bitter lies.

I think about telling her to stop. I even open my mouth to do it, or at least to *try* to force the words out. But then her other hand is in my hair, threading through the damp strands. It feels too damn good to tell her to stop.

Until it doesn't.

She grasps a handful of my hair and tugs my head back, causing me to cry out and tears to spring to my eyes. At the same time, she slips her hand into my underwear. What she finds makes her groan as her fingers tease over my wet slit.

"What is it, Elise?" She pants, her hot breath fanning over the side of my face. "Is it me or the pain?"

Fuck.

It's both. It's fucking both.

I don't remember the last time I was this turned on. How did I never know this about myself? That I like pain, like to be controlled, dominated.

That I…like girls?

I certainly like *this*. So maybe that's true?

Right now, it's easy not to freak out about the possibility that I might be bisexual. It feels too good to panic about it. If it comes later, so be it. But maybe, on some level, I always knew.

Maybe I just kept it all repressed, too busy with school and planning the rest of my life to let myself give into that part of me.

Well, I'm giving into it now.

I'm shamelessly rocking my hips into her hand, desperately seeking more of her touch as my hands grip her waist.

"Logan," I whimper as I widen my legs on instinct alone.

She moans before biting into the side of my neck as though to hide the sound. Her fingers explore me deeper, pushing past my folds. Her teeth scrape against my skin as she whispers breathlessly, "You're fucking soaked."

She sounds as wrecked as I feel, and if I could think past this haze of lust swirling around in my head, I might wonder if it's genuine. But I'm too elated by the idea that she wants me as badly as I want her.

Even if she does still hate me.

But her touch is still too soft, not where I need her most.

"Logan, please."

"You want me to fuck you with my fingers? You want to come all over my hand?"

"Yes."

It's the quietest *yes*, but the most sincere *yes*.

I shouldn't be surprised she has such a dirty mouth, but it does things to me I never would've expected.

"Beg me for it."

I groan and try to move my head away in frustration, but she still has a tight hold on my hair, baring my throat, her mouth brushing my skin. Two fingers continue teasing my opening, easily slipping through my arousal. The heat in my core flares hot, flames licking at the tension that's almost unbearable.

Maybe this is exactly what she wanted. To be the reason I fall apart, come undone. To make me beg. All so she can taunt me about it later.

But I don't care.

I'm too far gone.

"Please, Logan," I whimper again. "Please make me come."

She bites me again as she thrusts two fingers inside me. The moan I unleash is unlike any sound I've ever made. Her thumb presses against my clit, and I buck frantically as she starts rubbing slow circles while fucking her fingers into me.

Her mouth moves up, and she nips at the shell of my ear before commanding in a husky voice, "Come for me."

This time, I don't lie to myself.

It's her voice. Her fingers in me, on me. Her touch. Her mouth hot against my skin. The little bite of pain she's still giving me from the grip on my hair.

It's *her*.

And I just shatter.

My entire body shakes with the force of the most powerful orgasm I've ever experienced. Wave after wave of pure euphoria crashes into me until I think I'll drown in it. I'm still floating somewhere in that sea of bliss when I feel fingers brushing against my lips, wet with my own release.

"I think you have some self-reflection to do, straight girl."

I open my mouth, but all that comes out is a quiet whimper. I'd tell her the truth if I could—that I might not be so straight after all. But I can't speak. I can barely hold myself up right now, my legs weak and still trembling. She's let go of my hair now, her hand on the nape of my neck as my head rests lazily against the wall.

Logan brings her fingers to her own lips and sucks them into her mouth, moaning around them. Her eyes stay locked on mine as she licks them clean. "Fuck, you taste good. You're doing that on my tongue next time."

"Next time?" The effort it takes to talk causes the words to come out as an embarrassing squeak.

"I figured out what you can give me in exchange for more of my paintings. You don't want tattoos? You can come for me again, just like that, so beautifully."

Her mouth is going to be the death of me.

The heat of her body disappears as she steps back. I suck in a ragged breath like the oxygen we just spent so much time sharing was toxic and I was suffocating without pure air.

She runs her hand through her hair, eyes raking over me as she smiles. No, *smirks*. How the hell is she so composed, so steady, while I'm still trying to figure out which way is up?

"I'll let you know when I have another piece for you."

And with that, she leaves, the soft snick of the door closing behind her making something in me snap.

I wasn't freaking out before, but now my insides are feeling all twisted up. Confused. I let a woman touch me, make me come all over her hand. I *begged* for it. I got off on her control, on the pain she inflicted.

What the fuck is happening to me?

I don't know. But I do know one thing.

This is exactly what she wanted.

7

LOGAN

I couldn't stop. I couldn't fucking stop even when I knew I should have. I didn't *want* to.

Sure, this was all part of the plan. Just the first step.

There's just one little problem.

The moment that first moan escaped her lips, alarm bells went off in my head. Screaming at me to abort mission. It knew something I hadn't considered up until that moment.

How fucking addictive she could become.

How easily I could become obsessed.

But no matter how loud those warnings blared, they were drowned out by my fascination with her, my insatiable need to possess her. No woman has ever been that responsive, like putty in my hands. So willing to let me have my way with her.

I could ruin her so easily.

And I will.

I just need to remind myself why.

Which is why I'm currently making the long drive to see Landon. I need to clear my head and remember why I wanted to knock Elise down to begin with.

I don't regret leaving right after I made her come. I hope the memory of what she let me do to her, of what she begged me to do, kept her up. The thought of leaving her in the midst of an existential crisis gave me some depraved gratification. Almost as much as making her come all over my fingers.

The sunglasses over my eyes do little to block out the glare of the sun shining brightly in the sky. I'm not used to being awake during this time of the day, the sun too hot against my skin.

Heating me up like Elise did yesterday.

The fucking sunshine I'm not used to. Scorching me inside and out.

It's the little things that are throwing me off balance. The way she admires my art. The way she says things that make me angry because they're what I need to hear, not what I *want* to hear. The way she stands up to me until I take all of her control. The way my name sounds on her lips. The way she feels pressed against me and squeezing my fingers. The way she comes apart for me.

The way she fucking *tastes*.

Fuck, that taste.

Consider me addicted and obsessed.

I don't know what compelled me to paint something I knew she'd love, what made me *want* to see that look in her eyes when she first saw it. Even that did something to me.

For five nights straight, I labored over it. From the time I got off work at the studio until I went to bed the next morning,

I was working on it, ignoring all the other projects currently taking up space in my living room.

At least that house is good for one thing. It makes a decent art studio.

Pulling up outside the prison, I park my car and get out. The sun beats down on me, and I almost wish for rain. But it's still too early for those end-of-summer storms.

After I go through the multiple steps of security, I'm directed to take a seat in front of the glass partition. I'm a little surprised that Landon accepted my visit considering it's been so long since I was last here and he hasn't called in several weeks.

When I see him come through a door on the other side of the glass, I understand why.

A fading bruise of mottled yellow and purple circles his left eye, and he has a cut in his bottom lip that looks like it was probably pretty deep.

I pick up the phone on the wall beside my head before he even sits down.

His dark hair is longer than it was last time I visited, hanging partially in front of his eyes like he's trying to hide the bruise. That haunted look in his gaze that's become more and more pronounced with each of my visits is even more prominent. My deepest fear has always been that he'd lose himself in here. At least he's not wasting away. He's bigger than he was when he first went in, probably passing as much time as he can working out.

He sits down, and for a long moment, he simply stares at me through the glass. Like he's debating if he even wants to talk to me because he knows I'm just going to interrogate him until I get answers.

I raise a brow at him sternly, and he visibly sighs before finally picking up the phone on his side. I don't get the chance to say a word before he's already responding to my unspoken question.

"It's not a big deal," he says, his tone laced with exasperation.

"Tell me what the fuck happened."

He runs his hand through his hair and then rests his elbow on the counter. "I was defending another inmate. It wasn't about me. I barely got a slap on the wrist."

That makes me feel marginally better.

"I just don't want you to do anything that makes you stay in here longer."

"I know, Logan. I'm getting out of here as soon as I can. Okay?"

"Does that mean you're coming home?" I hate how my words come out choked as my throat clogs with emotion.

He gives me a small grin. "Where else would I go?"

"It's just…we haven't talked much. Not since Mom died. Not that we did much before that either. We've lost our entire fucking family, Lan. You're here, but you're…not. I don't want to lose you too. I don't—"

"Hey." He stops my frantic rambling in its tracks and leans closer to the glass. "I'm coming home, Logan. I'm up for parole early next year. There's no reason they shouldn't grant it. I'll be home soon, promise. I guess I just…I haven't called much because I'd rather think about you out there not worrying about me. If I don't call, then maybe you can forget I'm in here."

I clench my jaw. "I *never* forget."

He sighs and nods. "Then I promise I'll call more often."

That almost makes me smile. Almost. "Thanks."

We talk a little after that. I don't ask him how he's been because he hates that question. But he asks me about my tattooing and art, and I ask him if the other guy looks worse. The easy way he laughs has me finally feeling a bit more relaxed.

"I see you're keeping my jacket safe for me," he points out, nodding at the black leather jacket I'm wearing despite the summer heat.

I don't go anywhere without it. Just like Landon used to never go anywhere without it. It's one of the only things I can bring myself to keep with me that belonged to someone I loved and lost. Maybe because it reminds me he'll return one day.

I shrug. "It looks better on me. You're not getting it back."

He chuckles, and as I lower my head to try to quiet my own laughter, I feel something…odd. A kind of electric current tingling in the base of my spine.

At first, I think my phone is vibrating in my back pocket until I remember I had to leave it with security. It doesn't happen again right away, so I let it go.

A couple of minutes later into our next conversation about what's been changing around our hometown, I glance down and feel it again. I look behind me, expecting to see someone or something bumping into my chair, sparking this phantom-like sensation. But no one's there.

Am I becoming so in sync with my tattoo gun that I'm starting to feel its vibrations everywhere?

"You okay?" Landon asks.

"Yeah," I mutter, my brow pinched.

Testing a theory, I bend my neck, and there it is again. It zips across my lower back, an annoying vibration in my tailbone.

Fucking lightning arcing up my spine.

Grimacing, I reach up and rub at my neck. I must have a pinched nerve or something. I've probably been overdoing it with all the tattooing and spending so much time on Elise's paintings.

I just need a break. And maybe a chiropractor.

Wanting to change the subject, I look back at Landon. "Guess who's back in town."

I had been debating telling him. I came here to try to get my mind *off* Elise. But maybe knowing I have her in my clutches will let me see more of his smiles and hear more of his laughter.

"Who?"

I smirk. "Elise Novak."

"Logan," he sighs. "Whatever you're thinking about doing, don't."

My smirk grows. "Too late for that."

He shakes his head, his frown the exact opposite reaction I was hoping for. "Seriously, leave her alone. It wasn't her fault."

"How would you know? You don't even remember."

By the way he winces at my words, a barely perceptible reaction, I know he's caught the trace of sarcasm in them. He recovers quickly, his hard stare fixed on me. "I told you I won't talk about it."

"No, fuck that." I lean in and lower my voice. "You expect me to believe that Declan is the *only* one who remembers anything about that night? So which one of you is lying, Landon? You or Elise?"

He says nothing, staring at me from across the glass with a silent scowl.

"Fine. Talk to you again in another few months I guess."

"Logan—"

His voice is cut off as I slam the phone back on the receiver. He stands at the same time I do, his mouth still moving, but I don't stop to attempt to translate it. I spin around, walk right out of the visitation area, and go back through security and out to my car.

Sliding into the driver's seat, I slam my door closed and strike the top of the steering wheel with a fist. My hand throbs. A familiar chasm in my chest threatens to open. I lower my head, but that only makes things worse when another electric shock hits me in the back.

If I ever let myself cry, I know the tears could spill free easily right now. But I won't let them. I never do.

After taking a few deep breaths, I start the engine and drive away.

I hate the thought that my own brother is lying to me. It's easier to believe that he hasn't wanted to talk about it because he really can't remember and doesn't *want* to remember, that he doesn't want to think about Liam because it hurts too damn bad.

It's easier to believe that Elise is the one that's lying.

It's easier to hate her than Landon.

It doesn't matter that he told me to leave her alone. I can't, and I won't.

This trip succeeded in doing exactly what I needed it to. After seeing my brother beaten and bruised, I need an outlet for my hatred more than ever. Instead of being angry with him, I need someone else to direct my rage at.

After today, I want to destroy Elise Novak even more.

8

ELISE

Between shifts at the hospital that have increased from twelve hours to fourteen this last week and being too exhausted to do anything but squeeze in as much sleep as I can once I get home, I haven't had the time nor energy to have a full-on bi panic.

Even if I did, I'm not sure I would.

I think one of Logan's goals was to confuse me, wanting me to freak out about my sexuality. Maybe even feel shame. But the fact that I'm not feeling any of that isn't just a means to spite her.

What I felt ashamed of most when I made out with that blonde in college was that I got drunk enough to do that in the first place.

What I feel ashamed of most about what happened last week was that it was with *Logan*.

It's never been because they were women, and I'm not going to let it be about that now.

I'm bi.

And if I'm being honest, it feels good to shine light on something about myself that's been hidden away in the dark until now.

The fact that it was Logan that helped with that still kind of makes me itch, a creeping beneath my skin I can't reach. I try not to think about the last time I saw her, but...it's just about *all* I can think about.

It's like I can still feel her.

She might hate me, but damn did she know just how to play my body, like it was an instrument she was professionally trained on. Fingers and tongue and teeth moving gracefully, skillfully, as though those few caresses were touching every inch of me.

I've always been an expert at remaining fully concentrated on my work when I'm wearing my white coat, but I realize I've been slipping when the door to my mother's office opens. She peeks her head in, smiles, and then steps inside.

"You should head home early," she says.

"Really?" I glance down at the stack of documents I've been working on for the last hour. "I still have a lot of paperwork to do."

"Declan wants to take us both out to lunch today. You've been working hard this week. You should try to get some rest and come with us."

"Rest? What's that?"

We laugh, but I go ahead and set the papers aside, standing and rounding the desk. We both hang up our lab coats and walk out of the hospital together. My mom tells me when and where to meet her and Declan, and we part ways.

At home, I get a quick shower and crash on the couch because I'm worried I won't want to wake up if I fall into the comforting embrace of my bed.

I'm surprised that I manage to get a few hours of decent sleep. After my nap, I dress in jeans and a light sweater before heading out. I decide to walk since I'm meeting them at The Village just down the street. And it's a nice day.

As I approach the café, I spot them at a table outside. Declan stands and gives me a hug. We haven't seen each other since dinner a couple of weeks ago, so it's good to see him.

"Thanks for taking us out to lunch," I tell him before taking a seat. "How's Sarah doing?"

He shrugs. "We broke up."

My mom and I share a look.

Not surprised.

"Sorry to hear that, sweetie." My mom still sounds sympathetic and sincere. "She was nice."

Declan simply nods.

We order our food, and neither of them are shocked when I order the same thing I get every time. But I add a coffee today because I'm not sure if I'll be able to get more sleep before my shift tonight.

While we wait for our food, we fall into easy conversation. My mom tells us a funny story about how our dad came home the other day smelling like he had spent the entire night in a hotbox. Apparently, that's what some underage kids were doing in their vehicle, and when they opened the door, my dad choked on the smoke. My mom swears his eyes were a little bloodshot.

Our food arrives, and I dig into my sandwich, ravenous. I usually eat a snack or a small meal when I get home from the hospital, but I saved my appetite for this.

"So have you had the time to do anything fun since you've been home?" Declan asks me before taking a bite of his pasta salad.

My mom swallows a spoonful of soup and laughs. "She probably spends all her free time sleeping."

I laugh with her and nod. "Mostly. Although..." I set down the half of sandwich in my hand and peer between them. "I did get a tattoo."

My mom's eyes go a little wide, but I'm almost a hundred percent positive it's because she thinks it's so unlike me. It's not that I think she minds if I get tattoos, even though she doesn't know about the one I already had. Besides, Declan has many. Not as many as Logan, but he has plenty that are visible.

"Oh yeah?" Dec grins, then it falters. "Where'd you go?"

If what he told me several years ago is still true, he goes to a studio in another town to get all his work done. Knowing now just how much animosity Logan still harbors toward me—and probably toward my brother—I'd be willing to bet it's to avoid letting her come near him with a needle.

"The studio here in town, A Touch of Ink. Logan did it."

"Delaney?" my mom asks.

"Yeah. She did a really good job."

"Well, can I see it?" She's smiling now, a curious glint in her eyes.

"It's on my leg. I'll have to show it to you later. But I think you'll like it."

My mom accepts that and picks up her spoon to continue eating.

On the other side of the table, Declan holds his fork in the bowl but doesn't move. He stares at me, eyes narrowed, brow furrowed. Like he's trying to search for something on my face. "So, are you two like…friends now?"

I quickly shake my head. "Definitely not."

Even though it feels good to know myself a little better, I'm not quite ready to tell my family about my newly discovered sexuality. It's not that I think my parents wouldn't accept me no matter what, but it's still too new even to me. And I especially won't be telling them anything about what happened between me and Logan.

"She's doing some paintings for me to help decorate my apartment," I add as I pick my sandwich back up. "That's all."

He nods again. "Just be careful."

"Why?" I ask, my expression mirroring his that hasn't changed.

"Because she's a bitch."

"Declan James!"

My brother's face relaxes, and he chuckles. "Don't middle name me, Mom. I'm just speaking the truth. I can't run into her anywhere without her glaring at me like she's trying to cast some hex to turn me into a cockroach or something."

"That poor girl has had it rough." Mom looks at me with a warm smile. "She could probably use a friend."

"We're not friends."

Even though it's not a lie, I feel bad for some reason. I know I shouldn't. She's made the nature of our agreement crystal clear. She's never hidden her contempt for me. If I so much as claimed we were friends, she'd probably skin me alive.

We all return to our meals as my mom changes the subject, asking Declan how the shop's been doing. The occasional glances he gives me between bites of his food unsettle me as I try and fail to translate what's there just beneath his gaze. It couldn't possibly be suspicion. There's no way he could know what Logan and I have gotten up to. But I still have to keep from squirming beneath his disconcerting scrutiny.

Once we've finished eating, Declan pays for lunch, and Mom and I thank him again as we all exchange hugs. Then Dec says he has to get back to work and leaves. Mom says it's a nice day for a walk, so we stroll through downtown to my apartment together. Once we're upstairs and inside, I excuse myself to go change.

When I come back out of the bedroom in my pajamas, I find my mom standing in front of the newest addition on my wall.

"This is beautiful," she says, and I can tell she means it.

"She did that one after I got this."

She turns to face me, and I lift up the left leg of my shorts to show off the delicate stargazer lily tattooed there. Tilting her head, a wistful smile slowly spreads across her face. "That's beautiful too, Elise. You're right. I do like that. You've always loved the flowers your dad brings me as much as I do."

"He just loves you so much it makes me sick," I say jokingly as I move to stand beside her to stare at my new painting.

My mom turns back toward it too. We share a comfortable silence for nearly a minute while we study it together. I start to wonder what she thinks about it, almost a little nervously as though her thoughts and feelings toward it might be a direct reflection on me.

"Why do you think she paints storms?" she eventually asks.

"Probably because she is one."

My answer is followed by both of our quiet laughter.

But the truth is I wasn't completely joking. Logan is the storm that came blowing violently into my life. I always thought my foundation was strong and steady, but she proved just how fragile it really was, rocking in the face of her fierce winds. Making me sway just like the flowers in this new piece.

Is that what she was thinking about when she painted it?

After my mom leaves, I crawl into my bed, burrowing beneath the covers. During the few hours of sleep I manage to get, I dream of a single lily standing alone in an empty field.

Thunder booms, and it trembles.

Wind gusts, and it's nearly uprooted.

Lightning strikes, and its petals burn and turn to ash.

9

LOGAN

I decided to paint something a little different this time. Yes, there's still a storm. It wouldn't be one of mine if there wasn't.

Instead of a field or mountains, a vast sea takes up the entire bottom half of the canvas, fraught with turbulent, foaming waves that rise up into the horizon. Instead of heavy, dark clouds filling up the sky, they're only along the outer edges, spilling rain and conjuring white lightning. Between them is a sunset, painted in strokes of pinks and oranges, reflecting golden flecks in the water.

Like the eye of the storm.

A sense of peace.

A trick, a deception, as the storm closes in.

I hold it tucked under my arm as I knock on Elise's door. It takes her a little longer than usual to answer. When she does, I can't help but grin at the pink and purple striped pajama pants she's wearing.

"You think that'll stop me?"

The rosy tint that stains her cheeks is almost instantaneous as she shifts on her feet.

I take a step forward, leaning into her space and lowering my voice. "You should know I don't need to see your legs to make you spread them."

"For fuck's sake, Logan," she mutters as that blush deepens. She peers nervously out into the hallway and then takes a step back. "Just get in here."

I move to pass her but stop when my shoulder is brushed against hers, leaning in again as I whisper in her ear. "I'll get in wherever you want, sunshine."

Sunshine?

Where the fuck did that come from?

She snaps her gaze to me and scowls.

Whatever.

It helped rile her up. I won't second guess it.

"You're cute when you're angry," I say casually as I slip past her.

Judging by the loud bang of the door slamming shut behind me, that riled her up too. She stands there flustered and fuming while I start unwrapping the painting, smirking the entire time even though I'm trying to ignore those damn sparks lighting up my spine as I'm bent over. Like last time, I reveal the piece by leaning it against the back of the couch.

Also like last time, her reaction catches me completely off guard.

The subtle parting of her lips. The tension relaxing in her entire body. The look of utter awe in her eyes.

"I hate how talented you are," she says quietly as her gaze drifts up to mine. There's a faint frown on her face, adding to the truth in her words.

I couldn't even begin to explain why that bothers me.

I can feel the deflection in the next smug smirk I give her. "Are we talking about the painting now?"

She rolls her eyes, and I can't tell if she blushes again or if the same one flushing her face before just brightens. "How much?"

"One orgasm." I nearly laugh with how big her eyes get. "Actually, make that three."

Shaking her head, she mumbles, "You're fucking ridiculous."

I decide to show her a little mercy and give her my price. In dollars. She transfers the money from her phone, and I help her hang the painting.

The moment it's secure on its hook, I spin Elise around and trap her against the wall, my hands on either side of her. Her fresh scent invades my nose. Her damp hair has left wet spots on the shoulders of her shirt.

"Now, about those orgasms…"

She presses herself tightly against the wall like she's trying to keep as much space between our bodies as possible. She lifts her chin in the air, but I detect a slight tremble in it. "I'm not letting you manipulate me again, Logan."

"But you enjoyed it so much," I taunt, leaning in until I know she can feel the warmth of my breath on her face. "I believe I said you'd be doing it on my tongue next time."

"And I'm saying no," she says, standing her ground.

"Still want to claim you're not queer after what you let me do to you?" I tug my bottom lip between my teeth as I let my eyes sweep down to her breasts that I really wish weren't covered by that damn oversized shirt. "What you *begged* me to do to you?"

Just replaying that memory has heat pooling between my legs.

"No. I'm bi. Happy now?"

I narrow my eyes. "That easy for you?"

"Oh, I'm sorry," she says, not sounding sorry at all. "Did you want me to freak out?"

Did I?

Okay, maybe just a little. I would have enjoyed her confusion and suffering, watching her fight something she didn't want. I guess I just hate her *that* much.

"Maybe," I answer honestly.

"Happy to disappoint."

My glare turns into a full-on scowl. "So what then? You have a bi-awakening, realize you like girls, come all over my fingers, and you *don't* want a repeat?"

"Not with you." She says it easily, *too* easily.

My face starts to fall, but I catch it and quickly clench my jaw.

What the fuck?

It's not her brutal honesty that catches me off guard. It's my reaction to it. It's the way it feels as though she stabbed a knife in my chest and twisted.

I'm not used to rejection. That's all it is.

"You sure about that?" I ask between gritted teeth.

Taking one hand off the wall, I wrap it around her throat, not lightly but not tight enough to cut off her air. I bask in the way her eyes widen, her breath hitching.

"What are you doing?" she asks, her voice far less steady than before.

"Proving a point." I press my body into hers and roll my hips. Her pulse beats faster beneath my hand. "That you *do* want me. Even if it's just what I can give you."

When her gaze dips down to my mouth, mine instinctively finds hers too. Her lips look so soft—a beautiful, natural blush pink. Biteable. Kissable.

But I won't be doing that. I'm already way in over my head as it is. At risk of getting sucked into her orbit and never being able to hurl myself back out.

Instead, I lean in and nip at her jaw. Lightly at first, then harder until she gasps. I continue rocking my hips, grinding into her, as I bite and lick my way up her jaw. Her chest heaves against mine, her panting breaths warm against my cheek. The moment I sink my teeth into the soft flesh of her ear, she thrusts her hips forward to meet mine and lets out a slow, soft, whimpering moan.

"Fuck, you make pretty noises."

Having proven my point, I suddenly release her and step back out of her space. Her body slumps forward, like she's trying to chase after my touch. She stares at me beneath her thick lashes with a hint of betrayal and a lot of desire.

Biting back a smirk, I shrug with a mask of indifference. "But I guess if you have enough of my paintings…"

I turn my back on her and head toward the door.

"Wait."

This time, I let my mouth curl with all the cruel amusement I feel. But it's just for me. When I turn back to her, my arms crossed over my chest, it's back to the neutral expression.

"I was just kidding about the paintings. I'll still do more if you want them."

"I do, but…" She remains standing with her back against the wall, her chest still rising with quick, shallow breaths. When she finally meets my gaze, her brows are drawn tight. "Why?"

"Why what?"

She swallows and lowers her voice as though she's worried someone may overhear. "Why would you want to have sex with me? You hate me."

Damn her for always wanting to *communicate*.

I shrug again. "Haven't you ever had hate sex before?"

She shakes her head, a barely perceptible movement that I might have missed if I wasn't currently so fixated on her.

"Well, I haven't either. Thought it'd be fun."

For some reason, that causes her mouth to twitch. "You want to be my experiment?"

I drop my arms and slowly stalk back toward her. Stopping in front of her, I dip my head forward, my lips two inches from hers as I whisper, "I want to be your damnation."

Those pretty pink lips of her part on an exhale. I feel it on my face, the warmth of it soaking through my pores and traveling down to my core. The temptation to kiss her, to bruise those lips, returns, but I resist. Barely.

"You want company in hell?" she asks with a twinkle in her hazel eyes.

I grab her by the front of her shirt, fisting the fabric as I spin her around, her back toward the hallway, which I assume leads to her bedroom.

"What I want is you laid out on your bed, coming apart for me."

Her eyes widen, and a blush rises in her cheeks.

It's one of those things I'm obsessed with—the way she reacts to me. She's a challenging opponent, biting back with her own brand of venom. At least until I get my own teeth in her.

Releasing her, I shrug out of my jacket and drape it over the back of the couch. I'm wearing a black tank top underneath, and her eyes trace the length of my bare arms, most of the skin covered in black ink.

There are a few small flowers, dark clouds, silhouettes of trees, a moon peeking out from behind mountains. But what her gaze eventually sticks on is the shitty little lightning bolt on the inside of my wrist that I gave myself when I was seventeen.

Elise reaches out and brushes the tips of her fingers over the tattoo. The soft touch sends a shiver through me.

"This was your first one, wasn't it?" she asks in a reflective, hushed tone.

I yank my arm out of her reach and glare at her. I think my left eye even twitches. "This isn't a date, Elise." My voice comes out a little deeper as a result of my sudden irritation. "You don't have to *get to know me* or some shit. In fact, that's highly discouraged."

Her face falls.

Fucking hell. It's like I just kicked a puppy.

But then her demeanor shifts. She sets her jaw and lifts her chin. Her hands go to the bottom hem of her shirt, and...

And...

Holy fucking shit.

I think my brain short circuits as I watch her raise her shirt and slip it off over her head before dropping it to the floor at her feet.

As much as I wish I could hold eye contact and feign indifference, that's completely impossible.

I'm human.

I'm weak.

My gaze immediately drops as she bares her chest to me. It's not just the sight of her perfect breasts and dusky pink nipples that has my mouth watering. It's her surprising confidence too. I love those nervous blushes and wary looks she gives me as much as I do those moments she lets her courage shine.

When she fights fire with fire.

It's official.

Elise Novak fucking does it for me.

"Fine." She shrugs, the movement causing her chest to shudder. "Sex is just sex, right? That's what you want? I can do that."

I take one step forward because I think that's about all I can manage right now. "Can you?"

The corner of her mouth twitches. "Watch me."

And I do. I watch as she spins around and starts heading down the hallway. My eyes drift down the expanse of her back, all soft, creamy skin, and down to her ass still covered in those cursed pajama pants.

As I finally force my feet to move to follow her, I unscrew the ball from the bar in my tongue and remove the piercing, shoving it into my pocket. From the same pocket, I take out another bar, this one with a larger top on it. I can't keep the wicked grin off my face as I push it through my tongue and screw the ball on.

Entering the bedroom, I find her standing at the foot of the bed, staring down at the sheets. I step up behind her and sweep her now mostly dry hair off one shoulder. Leaning forward, I run the tip of my tongue up the column of her throat, and she shivers.

"Nervous?" I ask, speaking quietly because this particular piercing affects my speech a bit.

However, she doesn't seem to notice.

"No." Her voice trembles nearly as much as her body does.

"Liar," I whisper in her ear.

I move my left hand to her other shoulder, my fingers lightly brushing across her back and then down her spine, making her shiver again. My other hand travels over her waist, up her stomach, and stops to cup her right breast. When I roll her already hard nipple between my thumb and forefinger, she gasps, and I wish I was swallowing the sound into my mouth.

Goosebumps rise beneath my palm as my left hand continues its path around her body, my touch turning rougher as I pause to grip her hip harshly, pulling her body closer into mine and crushing my chest into her back. As my hand dips lower, moving toward her core, her breaths come faster, shallower.

Her head is practically rolling back on my shoulder as I easily slip beneath the waistbands of her pants and underwear.

"Fuck. You're so wet for me."

She moans. "Logan."

The moment she whimpers my name, I release her. I swear my entire body is about to burst into flames.

I shove her, and she falls onto the plush white comforter with a quiet *oomph*. She rolls over onto her back and sits up, reaching for the hem of my shirt. I bat her hand away and glare down at her.

"You're not going to let me see you?" she asks with a cute as fuck frown on her face.

"You don't need to see me to come for me."

She groans and falls back on the bed.

Right where I want her.

She's clearly already pretty far gone if she hasn't noticed the larger piece of metal in my tongue, causing me to speak a little differently.

Good. She'll realize it when my face is buried between her legs.

It's not that I'm shy or self-conscious about my body. It's not that I don't like being seen or touched. I just don't want to be seen or touched by *her*. It's a little because I hate her and a little more because I have to proceed with caution lest this plan completely blow up in my face.

When I place a knee on the edge of the mattress, she widens her legs and scoots backward. I crawl onto the bed and hover over her. She stares up at me, hunger in her eyes as they find my lips.

I don't let her consider it for long before I lower my head and take one of her nipples into my mouth. The taste of her along with the soft moans that slip past her lips has the heat in my lower belly flaring so hotly that it negates any other weird sensations that may be happening in my body.

As I swirl my tongue around her nipple, my hands move to the hem of her pants, slowly pulling them down. She lifts her hips, and before my mouth leaves her, I bite. A cry escapes her, leaving me grinning as I sit up to remove her pants and underwear, wanting her naked right the fuck now. Her panties are soaked, so I'm not surprised to see her pussy glistening with wetness and need.

My mouth fucking waters.

Then I notice the tattoo, the only other one she said she had. It's a small turtle, done in a simple black outline on her hip, right above the crease of her thigh.

I'd ask her about it, but I already told her we weren't doing that.

That and I'm too fucking impatient.

I can't wait any longer, so I don't.

Settling lower on the bed, I push her legs further apart as I let my gaze linger on her—on this part of her that I've been dying to get my eyes, tongue, and teeth on for too damn long now.

Once my eyes have had their fill, it's my tongue's turn.

I lean down and swipe the tip of my tongue over her slit, lapping up a taste of her juices.

Fuck.

She tastes just like she smells—a little sweet and a little musky. Not at all in a bad way. Sweet like honey. Musky like bourbon.

Just a taste, and I'm already drunk off her.

I dive my tongue in a little deeper this time, ending with a teasing flick over her clit. Her moan fills the room. I peer up at her to see her thick lashes fluttering against her flushed cheeks and her lips parted, her chest heaving as she pants.

That wicked grin of mine returns as I reach for the bar in my tongue and tighten the screw on top.

Her eyes fly open at the sound it makes. "What—"

I dive back in.

"Oh, fuck!"

The vibrating bar hits its target as I press it to her clit. I keep it there even as she writhes beneath me, rolling her hips and bucking up into my mouth, crying out as though she's begging for mercy.

The vibrations aren't all that strong, but I suspect she's never experienced anything like this based on the response and all those delicious noises she makes.

It doesn't take long before her entire body trembles with the force of her climax. She's gripping my hair tight, but I let her get away with it. I don't mind the bite of pain, and I'm too entranced by the way she unravels.

After the wave of her orgasm passes, her body slumps on the bed, her hands falling to her sides. She's still jerking from the stimulation until I show her a little mercy and lift my head.

"Holy fuck," she mutters between heavy, ragged breaths.

"I want another one."

"Logan," she whines.

I shake my head, smirking. "I said three."

"Oh my—*God!*"

I go back at her like a starving woman, licking up all the fresh flavor she's given me. It's on my lips, my chin, soaking my face. But it's still not nearly enough.

I want more.

I want all of it.

As I press the bar back to her clit, reveling in the way her hips roll, rocking her pussy against my mouth, I bring two fingers to the heat of her, pressing them through her slick entrance. Her breathless moan fills my ears as I curl my fingers inside her.

Her second orgasm is even more satisfying than the first.

She lays boneless as she tries to catch her breath.

Well, can't have that.

With my fingers still inside her, I move them in a wave, pressing up against that spot that has her hips bucking again and something like a sob catching in her throat.

Fucking hell. My underwear are soaked. I can feel them sticky between my thighs.

"Logan, I can't."

"Yes, you can. You *will*."

I use my free hand to unscrew the bar in my tongue just enough to turn it off. I want this orgasm to be all because of me.

All mine.

My tongue is feeling a little numb, but that doesn't slow me down. I lick up as much of her arousal as I can, swallowing it down and savoring the taste, before shoving my tongue inside her along with my fingers. Like I can siphon even more out of her.

Her hands find my hair again, tangling in the strands, while mine that's not currently inside her lands on her stomach.

It moves rapidly beneath my palm as I sink my nails into her smooth, soft skin.

The noise she makes is a moan, a cry, a choked sob all in one.

As my tongue returns to her clit, flicking the sensitive bud over and over, my nails scratch up her stomach. I roughly grab her left breast, kneading it in my hand.

Her third orgasm takes a little longer, but I can be patient when I need to be.

And it's worth it.

With two fingers inside her, my tongue lavishing her clit, and my other hand rolling and pinching her nipple, she breaks for a third time with a soft cry, trembling even more violently than before. The way she clenches around my fingers drives me fucking wild.

I slip them out of her and suck them clean. Her pussy is so wet and swollen, I can't resist the urge to gently clean her up too, lapping the juices from between her slit.

She whimpers and hisses until I've finally decided I'm done with her.

Sitting up, I wipe at my face, mourning every drop of flavor I won't get to taste.

Elise has her arm thrown over her face that glistens with a thin sheen of sweat. Her bare chest rises and falls enticingly with each panting breath, and bright pink claw marks decorate her stomach.

More of my marks left on her.

"I *really* hate how talented you are," she mutters, repeating her sentiment from earlier.

I can't help but laugh at that as my ego does a little victory dance.

As I remove the vibrating tongue piercing and replace it with my usual one, she drops her arms and stares at me. The longer she does, the deeper the crease between her brows gets.

"What about you?"

I tilt my head, my mouth curling at one corner. "You want to make me come?"

"Yes," she breathes, so desperately like she wants nothing more in the world than to give me what I just gave her.

If I didn't hate her, I might just let her.

Just the thought of her mouth or fingers—or any part of her—on me has me shifting on the bed and realizing just how fucking wet I am. There's an ache in my core that I can't wait to relieve.

Later.

I shrug. "No thanks."

She scoffs as I climb off the bed. Scooting back against the pillows, she grabs the corner of the comforter and throws it over her naked body like I didn't just spend the last twenty minutes with my face buried in her pussy. Like she didn't just come all over my fingers and tongue three times in a row.

I stare at her and lick my lips.

Fuck, I can still taste her on me.

"So…five for the next painting?"

She rolls her eyes, but she can't hide the grin she's clearly trying to suppress. "Get the hell out of here."

"You're welcome," I say with a wink before turning and leaving her bedroom.

On my way out of her apartment, I grab my jacket and stop to take one last look at the newest painting hung on her wall. Somehow, it looks different to me.

Like maybe it's not a sunset, but a sunrise.

Like maybe the storm isn't closing in, but receding in the midst of daybreak.

I wonder if Elise Novak is strong enough to hold back the rain and thunder and lightning.

10

ELISE

I've never come that hard in my entire life. Or that many times.

It's like I can still feel her down there.

Everywhere.

It's been a week, and I can't get that morning out of my head. I can't get *her* out of my head. For someone who claims to hate me, she sure did enjoy making me feel good. Even if she did hurt me a little as well. Though…I won't deny I liked that too.

She said she wants to be my damnation, and it looks like she's getting exactly what she wants.

I have a more difficult time than ever concentrating at work, but just while I'm in the office doing paperwork and clinical documentation. When I'm helping my mom on cases, I somehow manage to focus and not screw anything up.

Before Logan left that morning, I almost asked her for her phone number. Only because she keeps showing up and

I never know when to expect her. She could at least text me first. But then I realized what we're doing is supposed to mean nothing, and I didn't want to give her more ammunition to be cruel about it.

Is it really going to happen again?

Do I *want* it to happen again?

Yes.

Undeniably yes.

But, unfortunately, I want more. I want to touch her too. I want to explore her body the way she explored mine. If this is supposed to be an experiment of my sexuality, shouldn't I get to find out how it feels to be on the other side?

I know I shouldn't want anything with her. I give into her too easily. But there's this pull I feel when I'm near her, not unlike the first time I saw her painting. Except, with her, it's like I'm trying to find what my eyes can't see, what's not as clearly visible. Maybe that's just me *hoping* something exists where it doesn't.

If I never find it, at least it'll be that much easier when she finally decides to leave me behind in the dust.

And she will. Because I'm well aware of the game she's playing.

When I get home from work a week later, I don't immediately hop in the shower like usual. I'm expecting a call from Darcy this morning. We haven't had a chance to really talk since I moved back home, and considering we're both in residency, we have to plan our calls in advance with how many hours we're putting in.

I decide to kill some time while I wait by cleaning the apartment a little. I turn on some music and take care of the few dishes in the sink, leaving them to dry in the rack. I'm in the middle of dusting when my phone dings with a notification. I half expect it to be Darcy texting me to tell me she has to reschedule the call because she's working late or something. Instead, I find a text from Declan.

Dec: So what are you doing for me for my birthday next month?

I grin and shake my head as I text him back.

Me: Lol. What do you want?

Dec: A tattoo.

I roll my eyes but then narrow them down at my phone screen. Between the way he reacted last week when I told him and my mom that Logan gave me a tattoo and now this text, I can't help but be a bit suspicious.

Me: I could talk to Logan.

Dec: She's not coming anywhere near me with a needle. We should go to my guy and get tattoos together.

Me: She did a good job on mine.

Dec: She probably has the hots for you.

Me: So what if she does? She's not that bad.

Okay, so she *is* bad.

But there's a part of me that wishes we could all get along. Maybe it's that naive part that wants to see the good in everyone and believe that everything will eventually work itself out.

We may never have been close with Logan, but that wasn't our fault. Declan and I got along well with Liam and Landon, but Logan was the black sheep of the family. We could have tried harder to include her, but I don't think it would've changed anything.

When my phone goes off again, I look away from my newest painting I was just staring at and down at my screen.

Dec: Don't be gross. Let's just go to my guy.

Gross?

Maybe the comment was based on the animosity between them and not because Logan is gay, but it still gets under my skin.

Me: Fine. But I wish you'd get over this Logan thing.

Those three dots appear to show that he's typing. Then they stop. They start again only to disappear a couple more times before my phone rings.

I smile, forgetting all about Declan, and answer the call.

"Hey, Darce."

"Hey, Dr. Novak."

I laugh quietly. "How have you been?"

"Just as busy in my second year of residency as my first. I feel bad I haven't had a chance to talk since you graduated."

"Don't even worry about it. I haven't had much time either."

"Do you regret it yet?"

"Just the student loans."

Her laughter reaches my ear from the other line. "Tell me about it!"

As we fall into easy conversation for the next twenty minutes, I settle on the couch, lying on my back with my feet hanging over the armrest. We talk for a while about how residency is going for us, how busy and tired we often are. We talk about how nice it is to be back home and closer to our families. As we move on to reminisce about college and share stories, a particular one of mine comes back to me.

"Did you ever…experiment while you were in school?" I ask hesitantly.

"As in?"

I take a deep breath in. "As in…with women."

"Oh." The amusement in her voice tugs at my already frayed nerves. "Did you?"

I laugh, expelling all that nervous air in my lungs. But it still lingers. "Don't avoid the question."

"No, I didn't." There's nothing in her tone to make me suspect she's lying. "I guess I missed out on that particular experience." When I don't respond right away, she says, "Your turn. Did you?"

"I mean…" I clear my throat. "There was this one party I was at. I got drunk and…might've made out with another girl."

"Woah." When she laughs, there's no trace of judgment or disgust, which has the tension in my shoulders relaxing. "Innocent little Elise isn't so innocent after all."

"The thing is...I don't think it was just an experiment."

"Oh. So are you..."

"Bi."

"Oh, okay. Well, I'm glad you knew you could trust me with that."

I didn't, but I guess I should've since she's my best friend. It feels good to tell someone too, to admit it out loud. At least to somebody who isn't intent on hating me until the end of days.

Darcy and I talk for a while longer, and I'm thankful she doesn't pry too deep. While I'm starting to open up and accept my sexuality, Logan is an entirely different beast. She might be responsible for my bi-awakening, but she's temporary. There's no point in telling anyone about her.

For some reason I can't quite explain to myself, that leaves me a little sad by the time I end the call with Darcy.

Did I *want* to tell her about Logan?

Maybe. But I know it would've been a bad idea.

After I'm off the phone, I pull up the new text I have.

Dec: I just don't trust her, Elise. You shouldn't either.

I consider pointing out that she doesn't trust him either. Or me, for that matter.

Instead, I turn my screen off and drag myself off the couch to go get a shower. I'm suddenly mentally and physically drained and can't wait to shut my brain off for a few hours and get some sleep.

Having a bi-awakening during my first year of residency is exhausting.

11

LOGAN

I went to the doctor last week. The only reason I did was because I did what everyone's guilty of doing—I searched my symptoms online. That really strange and annoying vibration I get in the base of my spine every time I bend my neck forward only seemed to lead to one diagnosis. Surprisingly, it wasn't cancer like ninety percent of symptoms always point to according to the internet. But it was still…scary.

However, when I told my doctor about it, she said what I first suspected, that it was most likely a pinched nerve. Maybe I should've asked for some testing or to see a specialist. Something in my gut was telling me we were both wrong. But honestly…knowing is just as scary as not knowing.

Besides, if I ignore it, maybe it'll go away.

And it did.

I haven't felt it in the past few days, so the nerve thing was probably right.

See. It's always best to just ignore your problems.

Which is exactly what I've been doing with another *problem* of mine.

Elise fucking Novak.

I can't deny that she's gotten under my skin.

I'm like a moth to a flame.

I've had to resist the temptation to show up at her apartment before I even have a new painting for her. But without an excuse to see her and do more dirty things to her, I'd be giving myself away.

I might be purposefully taking my time with this next painting. The longer I can stay away, the more time I have to try to desensitize myself to the effect she has on me.

If I wasn't so weak, I would've kissed her that day. With how intently she was staring at my mouth, she clearly wanted me to. And I *am* supposed to be giving her reasons to trust me—to maybe even *like* me enough so that I can ruin her.

But it's so fucking damn hard to be *likable* around her.

If this plan doesn't work, I'll only have myself to blame.

Heavy metal blares through the house as my brush moves across the canvas. I go back to my palette, mixing a little of the gray paint with the white, before making a few more strokes across the landscape of snow.

Instead of a rainstorm this time, it's a blizzard.

I didn't really think or plan this one out before I started. I just knew I wanted to do something different. Everything is gray and white and black. Thick, gray clouds. Heavy, white snow. Silhouetted, black trees.

Everything is cold.

Like how I've been toward Elise, how I need to continue being for my own fucking sanity. Safe in my cold, unfeeling shell of stone, the one I've spent years building. I'll be damned if Elise Novak is the one to crack it.

Okay, not everything is without color. I know that's one element that made Elise come to me for more. I still want her to buy this one. I still want her to like it, to *admire* it.

However, what little color exists is almost completely buried beneath the weight of snow. Indistinguishable flowers with petals of yellow and orange and pink bow under an icy blanket of white.

The painting is nearly finished. It just needs a few finishing touches.

Suddenly, the deafening music booming through the house abruptly stops. I turn to find Tate leaning against the wall beside my sound system.

"I was knocking, but I'm not surprised you couldn't hear shit with all that god-awful noise."

"It's not noise," I mutter as I go back to painting.

Sometimes, I need the loud, angry music to drown out my angry thoughts.

"What are you doing here?" I ask as I collect more paint on my brush.

It's Sunday night, my night off from the tattoo studio. It's late, nearly midnight I think. I tend to lose track of time when I paint.

"Just got off work. Thought I'd stop by and see if you wanted to hang."

"I want to try to finish this tonight."

"That's cool. I don't mind chilling here." He comes to stand beside me, arms crossed as he stares at the image I've created. "You've been working on this one for a while, haven't you?"

I nod and resist the urge to gouge out his eyes. For some reason, I hate that he's seeing it before Elise.

"You already got into her pants. Why keep trying so hard?"

I clench my teeth and breathe in through my nose. "I regret telling you anything."

I really do. But it was his idea, after all. Besides, I had hoped if I told him, he could help keep me on track. Except when he makes his crude jokes and reminds me how close I am to the sweet taste of victory, it makes it all feel so cheap. Like it was a secret that would've been better if it was all mine.

Tate laughs and moves away toward the couch. He plops down on the threadbare cushions and rests his feet up on the coffee table. He knows I don't particularly care for this place, so he's never really treated it with respect. Which is perfectly fine with me.

The carpet and furniture in the living room are splattered with paint because I never bothered to cover anything when I converted it to a makeshift art studio. Blank canvases and forgotten, unfinished artwork are propped up against the walls. It's not that the house is dirty. I keep it clean. I just don't bother to try to make it feel like home anymore.

As I continue my work, I feel Tate's eyes on me. Without my music, it's more difficult to concentrate.

Giving up, I set my palette and brush down on the table and finally give him my reluctant attention. The curious, amused look he's pinning me with has me bristling.

"What?"

He shakes his head and shrugs. "Nothing."

I roll my eyes and stalk into the kitchen as I wipe my hands on my paint-stained basketball shorts. "Want a beer?"

"Sure."

I come back into the living room with two bottles, handing him one as I sit beside him. As I take a drink, I stare at my work in progress. I'm surprised to see that from farther away, the color stands out more, vibrant hues popping against the otherwise monochrome scene. I scowl at it, like the stubborn colors exist without my permission.

"Jacklyn said she and her husband found a place in Oregon."

My head twists to the side to look at Tate, grasping onto the change of subject. "Did she say what she's doing with the studio?"

"Not yet." Tate takes a swallow from his beer. "Probably selling it though. I think she's waiting to talk to you."

I smile at that. Jacklyn and I have always been close as far as boss and employee go, maybe even something closer to friends since we spend time outside of work too. I don't think it would be all that difficult to convince her to let me buy it from her. As long as I can get a loan.

Or, hell, I'd sell this fucking house if I had to.

"Know any good Realtors?" I ask Tate with a grin.

"Me?" He lets out a loud laugh. "No. But I can ask around."

"Do that."

With happier thoughts manifesting in my mind, I peer around my living room slash art studio. My gaze drifts to the hallway that leads to the bedrooms.

Landon's room.

Liam's old room.

And just like that, the doubt creeps in.

Am I ready to let go of the past?

I couldn't stall any longer. There was no work left to be done. As much as I wanted to paint over every last flower, to dull their colors, I couldn't bring myself to do it. They had survived the blizzard for a reason, so I let them be.

But also…I wasn't sure how much longer I could go without seeing Elise.

Which pisses me the fuck off.

I'm still obsessed. Still addicted. And going through withdrawals.

I wonder what would happen if I just gave into all of that. If I chose to let the shit go and let myself have something without putting an expiration date on it. If I didn't have to think about this effect she has on me ending.

If I have to consider selling my family's house, I'd have to let go of a lot. Could I do that with her?

Do I *want* to?

I don't know, and I'm not sure I want to know.

Yet here I am, again, standing outside her door.

She answers it a few seconds after I knock, looking a little surprised to see me. It's been nearly two weeks since I brought her the last painting, so maybe she thought our deal was done.

Not even close.

She's back to wearing her little shorts, still with the oversized T-shirts. Her hair is mostly dry, and her fresh shower and eucalyptus scent hits me immediately. Like a damn Pavlovian dog, my mouth begins to water.

Maybe I should start choosing a different time to show up.

I push my way past her into the apartment before I pounce.

The door closes behind me as I start unwrapping the painting. We both know the routine by now and feel no need to speak. As I reveal the new piece of art to add to Elise's collection, propping it up against the back of the sofa, the silence hangs even heavier in the air.

I swear I see her shiver.

Like the gloomy winter wonderland has pierced through her exterior and formed ice crystals in her veins.

But then a small smile curls her lips. "It's different."

I clear my throat and shift on my feet. "Bad different?"

She shakes her head and meets my gaze. "It's beautiful."

The tension in my shoulders eases. I think it's safe to say any self-confidence issues I might have are limited to my art.

After we hang it on the wall and she transfers the money, she leans her ass against the couch and studies the painting. Her head is tilted, her full lips parted. I can practically see the flowers reflected in her eyes, color swirling within the golden halos. The pensive expression she wears makes her look even softer somehow.

"It kind of reminds me of skiing in Vail."

I look away, realizing I had been staring, and take in the wintry scene with her. I can see how she would associate it with Vail, with its hills in the background, atmospheric perspective done in whites and grays.

"I went with my family a couple of times," I tell her, not even sure exactly why I'm sharing. "I preferred snowboarding."

I told her I didn't want her to try to get to know me, and here I am offering up information without hesitating.

"We should go sometime."

My entire body freezes, my muscles stiffening, my spine going rigid.

"I'm sorry." Elise laughs like she's not even a fraction as uncomfortable as I suddenly am. "I forgot who I was talking to for a second."

Before I can even think of a response, Elise moves to stand in front of me. On instinct, because my body knows exactly where it wants her, my legs widen, and she settles between them. The moment her hips are flush with mine, my core throbs and aches with need.

The time I purposefully spent away from her did fuck all.

If anything, my body is screaming at me for denying it this glorious contact with her soft, warm one for too damn long. The problem, however, is the bold initiative she's taking. Her making the first move is throwing me off.

I open my mouth, but my words get stuck in my throat. I clear them away and try again. "What are you doing?"

"You painted something for me. I thought…"

"Maybe you thought wrong."

"Oh." Her face falls but only by a fraction. "Okay."

I can't tell if she's sad or disappointed. If she's either, she hides it well.

When she takes a step back, I don't let her take more. I grab both her arms and pull her back, crushing her body to me. Her mouth ends up about two inches from mine.

"I said maybe," I say, my voice a little deep and assertive.

I make a split-second decision.

No second thought.

I claim her mouth with mine.

Our lips crash with brutal intensity. Our kiss is fierce and feral. At least it is on my end, desperate to taste her. Her lips are softer than I imagined they'd be, and they move compliantly under mine. She makes a little gasp, and I swallow it, taking the opportunity to drive my tongue into her mouth, licking against hers with a kind of eager fervency I didn't know I possessed.

My left hand travels to her hip, holding her flush against me with a harsh grip, while my right hand moves to the back of her neck, my fingers tangling in her hair. All the while, I continue ravishing her mouth with mine.

All I feel is the heat of her, the softness of her skin, her hair.

All I smell is her scent.

All I hear are her quiet moans.

All I know is that I never want to stop.

Then she goes and fucking ruins it. She places her hands on my waist and pushes herself back half a step, breaking our connection. She's panting heavily, her chest still brushing against mine with every breath, eyelashes fluttering against her flushed cheeks as she keeps her eyes closed.

"Have you never heard of breathing?" she asks with a small grin at the corner of her red, swollen lips.

"Not when it comes to you."

Fuck.

Why the hell did I just say that?

Because it turns out I don't care so much about air when I can breathe her instead.

Her eyes fly open, already locked on mine. There's so much behind those bright sunbursts, silent thoughts so close to the surface that if I stared hard enough, I could probably coax them out.

If she said what she was thinking right now, would I like what I heard?

When the fuck did I even start caring?

Before either of us can think more about my careless declaration, I shove her backwards. "Bedroom. Now."

She stumbles but then plants her feet, rooting herself so I can't advance. When I try, she lays her hand flat on my chest. I wrap my fingers around her wrist and pull her hand away, twisting her arm behind her back while hauling her forward. She lets out a soft cry, and, once more, her breasts end up pressed against mine.

There's an irrational anger coursing through me, different than the more rational kind I usually feel toward her. This time, I'm pissed at *myself*. Like I continuously grow more and more furious at my lack of control with each little brick of my wall she chips away.

I probably shouldn't take it out on her. But judging by the way her lips part, the way her breaths come quicker, the warmth of each exhale fanning across my face...

She likes it.

"Logan," she whimpers.

I tighten my grip around her wrist, hard enough to leave bruises. "What, Elise? Tell me what you want."

Breathless words whisper across my lips. "I want you naked."

Well, I wasn't expecting *that*.

But when I feel that throbbing ache deep down in my core, it's pretty clear I want nothing more than to roll around naked with her.

Releasing her, I shove her backwards again. "Then you'll have me naked."

12

ELISE

"*Then you'll have me naked.*"

Those words light me up from the inside out, flames licking their way across my skin and between my legs. It could also be the way she looks at me as she stalks after me while I back away toward the bedroom, a predatory gleam in her eyes.

I watch, enraptured, as she shrugs out of her leather jacket and drops it on the floor of the hallway. Her black tank top comes next, revealing a black sports bra and even more pale skin, decorated with black ink and only the occasional color.

Her eyes stay locked on mine as she leans over to untie the laces of her boots, like she's afraid I might run off if she looks away for even a second.

My heart is pounding so fast, the risk of that may not be zero.

After her boots are off, she continues her hunt, pursuing me down the hallway as her hands go to the buttons of her black jeans.

"I'm starting to feel a little left out here, Elise," she purrs as she pushes her pants past her hips and down her thighs.

That fire in my core grows hotter at the sound of my name on her lips. And then it's fucking scorching the moment I see those black boy short underwear.

The fever in my body must have caused some short circuit in the wiring of my brain, but my mind finally registers her words. I quickly pull my shirt up and over my head, tossing it away onto the floor. My nipples are already hard as they greet the air. I didn't think it was possible, but Logan's eyes darken even more.

"Your body is fucking glorious," she hums as she takes another step toward me.

The heat spreads to my cheeks. I've never loved my body, but I've never hated it either. I just exist in it. I've never thought of myself as sexy before, but the way this woman looks as though she wishes she could fuck me with her eyes makes me feel desirable.

The dangerous problem that's quickly developing the more we're together is that I only long to be desirable to *her*.

I know the game she's playing with me, despite what she said earlier. I know whatever it is we're doing is temporary, but I can't deny she makes me feel things I've never felt before. And it's not just because she's a woman. She turns me on more than anyone ever has. I don't think I've ever had to change my underwear in the middle of the day because of how wet I got. The orgasms she gives me are explosive.

Being with her is...*easy*. Which probably doesn't make much sense considering how much she hates me.

Maybe I should feel bad that she's Liam's sister, but I don't. What Liam and I had wasn't anything like this. We were two best friends who thought we owed it to ourselves to try to be more. Since he's been gone, I've always remembered him as the guy I could be myself around, my friend who was always there for me.

By the time she's backed me all the way into the bedroom, I'm down to nothing but my soaked panties while she stands there in matching black bra and boy shorts.

Her eyes flick down to the evidence of my arousal, then up again. They linger around my hip where just the top of my tattoo peeks out above the hem of my underwear. "Why a turtle?"

"You're not naked yet," I say, purposefully deflecting the question.

Her gaze meets mine, darkening even more. "Just for that, you first."

I huff. "That's not fair."

"Elise." Her tone is harsh and husky. A warning.

A shiver snakes up my spine. I never would've thought I'd enjoy being dominated, to submit to someone, especially to someone like Logan.

I was never obsessed with the bad boys.

Apparently, a bad girl is my weakness.

Besides, she's made me realize a lot of things about myself. Why not that too? I've always felt like I have to have control over every aspect of my life. Perfect daughter. Perfect student. Perfect doctor.

Being with Logan is...freeing.

I don't feel like I have to be perfect. I just have to be whatever she tells me to be. Whatever she wants me to be.

Slowly, I slip my thumbs into the waistband of my panties and slide them down my legs, the fabric sticky against my skin as I take my time. It's not until Logan's eyes are damn near black that I finally step out of them.

"Good girl."

I rub my thighs together, even wetter than before.

Then she attacks.

Her left hand is at the back of my neck, fingers threading in my hair and tugging roughly by the roots. She turns my head where she needs it so she can ravage my mouth again. Her tongue dives past my lips at the same time two fingers of her other hand thrust inside me. I'm lifted onto my toes as I moan into her mouth.

My hands go to her hips—both to help keep me steady and because I'm dying to touch her—while she sets a brutal rhythm of fucking me with her fingers.

Tapping into some of that courage from earlier when I told her I wanted her naked, I dip my fingers into her underwear, reveling in the feel of her soft skin. I skim one hand over her waist and around to the front between us. Just as my fingertips begin to venture between her folds, she withdrawals hers, leaving me a little sad. But before I can focus too much on the emptiness I feel without her inside me, she shoves me backwards. Again.

I crash onto the bed, not even getting a chance to move back before she's spreading my legs and kneeling between them. The first touch of her warm, wet tongue over my clit has me throwing my head back and panting. She flicks her tongue over that sensitive spot several times, bringing me dangerously close to orgasm, before her mouth moves.

A cry rips from my throat when her teeth sink into the flesh of my inner thigh. Then another one as she bites just over my hip bone.

I'm squirming and writhing on the bed, just wanting her to go back to where she was and finish what she started. Instead, her mouth travels north, licking and biting and sucking at what feels like every inch of skin.

Her lips close around my left nipple, sucking it into the blissful heat of her mouth. I moan as my back arches off the bed.

She hovers over me, pressing her weight down on me as she moves to suck on my other nipple. My hands tangle in her long hair, holding her to me like I could bring her even closer.

As my legs wrap around her waist, I realize she still has her underwear on. I'm determined to fix that immediately.

While she continues her ministrations on my breasts, occasionally biting down on my nipples, forcing lustful and tortured noises to escape me, I move my hands down to her back. My fingers slip beneath the hem of her sports bra, pushing the stretchy fabric upward. When she comprehends what I'm trying to do, she sits up just long enough to help me get it off her.

Her breasts are a little smaller than mine, her nipples darker. She tosses the bra away onto the floor, then comes back to lick a scorching path up between my breasts, over my collarbone, stopping at my neck. She comes back down on top of me, pressing her weight on me, and I love the feel of her breasts heavy against mine. She peppers hot kisses up the column of my throat, her teeth scraping across my skin.

Her hips grind against me, her pussy rubbing against mine through the thin fabric of her underwear. I moan, and the sound turns into a choked cry when she bites into the side of my neck.

"Fuck," I breathe, the sharp sting of pain only spurring me on as I lift my hips to thrust against her again.

The friction of her underwear feels good against my clit, but I still want so much more.

"Logan," I whine.

She chuckles, her face buried in my neck. "What do you want?"

All I can do is groan as I grab her hips and rock mine some more.

"Use your words, baby."

How am I still alive? This woman's mouth is a deadly weapon. Even though *baby* sounds more derisive than endearing coming from her, it still makes my throat go dry.

"I want to feel you," I answer breathlessly.

She wraps her arms around my middle, tucking them beneath me. Holding onto me tightly, she rolls us over the mattress until I'm on top of her. I can't help but laugh because I don't think any of the guys I've ever been with have even pulled that move.

Logan maneuvers us up the bed, settling back on the pillows. She places her hands behind her head and grins up at me.

"Show me what you got, sunshine."

That's the second time she's called me that. It's also the second time I've had a reaction to it that concerns me. It's a tightening in my chest, like my heart literally skips a bit. It's a twisting of my insides, everything so tangled that if someone were to cut me open, nothing would be identifiable.

Considering I'm already under whatever spell she's cast on me, all of that is heightened.

But if there's one thing I like about being with Logan almost as much as the orgasms, it's rising to her challenges.

I crawl down her legs, once more slipping my fingers in her underwear. As I slide them down, her eyes remain locked on mine, dark with desire, her lips parted as her breathing grows heavier.

When I have her boy shorts off, I forget all about the challenge and break eye contact, sweeping my gaze down her body as her legs fall open. Where I have a light dusting of blonde hair, she's completely shaved down there.

I can feel her eyes on me as I lean down to get my first taste of her. A soft hum echoes from somewhere above my head, but all I can focus on is exploring her.

She has no room to taunt me for how wet I get.

She's fucking soaked.

The taste isn't what I was expecting. Then again, I don't know *what* I was expecting. It's a little sweet but not much else other than the taste of skin.

I kind of love it.

Both her hands find their way into my hair as I brush my tongue over her clit, again and again. Her hips start swaying sensually back and forth, grinding herself against my mouth as I grab onto her thighs.

I've never done this before, but if I had to guess going by her pants and soft moans filling my bedroom, she at least doesn't hate it.

Her hips start moving faster, so I flatten my tongue and add more pressure. The muscles in her thighs eventually tense beneath my hands, letting me know she's close.

"Fuck, Elise. Fuck...you."

I want to laugh but decide it's probably not a good time for that. As she comes, her body spasming from the force of her orgasm, I imagine she hates me even more for being the one to give her that kind of pleasure.

After the waves of her release recede, she tugs on my hair. "Get the fuck up here."

I climb back up her body, settling between her legs. Her pussy is slick against mine, and my hips move of their own accord, grinding against her.

Then her hand wraps around my throat, her intense eyes demanding my full attention. I stop moving, my breath catching. Her hold on me isn't tight enough to cut off my oxygen. I'm breathless for an entirely different reason.

This close, I can make out every fleck of blue within the gray of her eyes. I could count her eyelashes. Her skin is pale, making the flush in her cheeks appear an even deeper pink.

I can't stop my next thought from blurting out.

"You're beautiful."

Her eyes widen, only by a fraction. The even more noticeable reaction to my words is a visible relaxation of her entire body, like all the tension she's been holding for years is finally given a reprieve.

It lasts all too briefly.

"Shut the fuck up, Elise," she says, back in that husky tone of hers. She hauls me even closer by my throat until our lips are brushing. "Now come all over my cunt."

I've stopped feeling as embarrassed about the noises I make when I'm with her, but my next moan might be the loudest of them all.

Giving into the fierce throbbing between my legs, I start rocking my hips again, grinding my pussy against hers. I'm already so close, and the friction on my clit has me quickly reaching a peak.

Keeping one hand around my throat, Logan grasps my hip with the other, squeezing hard until pain joins the pleasure, both mingling into a state of pure ecstasy. She's panting beneath me again, her warm breath licking at my lips like flames as my eyes flutter closed.

I want to hold off, to wait for her to join me. But the pressure is building with every thrust, every intense stroke of our clits, every moan that tangles in the hair's breadth between our mouths.

Her hand clamps a little tighter around my throat as I get close, robbing me of oxygen. My eyes shoot open to meet hers.

"Look at me while you come."

I don't know if it's the demand or the way I can hardly breathe that does it. Maybe it's a bit of both. I come so hard that everything goes black. Little spots dance at the edges of my vision, bursts of color like in Logan's paintings.

Whether it's in art or orgasms, she always has a way of making me see light where it shouldn't exist.

It's then that I realize when she decides she's done with me, it's going to hurt a hell of a lot more than I thought it would.

As she eases her hold on my throat, I suck in air. I'm not sure if it's the same orgasm or an entirely new one that has me finally understanding the meaning of *le petit mort*.

Logan takes advantage of my completely weakened state, moving her hand from my throat to the back of my head and bringing me down to crush our lips together. My hips are still rocking between her legs, determined to make her come again even through this post-orgasm haze. She slips her tongue into my mouth, kissing me fiercely, desperately.

Her second orgasm has her body shuddering beneath me as she moans into my mouth. I've never known a sound to taste so sweet.

We both fall still, the touch of her hands gone as her arms flop to the bed on either side of her like they're made of jelly. I feel the same, but I really don't want to lay all my weight on her. When I go to roll off, her arms come back up and wrap around me.

"Where do you think you're going?" she asks, eyes closed and voice sleepy.

"You don't strike me as the type of person who cuddles after sex," I say, evading the whole truth that I'm a little self-conscious about lying on top of her.

"I'm not. Just…give me a minute."

Once again, I notice the relaxing of her body. Her face too, her eyes still closed, even a slight upward curl at one corner of her mouth. It's as though I'm acting as a weighted blanket, providing some sense of comfort and calm that she hasn't known in too long a time.

Or maybe it's all in my head.

But she does look peaceful. Her breathing has evened out, her chest rising and falling in a slow, steady rhythm under mine. The ruddiness in her cheeks has mostly faded, her eyelashes fluttering. I'm tempted to count each and every one.

Before I can decide to do just that, she *snores*.

I don't know what I'm more surprised about. That she fell asleep or that she snores.

Now that her hold on me has relaxed, I roll over onto the mattress on my side next to her. She stirs but doesn't wake. I doubt she meant to fall asleep, and I'm not sure if she had plans today. But I don't have the heart to wake her. So, instead, I carefully reach for the blanket at the foot of the bed and pull it up over both of us.

This is around the time I usually go to bed for the day, so I'm especially tired after that new vigorous sexual experience. One I'm sure I'll never forget.

However, I lie awake for a while longer, watching Logan sleep like some kind of creep. Her snoring doesn't bother me. It's quiet, a little bit of white noise. Her pale pink lips are parted, and I think back to how it felt to kiss them.

How could something so soft be excruciatingly brutal at the same time?

And how could I love everything about it?

I touch my fingers lightly to my bottom lip, wondering if it'll bruise from her vicious kisses.

She already has her marks on me. What's one more?

13

LOGAN

Fuck fuck fuck.

I fucking fell asleep in Elise's fucking bed.

What the fuck was I thinking?

That's the problem. I wasn't. I was completely blissed out and exhausted from spending the night before trying to come up with something else to do or add to the painting, to give myself any reason to stay away from Elise just a little longer.

I should've tried harder.

She was nothing short of perfect that morning, pleasing me and taking her own pleasure. Falling asleep with her on top of me, holding her in my arms, was the most content I've felt in a long time. It was a comfort I shouldn't have allowed myself, one I shouldn't allow myself again.

But…fuck, I want to.

It's only been a few days, and I'm already going through withdrawals again. I've spent much of my life avoiding drugs of any kind after watching my mother slowly kill herself, but I think I've found one I can't resist. One that's potent and intoxicating and addictive. One I'd gladly overdose on if it meant having her all to myself.

Days later, and I'm still a little jelly-legged after those two orgasms. Or maybe…

No.

It's the orgasms. Nothing else.

Certainly not some scary ass disease eating away at my nerves.

Denial is my best friend.

Of course, when it comes to Elise, I'm not sure I can deny things for much longer. I only slept a few hours and then slipped silently out of her apartment while she was still sleeping. But fuck if I didn't want to stay in that bed all day with her. She was agonizingly beautiful, like an angel with her blonde hair splayed out on the white pillows. Peaceful.

I hate that I can't stop thinking about her.

I hate that I want her more than I've ever wanted anyone.

I haven't been able to even start on the next painting because she consumes my every waking thought. And dreaming one. Every time I get a flash of an idea, a hint of an image, it's not…right. It's too bright, too much color. Because of *her*. Because I want to paint something that's more her than it is me.

Even the tattoo I'm doing right now has me thinking about her.

The needle of my gun pierces the skin of the woman's upper arm, working around the clock face that's already done to outline the flowers that surround it. A bouquet of petunias and chrysanthemums.

They're not lilies, but they still remind me of *her*.

I've tried so hard these last few days to talk myself out of this. Out of wanting her. Out of forgiving her for whatever role she played in Liam's death. Out of choosing to believe her when she says she doesn't remember how it happened.

But fuck if I don't want to do all of that.

Between having to consider selling my house and wanting Elise for other reasons, maybe it's time to throw that stupid plan of destroying her out the window.

Maybe it's time to finally let things go.

I just don't know if I'm strong enough.

Almost two hours later, the tattoo is finished, everything shaded, wiped down, and covered. I give the client all the aftercare information and tell her she can pay up front with Tate.

After I get everything cleaned up, I start setting up for my last client of the night.

I'm sure I'm just tired, but as I walk around the studio, my legs feel even weaker than they did a few hours ago, my right more so. It makes me sick to my stomach. Not the feeling in my legs, but the fear of what it means.

I hate myself a little for what I'm about to do, but I don't have much of a choice.

Leaving the room, I head down the hallway toward Jacklyn's back office. The door is cracked, but I still knock.

"Come on in," I hear from the other side.

I push the door open and step into the office. Jacklyn sits behind her desk doing paperwork, and she looks up as I enter.

She gives me that kind smile of hers that immediately makes me feel guilty.

"What's up, Logan?"

I take a few more steps into the room. "I have one last client for the night, but, um…I'm feeling a little off. I can call him to see if he'd be okay with rescheduling unless you wanted to take him?"

She sets her pen down on the desk, her brows dipped low. "Everything okay?"

"Yeah, of course." I wave my hand in the air. I *hate* this part. "I'm just not feeling too great. It's no big deal."

"Okay." She nods, but I can still see the concern in her eyes. "I can take him if you and him are both okay with that."

"I'd rather give him the option than have to reschedule him."

"All right. Well, get out of here then. I wanted to talk to you about something, but we can do that later. Yeah?"

"Sure."

I suppress the smile threatening to break free at thinking of what she wants to talk to me about. I need to stop getting my hopes up, dammit.

"Feel better."

"Thanks."

I leave Jacklyn's office, still feeling a little guilty, even if the sympathy in her eyes did make my skin crawl. I know it's just her compassionate nature, and I should probably be more thankful for it. It's just something I've never been comfortable with. At least when I tell Tate I'm leaving for the night, all he does is blow a bubble with the gum he's chewing and waves me out the door.

When I get home, I take a shower and go straight to bed. Maybe I'll try to sleep all night and day. I haven't been sleeping much, so maybe all I need is some fucking rest.

It happens slowly. My right leg starts to feel more weak, leaden and clumsy, like it doesn't want to listen to the signals my brain is sending it. It's subtle at first but becomes more noticeable when I go up and down the stairs of my front porch.

The damn leg still *works*, but it just feels…weird.

I can't describe it much better than that.

I go back to work though, mainly because Jacklyn is off at the beginning of each week, and I don't want to have to reschedule any of my clients.

But after a couple more days, my leg works even less. It becomes a chore just to make it up the steps. The unexplained extra weight of my leg starts to settle in my foot until it doesn't want to work *at all*. My foot is weighed down like a sack of bricks. My left leg still functions normally, so when I walk, it's like…

Step. *Stomp.* Step. *Stomp.*

It's annoying and embarrassing as hell.

When I look it up, I discover it's called foot drop. Which is fitting because my right foot just…*drops.*

After that shit starts, it doesn't take long for me to cave and make another doctor appointment. However, the earliest I could get in was three weeks from now, so I guess I get to deal with it until then.

Fucking perfect.

At least I don't have to walk around too much in front of my clients, and when I do, they don't mention it. I'm sure they notice—it's difficult not to with the fucking thunder slaps my foot makes on the tile—but they're polite enough not to bring it up or ask about it.

Tate, however, didn't bother censoring himself when he first noticed.

"What the fuck is going on with your foot?" he had blurted out the day it started.

I told him to go fuck himself, but then I told him I didn't know. Which isn't exactly the truth. But no one needs to know I've already diagnosed myself before I've even talked to a doctor, at least since these new symptoms have started.

He's left it alone since then, but I still catch him glancing at me when I'm walking across the lobby. He's never been one to show too much sympathy for anyone, and not just because that's kind of a trait of his. He knows how much I hate people feeling sorry for me because that was one of the reasons it took me so long to confide in him about my past. I made sure to tell him if he tried to console me—or God forbid, give me a hug—I'd punch him in the face.

But I still see it in his eyes from time to time, the concern that I'm barely capable of walking without creating a fuck ton of noise. I choose to let it go because I have enough to deal with as it is. Besides, he's my best friend. I *guess* he's allowed to worry about me a little.

"Oh, I should probably warn you," Tate says as we start shutting down the studio for the night. "Elise called while you were with your last client."

I turn to glare at him after shutting off the computer. "What the fuck for?"

"She asked for your number. I gave it to her."

Okay, so he's no longer my best friend.

"What the fuck, Tate?"

He's not looking at me, but I can see that one side of his mouth is curled in one of his wicked, mischievous grins. They don't usually make me want to punch him, but this one does.

"What? You two are a thing, right? She should have your number."

"We're not a thing," I mutter, even while there's something inside me doubting if I want those words to be true.

"Well, you and I know that, but she doesn't. But that's what she's supposed to think, isn't it?" He finally meets my gaze and arches a brow. "Unless something's changed?"

He stares at me like he dares to believe he knows something I don't. What he doesn't know is that I *do* already know it. I just don't want to fucking admit it, to him or to myself.

I avert my eyes and stand. "Fuck off, Tate."

His laughter follows me, helping to drown out the sound of my defiant right foot dropping heavily onto the floor as I hobble around the counter. I snatch up Landon's old jacket and shrug it on.

"Hey, seriously, Lo. You know you can talk to me, right?" Tate says after we turn off the lights and exit the studio. He still wears a smile, but it's relaxed and a bit more serious now.

"Yeah, I know."

I lock up, and we head down the sidewalk to our vehicles together, Tate walking a little slower than usual to keep up with my hindered pace. It's not that I don't know I can talk to him if I need to. He might be a little shit most of the time, but he's actually a good friend.

We stop in front of my car, and I sigh as I turn to look at him beneath the amber glow of the streetlights.

"I just don't know what the fuck I'm doing, Tate."

He nods with understanding, or at least as much as he possibly can understand. "Sounds like you got some shit to figure out."

"Yeah, no fucking kidding."

I walk away and open the driver door of my car.

"Hey," he says before I can climb inside. "You're okay to drive, right?"

I peer down at my fucking foot, the one that doesn't work right, the one that's responsible for working the pedals, half the job of driving safely. It's honestly not easy, but I've been cautious.

Shrugging, I look back at Tate. "I haven't died yet."

He rolls his eyes but still grins. At least I'm able to make light out of a shitty situation.

"Just be careful," he says as he starts walking away toward his car.

"With the way you drive, you're the one who needs to be careful," I call after him.

He flips me off, and I laugh as I climb into my car. Once the door is closed, my laughter dies. I start the engine and stretch my foot as much as I can, rolling my ankle with what limited movement I can manage. It doesn't help like I wish it would.

I drive home, being careful just like Tate told me to. It takes a little more concentration to get my foot to move just right, not letting it weigh too heavily on the gas pedal or slamming on the brakes.

When I make it home alive, I head inside, needing to use the damn railing for support on my way up the porch stairs. I move straight over to the couch, crashing down.

I never realized how much I should've appreciated having the ability to walk normally while I could. Now that I can't, I'd much rather sit on my ass. I wouldn't consider myself lazy—I actually *like* walking and being active—but fuck if I don't want to just lie here and never get up again. Never have to feel my foot freefalling or hear the impact on the ground. Never have to fight for control over my own body. And lose.

My phone dings, and I dig it out of the pocket of my jacket that I didn't even bother to take off. I know who it is the moment I see it's a text even though it's from an unknown number.

Unknown Number: Hey, it's Elise.

Me: K

I smirk as those three little dots start dancing, imagining her rolling her eyes.

While she types, I go to save her number in my phone. I pause at the name, hesitating. Common sense tells me I should save it under *Elise*. Or maybe even *bane of my existence*. But then I think back to what I've called her twice now.

Sunshine.

It fits her. All bright and warm and golden.

Hot.

Now *I'm* the one rolling *my* eyes.

I type in *Elise* and be done with it. I'm not wrestling with my mind right now while I'm busy wrestling with my own damn body.

Elise: I thought it'd be easier for you to text me instead of, you know, showing up unannounced like you usually do.

Me: If you wanted my number, you could've just asked.

Elise: A date and time would be helpful.

I let out a breathy laugh. I really enjoy pressing her buttons. However, since she came back into town, something about that enjoyment has changed. I loved watching her get flustered, maybe a little intimidated. Now…I don't know. I think it's cute when she gets all riled up. When *I'm* the one to rile her up.

Me: You want to know when your next orgasm will be?

I wish I could see her right now, see just how much I'm getting under her skin. But if I am, she pretends otherwise, completely ignoring my question.

Elise: I shouldn't be surprised you lack common courtesy to warn someone before showing up at their door.

Me: You think I care about common courtesy when it comes to you?

Elise: Is there anything you DO care about? Because it's not breathing apparently.

Oh, fuck her.

I should've known she'd throw that in my face. No way was she going to let me get away with that one.

Me: I care about making you come. Over and over and over and over…

Elise: I believe I only came once last time.

Me: Is that a challenge?

Elise: Maybe. When should I be expecting you?

When I realize I'm smiling down at my screen, I feel like a fool, like a fucking schoolgirl with a crush. Which I definitely don't have for Elise. And, yet, the smile doesn't go anywhere. At least not until I think about the answer to Elise's question. It fades as I type out my next message.

Me: I haven't started another one yet.

Elise: That's okay. I can wait.

Yeah, well maybe I can't.

I want to fucking see her again. I want to do dirty things with her. *To* her. I want to lie in her bed with her. But I haven't painted in days, and without another piece to sell her, I have no excuse to show up at her apartment. Or I guess text her *before* showing up at her apartment if she really insists on it.

I stare at our conversation, wishing I didn't need an excuse. I'm about to give in and try to make something up when Elise starts typing again. Those dots pop up, then disappear, then pop up again. I think I hold my breath.

Elise: Everything okay though?

No, everything is not okay.
I'm fucking obsessed with you and can't get you out of my head.
Oh, and my nervous system is having a nervous breakdown.

Me: Everything's fine.

Elise: Promise?

I'm tempted to ask why she even cares, but I'm pretty sure I already know the answer. She doesn't actually care. She's a doctor. It's in her nature to show a little human decency, even if it's toward someone who's made it clear they couldn't be bothered to return the thought.

She's being kind. Too polite for her own good.

Me: Sure, Elise.

Elise: Okay. Goodnight, Logan.

I don't respond again. I lock the screen and toss my phone away to the other end of the couch, not wanting to look at it any longer. Despite her saying goodnight, I know she'll be awake all night, a couple miles away at the hospital, probably just starting a twelve or fourteen hour shift.

But maybe it's goodnight for me. My mind is tired. My body's exhausted.

When it rains, it fucking pours.

14

ELISE

Everything isn't fine.

I may not know Logan all that well, but it's a gut instinct.

It's not that I expect her to finish a painting every two weeks or anything. But considering she's done three for me in less than a couple of months and hasn't started on another in the past week, something just feels off.

I hope it's not. I hope she's just taking a break.

Of course, after everything we've done together, I can't help but wonder if something's wrong because of me. It didn't feel like she was upset with me while we were texting—at least past her usual animosity toward me.

Then again…I didn't feel that either.

That's probably just my hope talking, that little voice inside me that tells me I want more. I don't *want* Logan to hate me anymore. I don't want her to keep playing this game of hers, the one where she gives me everything I want with the plan to rip it away and leave me empty and broken and alone.

I've known that's what she was doing from the beginning, and I still couldn't stop myself from falling.

I'll have to accept it when it happens. I know that.

So why not make it even worse on myself?

I realize that's what I'm doing when I get off work two days after our text conversation and find myself driving to her house. I didn't let her know I was on my way. That might make me a hypocrite, but I knew if I texted to ask if it was okay for me to come over, she'd tell me not to.

I don't want to give her the chance to push me away. I have no doubt she'll find opportunities to do that on her own.

As I pull up and park in the driveway, I look up at the house bathing in the early morning sun, a wave of nostalgia crashing over me. I haven't been here since high school. I didn't come often, just a few times to hang out with Liam. But it doesn't look like it's changed a bit, only a little older.

It's a nice house, not much smaller than my family's home. The paint is peeling in a few places, and there aren't as many plants thriving in the garden beds out front as I remember. Other than that, it looks like Logan's kept up with it.

I can't imagine that's been easy for her, physically or emotionally.

Turning off my car, I get out and walk up the porch steps to the front door. I hesitate briefly, wondering how much more Logan's going to hate me for showing up here.

I just want to make sure she's okay.

I wish I didn't care, but I do.

Sucking in a breath, I knock.

It takes about half a minute for the door to open, and when it does, all the air comes whooshing out of my lungs. It's a mix of relief and my usual reaction every time I see her.

I always knew she was beautiful. I wasn't blind to that. But her beauty affects me in an entirely different way than it did a couple months ago. I want to constantly be surrounded by it, consumed by it. If she's the storms she paints, she can drown me. She's already swept me up in her winds, and I'm suddenly terrified to see how far she carries me away.

She's wearing black basketball shorts and a black tank top, both of which are stained with paint. But it doesn't matter what she wears. She's always stunning.

Logan crosses her arms and leans her shoulder against the doorjamb, eyes narrowed. "A date and time would've been helpful."

I barely suppress a wince as my words are thrown back at me. "I know. I'm sorry. I figured you wouldn't have opened the door if you knew it was me."

"Look at that. You know me well after all."

I sigh and shuffle my feet uncomfortably. "I'll leave. I just wanted to make sure everything is really all right."

Her jaw ticks. "What makes you think it's not?"

"I don't know." I shrug. "Just tell me it is, and I'll go."

Her eyes move between mine, and I can see the wheels turning behind them, considering what kind of truth or lie she wants to tell me. I'm not any more of an expert at reading people than most. I don't have a built-in lie detector like some are gifted with. But there's something about Logan that's become easier to figure out, easier to translate her tells, to decipher that look in her eyes.

She's about to lie to me.

She leans forward an inch as if the closer proximity will convince me what she's about to say is the truth. "Everything's fine."

I frown. "You're lying."

"So what if I am, Elise?" Her fiery glare returns in full force. "The fact is it's none of your fucking business."

She's right, of course. We're nothing to each other. She's not obligated to tell me anything.

But if she hasn't figured it out by now, I can be very stubborn.

It's my turn to cross my arms. "What if I want to make it my business?"

"You don't," she says like she's already decided for me.

"Look, I know you hate me. But...I don't hate you."

Her face falls, the hard lines around her eyes and mouth relaxing. The gray clouds swirling around her pupils appear to lighten, the flecks of blue within brightening until they almost take over.

"You don't have to tell me what's going on," I say when she remains silent. "But you can."

She presses her mouth into a thin line, but it appears to be more out of exasperation than her previous hostility. "You're not going to let it go, are you?"

"I don't want to, but I will if that's what you want."

Dropping her arms, she rolls her eyes and takes half a step back. "Get the fuck in here."

I wasn't expecting her to invite me in, but I quickly move past her into the house before she changes her mind.

While the outside isn't all that different than it was nearly a decade ago, the inside sure is. I think most of the furniture is the same, but it's all worn, the couch threadbare. Canvases, large and small, some blank and some not, are leaning against nearly every available wall. Paint stains the carpet and the coffee table.

Once I'm a few steps inside, I turn back around to face Logan. She closes the door, then leans her back against it.

"I swear, if you go all doctor on me, I'm kicking your fucking ass."

I don't like the sound of that. Not the kicking my ass part, but the first part.

Instead of urging her to explain, I remain quiet and patient, letting her tell me on her own time.

"Do you want a drink?"

Again, I wasn't expecting that.

I stare at her for a moment, and something about the way she stares back tells me I'm supposed to say yes.

"Umm…I'll take a water."

She doesn't move right away, eyes locked on me as an intense and unsettling silence descends between us. It only makes me more curious and more concerned the longer it continues.

Finally, she pushes herself off the door and turns toward the kitchen.

It only takes me two of her steps to realize what's wrong. Her right foot doesn't land normally, not heel first like it should. It hits the floor with its full weight, making a quiet *thud* on the carpet. When she crosses into the kitchen, it turns into a *slap* against the tile.

She doesn't stop, and I quickly follow after her.

"Did you hurt your foot?" I ask as I stop on the other side of the kitchen island.

"I didn't do shit," she says as she opens the fridge, taking out a bottle of water. She turns back and tosses it to me.

I catch it but set it aside on the countertop. "You didn't injure your leg or your knee or something?"

Crossing her arms again, she leans against the opposite counter, her glare from earlier back in place. "What did I tell you about that doctor bullshit?"

"This could be serious, Logan. It could be a nerve injury. Or even some kind of muscle or spinal disease. Hell, you could've had a stroke."

"I didn't have a fucking stroke," she snaps. "You really need to work on your bedside manner."

I take a calming breath because…she's not wrong. But, then again, I don't feel this kind of unease for typical patients.

This is *Logan*.

I refuse to lie to myself and pretend I don't care about her, act like I'm not concerned when I really am. It'll hurt like hell later, but whatever. I'll deal with it when it's time to cross that bridge. One that will probably only lead to me working much longer hours at the hospital to forget what I felt for her, felt *with* her. How she *made* me feel.

I've only had one real breakup, and even though Logan and I aren't technically in a relationship, I have a feeling it's going to be a lot harder than that when she walks away.

I really did fall right into her trap, despite knowing it was there all along.

"I'm just saying," I start again even though she's looking at me like she'd love nothing more than to shut me up. "This is something you really need to get checked out."

"I'm seeing my doctor in a few weeks."

"If this *is* something serious, I don't think you should wait that long. You probably need a CT scan at the very least."

"Elise." Her tone is hard, a warning. "You're not my doctor. I'm taking care of it. Now drop it."

"I really think—"

"I don't give a fuck what you think."

With another deep breath, I reconsider my approach. All my education and training has taught me that with something like this, something that could have so many different possible causes, many of them quite severe, it needs to be evaluated sooner rather than later. Whatever the cause, treatment is important for a faster and more efficient recovery. The longer it's allowed to go on, the higher the chance of permanent damage.

But, again, this is Logan. I can't be a doctor with her. I have to be…whatever it is she needs me to be.

I only wish I knew what that was.

Taking a risk, I move slowly around the island. I stop a few feet in front of her, not because I'm scared of her, but because I'm scared of making the wrong move.

"Then what about how I *feel*?"

All that tension has returned to her body, her jaw tight and tense. "I don't give a fuck about that either."

I nod because that's exactly what I was expecting. "I'm going to tell you anyway, and you're going to fucking listen."

Her brow dips lower, and her lips part. But she doesn't speak.

"There's something about you, Logan. I see it in your art. I *feel* it when I'm with you. That light, that vibrancy. You try to smother it, even with the storms you paint. But you can't because it's still there. I don't want to see something else try to extinguish what's left of it."

She swallows, the hollow of her smooth throat moving with it. "Maybe you're seeing something that's not there."

I shake my head. "I see something that you believe isn't there anymore."

For a long moment, she stares at me, the storm in the gray clouds of her eyes brewing. I swear I see her bottom lip tremble, but it doesn't last long enough for me to be sure.

Then she moves, two steps forward, and stops. "I don't need your fucking pity, Elise."

"It's not pity," I say in a whisper now that she's standing so close. I can tell she truly believes that's what it is, but it's the farthest thing from it. "It's compassion. It's…affection."

This time, I *know* I see the slight tremble in her bottom lip.

"I know you said you don't care what I think, but…I think you're not used to those things. I think you can't tell the difference. People can care for you without feeling sorry for you. So, good news, Logan. You win. I *do* care."

It's not often that Logan is struck speechless, but she says nothing as I back away. She doesn't try to stop me, not that I expected her to.

Before exiting the kitchen, I give her a small smile. "Please consider trying to see a doctor sooner. Not for me. For you."

She remains silent and lets me leave.

As I show myself out, closing the front door behind me, I realize just how much I do care. I don't have to know everything there is to know about Logan. What I feel goes deeper than that.

I don't have to know her favorite color to know how undeniably talented she is.

I don't have to taste her favorite food to feel her passion.

I don't have to follow her around for an entire day to see her strength and courage and conviction. I may not know every one of her hopes and dreams, but if it's not something in the realm of art, I'd be surprised. And I know she has what it takes to claim whatever it is she wants.

She sure as hell claimed me.

I don't have to know what she thinks her weakness is to know her true weakness is a fear of trusting others.

I can't force her to trust me. She's the only one who can take that leap of faith.

I want her to trust me because I don't want her to walk away.

If I'm being honest with myself, I think I started falling for Logan the day I saw her first piece of artwork hanging in that shop downtown.

My eyes fell in love with the painting while my heart fell in love with the painter.

15

LOGAN

Elise was right.

And fuck do I hate that.

I hate when people feel sorry for me so much that I can't even deal with their concern. More than that, I hate feeling sorry for *myself*. And right now, I do a little. Not because of the way my body is fighting me when it comes to something as simple as walking, but because I want something I can't have.

Or something I can't *let* myself have.

It's not about the past anymore. I mean, the past is still there. There's no erasing it. But the fact I can't deny any longer is that I don't hate Elise like I did two months ago. I could pretend all I want, but that's exactly what it would be. Pretend.

And maybe that's what I should do.

While she was right about my deficiencies when it comes to accepting things like kindness and empathy, she was wrong about one thing.

There's nothing left in me that's redeemable. There's no light. No color. It was already extinguished a long time ago.

Whatever she thinks she's seen or felt, she's wrong. Whatever she believes exists in those paintings I've done, she's mistaking the truth for something else. She assumes those hints of vivid hues that break up the blacks and grays are there because they're still somewhere inside me. The truth is they're all a reflection of what's already been done. Everything good, all of my hope and innocence I may have once had, was swept away in the storm when Liam died. When Landon went to prison. When my father left. When my mother stopped being my mother.

Those paintings are only showing the inevitable, representing the storm closing in to wipe it all out.

Life has turned me jaded. At least I'm self-aware of that.

But I can't do that to Elise. I can't let the storm that is my life destroy everything good in her.

Even though that was my original plan…

But I can't do it. Not anymore.

She has so much good in her. The light she thinks she sees in me is dead, but hers is the one that burns bright and hot. I can't allow myself to be the reason it's snuffed out. When I saw her for the first time after eight years, that's all I wanted, a front-row seat to her ruination. Like I had to my own.

I can't have her because I'll just bring her down with me.

She doesn't deserve to be my casualty.

I probably don't have to worry about that though considering she wouldn't be very happy with me right now. I'm walking—as best I can—back into work and still haven't called or gone to the doctor. I know I should, but, dammit, I hate doctors.

Accept for one, apparently.

I've always been stubborn, but, for some reason, I'm being more obstinate than usual.

The nagging voice in the back of my mind tells me I'm scared. I know it's right, but I wish it would shut the fuck up.

However, it's only gotten louder over the past twenty-four hours. That weak feeling I had in my legs before the foot drop started has traveled to my left arm, mainly in my hand. Going into work where I'm supposed to be tattooing a permanent design onto someone's body probably isn't the best idea, but I'm not one to give up. I have to at least try.

When I enter the studio, Tate is busy speaking with a client. It sounds like they're setting up an appointment, so I don't interrupt, greeting him with a wave before heading back to my room, trying to make as little noise with my damned foot as I can. I take a seat at my desk and open up the email from my first client of the day on my tablet.

After going through the design examples and details they've provided, I get out my sketch pad and start drawing. I haven't been using my tablet to draw up designs for the last several weeks, and I think that's been helping since I haven't had as much eye pain.

But, this time, it's not my eyes I'm having a problem with.

The first few lines I draft end up looking shaky. I erase them and try again. The new ones are even worse.

Dropping my pencil on the desk, I shake my hand out, like maybe it's just asleep and needs to be woken the fuck up. I barely resist the urge to bang it against the desk.

Injuring it probably wouldn't solve anything.

I pick up the pencil, holding it a little tighter and leaning closer to the page. I've never had to try so hard to just create some decent fucking lines. But no matter how hard I do try, none of them turn out right. They're still shaky, even the pressure of the lines uneven.

If I can't draw something on paper, how the fuck am I supposed to do it with a vibrating tattoo gun in my hand?

I can't.

Frustration, fury, and self-pity swirl around in my head, twisting up my gut, until it all comes bubbling over.

I spin around in my chair and hurl the pencil across the room. It doesn't make me feel better.

Placing my elbows on my knees, I double over, grabbing fistfuls of my hair, gripping tightly until it hurts. I welcome the pain that shoots through my skull. I prefer it over everything else I'm feeling right now.

"Hey, Logan, I was wondering if we could have that talk—" Jacklyn's voice sounds far away as I'm drowning. "Logan?"

Her footsteps come closer until I sense her presence beside me.

"Are you okay?"

This is where I lie, where I say everything is fine even if it's not. But…I don't think I can do it this time.

"No, I'm not okay."

The words taste bitter on my tongue, but at the same time, that tight ball of tension in my chest eases a little. When I look up at Jacklyn, I'm at least thankful I'm not crying. I don't think I could stand for this to be any more mortifying than it already is.

"What's wrong?" she asks.

"I don't know." Except, I do know. I'm just not willing to say it out loud yet. "But something's definitely not right. My hand doesn't seem to want to work."

I pick up my sketch pad and offer it to her. She takes it, her brow furrowing as she looks down at the shaky lines and multiple eraser marks.

"I don't understand."

With a heavy sigh, I stand and walk across the room, the smacking of my foot against the tile reverberating off the walls. Turning around, I place my hands on my hips. "My whole damn body is out of commission apparently. Check engine light on and flashing."

"Okay," Jacklyn says slowly, nodding in contemplation as she places my pad back on the desk. "How long has this been going on?"

I shrug. "I don't know exactly, but it's been getting steadily worse over the past week or so."

"You need to go to the hospital, Logan."

Crossing my arms over my chest, I roll my eyes, my usual defenses rising into place. "Why is that such a popular opinion?"

"Because this is a loss of motor function, which could very well be an emergency."

"What about my appointments for today?"

"I'll take them or offer to reschedule. Tate might be ready to take on some clients soon too."

Looking away, I clench my jaw, that tension from before returning. It's different this time. Worse.

"Hey." Jacklyn takes a step toward me, forcing my gaze back to her. "We're not going to push you out. We're a family here, yeah? That means we take care of each other. So if I have to shove you in the trunk of my car and drive you to the hospital myself, I'll do it."

My throat clogs with emotion. It's an unfamiliar sensation that claws at my nerves—at least the ones that work—like nails on a chalkboard. But that same emotion also swells in my chest, warming the cavity where my heart sometimes chooses to reside.

Family?

Tate's been my best friend for years, and Jacklyn has always been amazing and supportive. She's taught me most of what I know about tattooing and the business side of things. I respect her more than I do most people. Family isn't a word I've let myself think or feel in nearly a decade outside of Landon, but the truth is they're the closest thing I have to one while my only brother is still locked away.

When I'm silent for too long, Jacklyn arches a brow. "Do I need to do that, Logan?"

I clench my jaw again, but this time it's an attempt to suppress a grin. "No. I'll go."

"Good. Now get out of here."

"Yes, ma'am." I start hobbling away, but at the door, I turn back. "Thanks, Jacklyn."

"I love ya, kid. I just want you to take care of yourself."

I nod, then leave the room, walking through the studio and outside to my car. Even if Jacklyn hadn't demanded I go, I most likely would have made the decision on my own. Not being able to draw or paint or tattoo is the last straw.

At the hospital, they get me through triage and into a room quicker than I would've expected. I guess my symptoms really do imply a possible emergency, and I don't say anything to contradict that. I'm not about to tell them I know exactly what's wrong with me before they run whatever tests they want. Which, unsurprisingly, is a CT scan.

I'm glad Elise isn't here to rub that one in my face.

It's the middle of the afternoon, so at least I don't have to worry about running into her here since I know she works nights. I just hope I'm not here long enough to see her when she comes in.

I'm sitting up in the small bed, waiting for the doctor to come in and talk to me, scrolling on my phone to help distract myself. However, I'm noticing that weakness in my hand even while doing that. Frustrated, I shove my phone in the pocket of my jacket and lean back in the bed to stare up at the ceiling instead.

A few minutes later, there's a knock on the door, and the doctor enters. He's not one I recognize. The fact that my first thought is wondering if he knows Elise annoys me.

Even at a time like this, I can't stop fucking thinking about her.

"Well, Ms. Delaney," he starts as he closes the door behind him. "Your CT scan came back clear, so it's definitely not a stroke."

Could've told you that.

I almost say it but manage to hold my tongue.

The doctor leans against the counter and gives me a small smile. It's the kind that most doctors seem to have perfected, the kind that's just shy of sympathetic, more leaning toward compassionate. The kind I'm supposed to be learning to accept.

"Looking at your symptoms and considering your age, what I'd be most concerned about is the possibility of MS."

Those Google results come back to me in a colorful montage.

Multiple sclerosis.

I wish I could say I'm surprised to hear that, but I'm not. Not even a little. If anything, I'm…relieved. It's not an official diagnosis, but it's the closest thing to answers I didn't get off the internet. I'm in that age range where MS is most commonly diagnosed, so I figured there'd be at least one doctor able to draw that suspicion.

All I do is nod.

"Seems like you already considered that yourself."

"I did my research."

The doc smiles again, and this time, it's the one that means he doesn't fully approve of self-diagnosing via Google but secretly knows just how helpful and informative it can be.

"So, what we can do is get you a referral to a neurologist. We can mark it as urgent so you can get seen as soon as possible."

That's the best case scenario I could've hoped for. I know had I waited to see my primary doctor, a wait for a specialist could've been months long. As much as I hate to hope, maybe this means I can get treatment that much sooner too. I would really love to be able to write and draw again, to tattoo, to fucking *walk*.

I thank the doctor and only have to wait a few more minutes for my discharge papers.

Leaving the hospital a couple hours after I arrived, I head outside to see the sun starting its descent behind the mountains. Golden rays split the sky and stream through gaps in the clouds.

I stop in the middle of the quiet parking lot, a little to take a break because it's exhausting trying to walk with one bum foot, and a little to stare out at the brilliant beams of light scattered over the tops of the mountains. I don't see a lot of daylight except for the short drive it takes me to get to work in the afternoons. That's something I fear may have contributed to this new disease currently ravaging my body.

But I don't want to think about that. I don't want to think about *anything*.

If I could, I'd sit down right in this spot, watch the sunset, and try to forget about it all.

Except...there's something that would be even better. I don't need the sun in the sky, the one that disappears every night. Not when I have *her*, my own personal sunshine.

Fuck it.

I continue off through the parking lot, determined not to talk myself out of this. It's still a little early in the evening, and she might still be asleep. But if she meant what she said when she told me she cares, then maybe she wouldn't be too upset with me for waking her.

Since when did I start giving a shit about upsetting her?

Probably around the time I stopped hating her.

Just don't ask me when exactly that was. I don't think there was any one moment but many that resulted in a culmination of stupid fucking feelings while she was standing in my kitchen, scolding me because she...*cares*.

I wasn't the least bit surprised when the ER doctor said he suspected MS.

Realizing I have feelings for Elise? There's the shock of my life.

If someone as good as her can care about someone like me, then maybe—just fucking maybe—I can try to be worthy of that. I can try not to ruin her like everything else in my life gets ruined.

I pull up outside her apartment, park, and fling the door open as soon as I cut the engine. If I give myself even a moment to stop and think about what I'm doing, I might change my mind. I might turn around and go home instead of letting myself have something I really want.

Not even want.

Need.

The fact is...right now, I think I *need* her. There's an overwhelming mix of relief and fear and uncertainty clouding my thoughts—and probably my judgment—and the only thing that stands out within all of that is *her*. If I don't get to her—if I can't see her or talk to her or touch her—then I might just fall apart.

Still...I hesitate at her door. Because this is *me*. Because I think I'll always doubt myself when it comes to grabbing onto something that would make me happy. Because it's what I do.

But all I have to do is picture her face and I'm knocking on the door.

Seconds pass, turning into a minute. I consider leaving, giving up. When the wait turns into a minute and a half, it feels like a sign. Like this was the wrong decision, like I don't deserve to be happy.

But then the door opens, and Elise stands on the other side. Her oversized, bright yellow shirt is wrinkled, and her hair is mussed with bedhead. She squints at me as she runs her hand through it. "Logan? What are you doing here?"

"Umm." I forgot, which is exactly what I was hoping for. "I'm sorry I woke you."

"Is everything okay?"

I shake my head, my next words coming out as a whisper. "I don't know yet."

She sighs. "Did you see a doctor?"

A smile almost breaks out on my face, but I contain it. I just woke her up, probably at least an hour or two before she'd normally have to be up to get ready for work, and she's worried about *me*. Yes, usually, I'd hate that. *A lot*. But, right now, coming from her, it feels good.

But I have to push her because that's what I do too. "If I say no?"

She rolls her eyes and starts to shut the door.

I can't help but grin, slamming my hand flat against the wood to stop it from closing. "Christ, Elise. I went."

With one hand still on the door, she places her other on her hip and stares at me like she's trying to decide if I'm telling the truth. "You did?"

I nod. "I just went to the hospital."

"And?"

I consider telling her all about it, about the doctor's suspicion and how it matched my own. But…

"Do I have to talk about it in order to come inside?"

She stares at me a few seconds longer, then releases a long breath. "No."

Without waiting for more of an invitation than that, I push my way in and slam the door shut. I take Elise's face between my hands and bring my mouth to hers.

16

ELISE

Logan's here. Here, *everywhere*. All over me. Surrounding me. Becoming my entire world as the rest of it is shut out.

I let her ravage me because I can tell it's what she needs. Her tongue slips past my lips like a thief in the night, the feel of silky flesh and hard, smooth steel from her piercing sending a wave of heat through me. The full length of her body presses against mine, and I moan into her mouth. Her hands move from my face, one traveling down my arm to grip me just above my elbow and the other tangling itself in my hair.

She starts to push me back, and again, I let her. Until I can kind of feel the limp of her right foot hindering her. Then I plant my feet and stop her, gently extricating my mouth from hers.

"Wait," I whisper between panting breaths. Because, once more, Logan has forgotten about the importance of breathing. I stare into her eyes that are full of...not quite desperation. More like determination. And desire. "Just tell me everything's okay."

The small smile she gives me is easy and genuine, something I'm not used to seeing directed at me. "It will be."

I want more. I want to know what happened and what she found out, but I don't want to pressure her to talk about it if she doesn't want to. Even if our relationship—situationship?—wasn't already so fragile, I couldn't bring myself to try to force it out of her. I'll just have to accept that it's a good sign they didn't admit her, that she's here now.

"What do you need, Logan?" I ask, reaching up with one hand to move a loose strand of dark, flowing hair away from her face.

She leans into my touch, practically purring. "Just you."

My heart damn near leaps out of my throat. I don't know what changed or when it did, but those are just more answers I'm not about to push for.

I press my lips to hers, a light, sweeping touch. "I'm yours."

The next noise she makes rumbles through her and into me. I swear it's a *growl*. "Fucking right you are."

She snatches up my lips in a brutal, demanding, *claiming* kiss. Her grip in my hair tightens as she begins to back me up again, moving us in the direction of my bedroom. I go easily, not caring what her plans are once we get there as long as *she's* there. I'm still a bit tired and groggy from having been woken up early, but I don't mind sacrificing sleep when it comes to her.

I'm so completely hypnotized by her that I don't realize we've made it to the bedroom until the backs of my legs hit my bed.

Blackout curtains over the one window in the room shroud any light from what I'm sure is dusk outside. The only light comes from the bulb in the hallway I turned on when I woke up to answer the door.

Mostly veiled in shadows, she pushes me down and then makes quick work of taking off her boots and jeans. I expect her to crawl on top of me, but instead, she climbs onto the mattress beside me, scooching us both back until our heads are on the pillows.

Then she wraps her arms around me, buries her face in the crook of my neck and shoulder and…just stays there.

I let her stay like that for over a minute before curiosity gets the best of me.

"What are we doing?" I ask, amusement seeping through my voice.

"I'm holding you," she says, like that should be obvious.

Which it is. But I guess I have whiplash from going from hot and heavy making out to cuddling. Not that I'm complaining. I'll take Logan whichever way I can have her.

"Are you sure everything's okay?" I can't help but ask.

"Shut up, Elise."

The way her curt voice is muffled in my neck makes me grin. "Okay."

Our breathing evens out the longer we lie here. A few minutes pass, and I think she's fallen asleep until she speaks again.

"I think we should go to Vail."

I pull back to look at her because there's no way I heard that correctly.

She doesn't move, keeping her eyes closed. I half expect to feel her tense, to regret the words that just came out of her mouth. But she doesn't.

"Together?" I ask on a breath.

"No. We'll take turns."

Usually, there's venom dripping off her tongue, so I'll gladly take the sarcasm instead.

"Please tell me they at least ran a CT scan because I'm seriously starting to worry about brain dam—"

I don't get the chance to finish my sentence before she's gripping me by my hair and yanking my head back, exposing my throat to her so she can sink her teeth into my skin, right at the junction of my neck and shoulder. A sharp cry tears out of me, quickly turning into a moan. Her leg comes up between mine, parting them so she can rub her thigh against my center. I wouldn't be surprised if I'm already dripping wet.

The sharp sting eases as she lets up, her teeth scraping down to my collarbone. My breath comes heavier as I rock my hips, chasing the friction of her thigh.

Suddenly, it's gone.

I whine, and she laughs, the raspy sound vibrating against my chest, the warmth of her breath feeling even hotter against my skin.

Her hand replaces her thigh between my legs, her fingertips ghosting over my pussy. It's a featherlight touch, barely there over the thin fabric of my shorts and panties. I roll my hips forward, but she pulls her hand back. I groan, but it doesn't stop her from doing that half a dozen more times.

"You want more?" she whispers, nipping at what skin she

can reach above the collar of my shirt. "Show me what you want."

I don't hesitate. I reach for the hem of her boy shorts and slip my hand inside them, immediately finding her wet. As I brush my finger over her clit, she finally gives me the pressure on mine that I was searching for.

I quicken my pace, rolling the sensitive bud between my fingers. She matches my rhythm for a few rolls of my hips until her hand glides smoothly beneath both layers of clothes until I feel her bare fingers. When two of them slide through my slickness and thrust inside me, I moan. The sound isn't even halfway out before she raises her head and swallows it down with a kiss.

The feeling of her fingers inside me, her tongue diving into my mouth to tangle with mine, is enough to make me want to feel her too. My fingers travel, finding her entrance and slowly pressing two inside her. I pump them in and out, using my thumb to rub circles over her clit. She moans into my mouth and does the same, copying my movements almost exactly until it's like there's a mirror between us.

Not that there's space for anything to fit, joined together like we are.

She breaks our kiss to nip at my bottom lip. "I fucking love being inside you. You get so fucking wet."

As always, her words make me burn hotter, igniting that throbbing ache between my legs until it's like I'm on fire, dying for release. Ready to beg for it.

Again, she bites my lip, harder than before. "I'm going to fuck you with my cock one of these days."

My eyes fly open. "Wh-what?"

"Would you like that?" Another bite. "If I strapped on my cock and fucked you real good with it?"

Oh.

Chances are I probably would've been able to guess that's what she meant if my brain wasn't currently offline, not able to connect with any sense of reasonable thought.

But when the meaning finally registers, an image conjuring in my head, I lose myself. I don't think I've ever known what it feels like to go feral for another human, but I do now.

Her lips are right there, brushing against mine, so I bite hers this time, taking her bottom one into my mouth. I suck on it, scrape my teeth across the soft, full, pink flesh. She groans, adds a third finger, and starts fucking me with them relentlessly. I match her tempo until we're moaning into each other's mouths, our hips rocking to the same rhythm.

I don't think it was meant to be a race, a competition to see who could make the other come the fastest. At least it wasn't for me, too wrapped up in her. Her reactions, her body. Fully submerged in pleasure.

But when she breaks first, muscles spasming around my fingers, I feel something like triumph.

I only get to enjoy it for a moment before her orgasm sets off my own, ecstasy coursing through my veins and my bones, every single atom. My entire body trembles and shivers with it, as though it's seeping out of every pore.

When I finally come down from the high and my eyes flutter open, I'm greeted by the sight of Logan's easy smile. A faint blush has risen to her skin, like light brush strokes across the apples of her cheeks. We never bothered to turn on a light, but the dim glow from the hallway illuminates half her face. I swear the gray of her eyes is the lightest I've ever seen them.

"Good to know you like the idea of me fucking you with something bigger than my fingers," she says, her relaxed smile turning into a smug grin.

"I never said that."

"You didn't have to."

She removes her hand from my underwear, and I do the same. Bringing her fingers that are glistening with my arousal to her lips, she darts out her tongue, licking the evidence of my release off of them.

If the flush in my face didn't give me away, that certainly did.

Holding her gaze, I complete our mirror effect by sucking my own fingers clean.

After she's finished, she wraps her arm around me again and pulls me in for another kiss. It's slower this time, our tongues lazily tangling together as we share each other's taste. My lip feels a little bruised from all the attention she gave it with her teeth, but I don't even try to stop her.

We break apart, and she rests her head on my pillow with what sounds like a contented sigh. Her eyes gradually drift closed, and her breathing turns slow and steady. I know she's fallen asleep when her hold on me relaxes.

I lie there for a while, wishing I knew what was going on inside her head. Why it feels like she doesn't hate me. At least not today.

It doesn't feel like the game she's been playing. If anything, it felt like she meant what she said, that she needed me. *Me.*

Maybe that's all it was. Maybe she just needed something to help her forget. Maybe nothing's really changed between us.

I don't want that to be the case, but I don't think I'd hold it against her if it was.

Not with everything she's clearly going through—a physical and mental battle she's not quite ready to share with me. I don't hold that against her either. If she needs time to come to terms with whatever she found out at the hospital, I'll give it to her.

I think I'd give her whatever it is she needs.

17

LOGAN

I woke up in Elise's bed sometime in the middle of the night. I vaguely remember her waking me to tell me she had to go to work and that I could stay there. I was too tired to move. So I stayed.

Once I was fully awake, I considered sticking around until Elise came home. Maybe snoop around a bit, maybe cook her something for breakfast. Dinner? Our schedules are both fucked.

Ultimately, that felt a little too fucking domesticated, so I left.

After last night, I'm even more turned upside down. Elise was perfect. No surprise there. I was scared she was going to push me to talk about my trip to the hospital, but as always, she knew exactly what I needed and gave it to me.

I don't fucking deserve her.

But, fuck, I want her.

She said she was mine, and I want to make her mine.

But that requires me to be selfish.

And...maybe I'm selfish after all.

I want more nights like that. I want her to give me what I need. Sometimes, that's giving me hell, showing me that spark in her. Sometimes, that's her orgasms or mine. Sometimes, that's falling asleep while holding her.

I want Elise Novak.

I make that decision sometime that morning while I'm making a bite to eat before I go get a few more hours of sleep.

I should've stayed and cooked for her instead of running away scared.

When my phone rings, I'm frustrated as it interrupts my daring, dumb, and determined resolution to officially make Elise mine. But when I see it's the doctor's office calling, I quickly answer, nearly burning myself on the stove in the process.

Okay, Elise probably wouldn't have wanted me to cook for her anyway.

The receptionist on the other end of the line tells me they can get me in with a neurologist the day after tomorrow.

Yeah, that's *a lot* faster than if I had waited to see my primary doctor first.

She also lets me know that the neurologist has already ordered an MRI and that they could set that up for me two weeks out. I guess I don't have much of a choice.

After booking both the appointments with the receptionist, I hang up and take my food off the stove. It's slightly burnt but still edible. I eat most of it while texting Jacklyn to let her know I need a few more days off but that I'm getting everything taken care of. She tells me to take all the time I need and to take care of myself.

Even though I have to practically drag one of my feet to bed, I feel a little lighter than I have in weeks.

I've stayed away from Elise the past two days, only because I'm not ready to talk to her about any of this. I want to have good news to share with her the next time I see her. I hope I get some today.

The clinic that my appointment is at is in the next town over because our small touristy town doesn't have a lot of specialists. At least it wasn't too far of a drive. I'm not sure if my right foot would've been able to handle it if it was. It takes too much energy trying to control the damn thing to work the pedals safely.

I pull up outside the clinic and head inside.

That familiar anxiety of being in a doctor's office creeps through me, especially considering all the noise I cause as I make my way through the lobby to the front desk, drawing too much attention to myself.

Why is it so fucking quiet in here?

After getting checked in, I make more racket as I walk over and take a seat in one of the hideous yellow chairs. I stare up at the door in front of me with large capital letters above it that spell out the word *Neurology*. My anxiety kicks up a notch.

I don't have to wait long before the door opens and a nurse calls my name.

Here we go again.

I'm so fucking tired of walking.

On the other side of the door, the nurse has me step on a scale before taking me to a room. She takes my vitals, then leaves me alone to wait for the doctor. The wait is only a little longer than the last one. When the doctor enters, he gives me a brilliant smile, striking white teeth against warm, golden skin.

"I'm Dr. Dharashiokar. You can call me Dr. D; everyone does."

He offers me his hand, and I shake it, his skin icy against my heated palm.

"So why don't you tell me what's been going on?" he asks as he takes a seat on his stool.

I do, starting with the vibrating in my tailbone I experienced a couple months ago, that bolt of lightning that would strike my spine every time I bent my neck forward. He's impressed when I already know what it's called—Lhermitte's Sign, a symptom almost exclusive to MS. When I tell him I mentioned it to my primary doctor who chalked it up to a pinched nerve, I get the feeling he's a little upset that I didn't advocate for myself better when I already knew what it was.

I get it. After gaining all these new symptoms, I'm upset with myself too.

Dr. D tells me that the best treatment for an MS exacerbation—what I'm currently experiencing—is a round of steroid infusions. My heart does this strange flip back and forth. Dropping with dread because...*drugs*. But also jumping for joy and immense relief that I'm able to be treated for this. And soon, judging by the sound of it.

"So...does this mean I for sure have MS?" I ask before the appointment is over.

"I can't give you an official diagnosis just yet without the tests we need to run. Blood tests, MRI, spinal tap. But I think it's safe to say that MS is the most likely diagnosis."

I don't know exactly what happens during a spinal tap, but I know I don't like the sound of it.

However, after all the research I've done, I'm aware that it takes some people months or years to get an official diagnosis of MS. I already really like this neurologist with how quickly he's trying to get that done. So I suppose I need to do what's necessary to help that along.

As we head out of the room and he's walking with me to the main desk of the neurology department, he asks, "You were scheduled for an MRI, right?"

"I was. They couldn't get me in for a couple weeks though."

"Well, that won't work."

The way his eyes narrow shocks me. He's genuinely *mad*. I don't think I've ever seen a doctor that angry before.

I have a doctor who truly, sincerely *cares*.

I think this is the easiest I've ever been able to accept compassion from another person.

At the desk, he tells his receptionist to call Radiology personally and get that MRI ordered "stat." I nearly grin because

I also don't think I've ever heard a doctor use that word. Still, I appreciate his urgency.

Before leaving the clinic, I make a follow-up appointment with Dr. D for after all my tests have been run, then head to the other side of the building to get blood work done. They draw several vials of blood, more than I've ever had them take, wrap an elastic bandage over a cotton ball in the crease of my elbow, and send me on my way.

I'm utterly drained, both physically and mentally, by the time I'm heading back out to the parking lot. It's not a huge lot, but it's big enough, stretching out before me. Mocking me.

But it's the last remaining walking journey of this exhausting trip. I've got this.

Except I don't.

I haven't even made it past the sidewalk when my right foot lands the wrong way with all its extra weight, rolling beneath me. I fall, literally and figuratively, tumbling to my lowest point of these past few months.

My knee hits the concrete, probably scraping the hell out of it. But the pain of that and the throbbing in my right ankle is dulled by my mortification.

I curse my defective nervous system to the deepest, darkest pits of hell.

Quickly grabbing onto the brick ledge of the garden beside me, I attempt to hoist myself up. But…I can't. No matter how hard I try, I gain no vertical distance. I take a beat and a breath. Give it another shot.

Why the fuck can't I just stand up?

It's like a mortal struggle against the force of gravity.

And gravity is winning.

It's beating me, holding me down until I just want to fucking give up. I'm tempted. I could simply fall to my ass and stay here to rot. It's the final betrayal of my body. It's won the last battle. I've been defeated.

Even with all these pessimistic and self-pitying thoughts running rampant through my mind, I don't stop trying. I don't stop fighting.

The driver side door of a small red car parked in front of the sidewalk opens, and an older man steps out. The first thing I notice is the windbreaker he wears, the color a much more bright and cheerful yellow than the unsightly chairs inside the clinic. He rushes over to me and offers his hand.

"Are you all right?"

"I'm fine," I lie as I take his hand, trying not to give him too much of my weight.

"Are you sure?"

The second thing I notice about him is his familiar face—dark skin, salt-and-pepper hair. I'm certain I've seen him before, but I can't place him.

"I'm okay. Thank you."

It's another lie because as soon as I rush away as fast as my body allows, more humiliated than before, I know I'm not even close to okay. A sharp pain radiates through my right ankle every time my foot drops to the ground. At least if it's sprained, it happened to the foot that might as well be broken.

When I finally make it to my car, I hurry inside, slamming the door behind me. I thought once I was safe within the confines of my vehicle I'd feel better.

I don't.

Pulling out my phone from the pocket of my jacket, I do my best to ignore the pressure growing in my skull, the wave of despair and hopelessness threatening to drown me. I look down at my screen, my trembling fingers mindlessly pulling up Elise's contact. My brain is too tired to admit how much I need her right now, the part of my body that still functions working off instinct.

My fingers hover over the call button. It's the middle of the day, so she's probably asleep.

But…I *need* her.

I press the call button.

I'm such a selfish cunt.

It rings once. Twice. By the third ring, my eyes are stinging. Every second that passes that I can't hear her voice on the other end has my vision blurring.

Finally, I hear her voice, but it's not the one I want. It's the recorded one, too professional, with none of Elise's warmth.

Fuck this stupid fucking pity party.

I'm over it.

Hanging up the phone, I toss it over onto the passenger seat and start my car. I sniff back the tears that I managed to keep from falling, blinking them away.

It's even more difficult to drive now because on top of barely being able to control it, I'm pretty sure my foot is indeed sprained. It hurts like a motherfucker. But I have to get home, so I'll deal with it.

As I pull out of the lot, I think about that man who helped me off the sidewalk. I wish I knew where I recognized him from, but I can't seem to find the right memory through all the chaos in my head.

How long would I have stayed on that sidewalk if he hadn't been there?

If I believed in them, I might have called him my guardian angel.

I'm nearly halfway home when I get a call from Radiology. They want me back there for an MRI in less than two hours.

Turns out I have a badass for a neurologist.

Since I haven't made it too far yet, I turn my car around and head back. I'll take a nap in my seat or something while I wait.

After my MRI, it's officially been the longest day of my life. I finally get to drive home, emotional and exhausted. Despite the earplugs I wore in the machine, I'm left with the lingering hums and knocks and pulses and beeps and buzzes ringing in my ears.

They stay with me all the way to Elise's apartment.

It's only when she's once more in my arms that they fall silent.

18

ELISE

I usually wake up to my phone when it rings. I like to be available in case the hospital or any of my family needs me. However, I went to sleep completely forgetting that I left it on silent. Declan had been blowing up my phone after I told him I couldn't go out of town with him to get tattoos for his birthday. When he asked if it was because of "that Logan bitch," I stopped responding and silenced my phone.

It's not *just* because of Logan. My first year of residency is already kicking my ass just a couple months in. I'm tired and simply not up to a trip like that.

But, also…it is a little because of Logan. I want to be around in case she needs me. And clearly she does.

I felt bad for not answering my phone when she told me what happened at the clinic. We stayed awake, lying in my bed together for a couple hours before I had to go to work while she told me everything.

When she said it's MS, my heart plummeted into my stomach like one of those drop tower amusement park rides. I wanted to cry, but I wasn't about to do that in front of her. She didn't shed a single tear while she told me all about this horrible thing that's happening to her.

I'll be damned if I let *her* be the only one who's strong during all this.

And she is. She's so fucking strong.

I could tell it's not easy on her. But it wouldn't be for anyone, no matter how strong they were.

I don't know everything there is to know about MS, but I at least know there are treatments available and therapy drugs that can lessen the amount and severity of flares. I want to be there with her through it all.

If she'll let me.

She fell asleep before we could get into anything deep like that. Once again, I let her stay in my bed while I went to work.

The stack of paperwork on my mom's desk in front of me never seems to get any smaller. Every evening I come in, I swear it's a few inches taller. Even when I spend most of the night working on it, I never get close to finishing.

Of course, tonight, I've been a bit more distracted than I usually allow myself to be.

I can't stop thinking about Logan and her future.

My future.

I don't dare think *ours*.

I've spent a couple hours researching MS and neurology in general. At least no one can say I haven't been using the computer for anything not medical related.

Fortunately, I've gone back to the paperwork when my mom walks into her office.

"Break time," she announces as she settles in the chair on the other side of her own desk. She opens a small Tupperware container of fruit and places it on the desk between us. "How's the grunt work coming along?"

I shrug as I take a slice of apple from the container. "It's fine."

"No complaining?" she asks with a grin.

"Do I ever complain?"

"Not out loud."

I bite my tongue because, yeah…my mom knows me too well.

"It's okay," she says with a knowing smile. "I know it feels like you're not really allowed to complain, but you always can with me if you need to."

"I don't need to complain, but…" I take the last bite of my apple and swallow it down. "I did want to talk to you about something."

She sits up a little straighter in her seat. "Anything, sweetie."

"I haven't made a definite decision yet, but I've been thinking." I take a slow, deep breath. "About maybe…specializing in neurology."

"Neurology?" My mom's eyebrows rise a little into her forehead, and I don't blame her for being shocked. I've never mentioned that as a possible specialty before. "Really?"

I nod, waiting to see more of her reaction.

"Well, I think that's great," she says with a genuine smile. "Is there a particular reason?"

I anticipated that question, but I unfortunately hadn't planned a more detailed answer than, "Kind of."

She doesn't press for more of an explanation, which I'm grateful for. I haven't told my mom about Logan yet, and even though I'm not ashamed, I'm still not quite ready.

Not only that, but Logan's diagnosis isn't for me to share.

It's not that I expect her to want me to be her doctor, but if she did, it would save her a trip out of town for every one of her appointments. If not, I wouldn't be upset. I'd drive her to her neurologist if she'd let me.

"You do know that means more like seven years of residency instead of the three you'd need for something like family medicine?"

"I know. I don't mind. But I'm still not fully decided yet."

"Okay." She gives me another smile as she plucks a couple of grapes from the container on the desk. "Let me know what you decide."

"I will."

If I'm being honest with myself, I've probably already decided.

When I get home the next morning, I see Logan's car is still parked out front of my apartment. I couldn't stop the way my lips stretch across half my face even if I tried.

I hop out of my car so fast I nearly forget to cut the engine first. I climb the stairs with much more energy than I'm used to having after a twelve-hour shift.

But when I reach the second floor, my pace slows, and my good mood evaporates.

Declan stands outside my door, leaning against the wall, staring down at his phone in his hand. When he hears my steps approaching, he looks up and gives me one of those boyish grins of his. "Hey."

"Hey," I say back, giving him my best tired smile. Which isn't all that difficult to fake. "What are you doing here?"

"Thought I'd swing by on my way to work. Wanted to check on you. Make sure everything's okay since you bailed on my birthday plans."

"Oh. Yeah, I'm fine. I'm really sorry. I've been slammed with work. I'm always tired. I just don't have it in me."

"Okay. I understand. How about we go inside and I make you a cup of coffee?" he asks like he's not inviting me into my own apartment.

Despite being a little put off, I try to keep the smile on my face. "I think I'm going to head to bed early. I'll make it up to you though, okay?"

He stares at me for an uncomfortable beat, then says, "So it has nothing to do with Logan being inside?"

My face falls.

"I know that's her car parked out front."

I cross my arms over my chest, suddenly feeling defensive. More so for Logan than for myself. "It's really none of your business, Dec."

He moves away from the wall to take a step toward me. "It is when she's treated our whole family like dirt on the bottom of her shoe for the past decade."

"She was grieving *her* family, Declan," I say, lowering my voice, *really* hoping Logan isn't pressing her ear against the door right now. "Can you seriously blame her? It was *her* brother who died."

"And she's probably using you for some sick, petty revenge plan that you don't even deserve."

I clench my jaw, remaining silent. I'm not about to tell him that's exactly what her goal was. Because that was in the beginning. Things have changed. I know they have. It's not some naive hope. I can tell there's more between us than that now by the way she holds me, the way she needs me even if she doesn't want to need me.

"We didn't do anything wrong, El. It wasn't our fault. It was Landon's. She can't accept that, and now she's going to take it out on you. But you can't see that because you've always wanted to believe the best in people."

"So what if I do? What if I do get hurt? It's not your problem."

His face screws up, and I can practically feel the heat of his disgust. "You're fucking her, aren't you?"

"That's *definitely* none of your business."

"So what? Are you fucking queer now?"

I've never been one quick to temper, but I can feel the pressure of angry tears behind my eyes. Or maybe they're just from hurt. Because I also never would've thought my own brother would be the one to judge me, to shame me. He doesn't have to say the words. I can feel his revulsion and see the indignation in his eyes.

It breaks my heart.

"This isn't you, El. She's a manipulative cunt, and you need to stay away from her."

That's fucking it.

"Leave, Declan. You're not welcome here."

His head jerks back like I just slapped him. His brows dip, and his eyes fill with hurt.

But I won't let *him* be the one to manipulate me.

"You're choosing her over me?"

"Logan and I are working on moving past everything. Until you can do the same, I think *you* should stay away from *me*."

His jaw ticks, but after a moment, he nods and takes a step back. "Fine, Elise. When you realize what a bitch she is and you're over this phase, I'll be around."

He brushes past me, his swift steps heavy on the stairs as he leaves.

All the air in my lungs I had been holding in for the last minute comes rushing out. I blink, and a single tear slides down my cheek. I quickly wipe it away.

"When you're over this phase…"

So if he knows that I'm bisexual with or without Logan, then…what? He *won't* be around?

I stay out in the hallway for a couple more minutes, taking deep breaths in an attempt to stave off the impending anxiety attack that's lingering on the horizon. I don't want to go inside and face Logan like this.

Once I'm calm enough, I unlock my door and step inside.

Logan's sitting on my couch, my worn copy of *The Invisible Life of Addie LaRue* in her hands and a steaming mug of something on my coffee table. Her right foot is propped up on the armrest with a frozen bag of peas over her ankle.

"How was your talk with Declan?" she asks without looking up from the book.

I frown. "How much did you hear?"

"Nothing. I'm not a snoop. I could tell it was him by his voice."

She peers up at me with a smile on her face, but as soon as her gaze meets mine, it falls. Shutting the book, she places it on the table and stands. She still has the foot drop and a minor sprained ankle, so when she walks around the couch in my direction, I meet her halfway.

Her arms are around me immediately, holding me tight in that way I've grown to love.

"What happened? Do I need to beat his ass?"

I wrap my arms around her waist, rest my cheek on her shoulder, and shake my head. "No. That's the last thing I need you to do. I want things to get better, not worse. I just…I guess I didn't think about how some people would react."

Her body tenses. "You told him?"

"He figured it out when he saw your car out front."

"Shit. I'm sorry."

"It's not your fault. Well, the bi-awakening kind of is…"

She laughs, the sound rumbling through me. "Not sorry about that one. I made coffee, by the way."

My laughter joins hers at the drastic change of subject. I peer over her shoulder at the mug on the coffee table. The liquid inside looks like a lighter shade of brown than a latte. "Did you drown the entire pot with cream and sugar or just your own?"

"Just mine. I wasn't sure how you took it."

"Do you still hate me?"

I blurt out the question, switching gears even faster than she had. I bury my face into the crook of her neck and shoulder because I can't stand to see the answer on her face. The sound of blood rushes in my ears. I inhale that faint, sweet sage scent of hers like it might be the last time I get to smell it.

Her chest rises and falls against mine with a sigh. "I want to, Elise. You were one of the last people to see Liam alive, and I want to hate you for that alone."

I pull back just enough to look into her eyes, desperate for her to see the truth in mine. "I swear, Logan, I don't remember exactly what happened."

"I believe you now."

She reaches up to brush a strand of hair off my face, and I lean into her touch, my heart still beating wildly. Waiting.

"So, no," she finally says. "I don't hate you. I *can't*."

And just like that, everything is fine. She presses her lips to mine, and everything is perfect.

All thoughts of the past, of Logan's diagnosis, of Declan's spite fade away as she holds me and kisses me. I cling to this escape she's giving me, reminding me how good it feels to be this close to her.

How can something that feels like this, that helps to mend my heart that's breaking over so much, be wrong?

19

LOGAN

I'm so tired of seeing the inside of hospitals. But I'm finally getting treatment for this flare, so I won't complain. Not this time at least.

As much as I hate pretty much all drugs and am not at all looking forward to getting these steroid infusions, I'm hoping they're worth it.

I've found myself full of hope a lot more lately.

It probably has something to do with my ray of sunshine sitting beside me in the waiting room.

She's on her phone, giving me space, I suspect, as I fill out the paperwork on the clipboard in my hands.

At least, I *try* to.

The pen shakes in my hand, writing nothing but squiggly marks. My hand has gotten much worse over the past few days, and every little scrawl I manage is illegible.

I take a deep breath and keep trying.

No matter how slowly I move the pen across the paper or how much effort I put into forming clear and smooth letters, no one's going to be able to read this shit.

The last thing I want to do is ask Elise for help. Not because I think she'd mind or make me feel bad about it. Asking for help is just as difficult for me as accepting sympathy or concern or compassion.

But if *I* can't even make out my own name through the shaky, aimless scribbles, no one else is going to be able to either.

"Fuck," I mutter under my breath, barely resisting the urge to throw the pen across the room.

Elise looks up from her phone, her brows pinched with—surprise!—*concern*.

I clench my jaw and offer her the pen and clipboard. "I can't do it."

She gives me a smile that's relaxed and caring, not pitying. "I've got you," she says as she takes the paperwork from me and starts filling it in with handwriting that's as bubbly as her damn personality.

Leaning back in my seat, I cross my arms over my chest, pick a random spot across the room, and glare at it.

I fucking hate this.

I hate this.

I hate this so fucking much!

I hate my nervous wreck of a nervous system. I hate the way my body's betraying me. I hate not being able to walk or write or work. I hate this itch that's developing in my right forearm. No matter how hard or how much I scratch it, it never goes away.

Most of all, I hate feeling sorry for myself.

The problem is I don't know how to stop. If I could, I would in a heartbeat. This feeling is gross. There's a tightness in my chest and a vise squeezing the life out of my stomach until I'm sure I'm going to throw up what little food is in there.

"I'll take this to the desk," Elise says as she stands and heads up to the front.

I was brooding so long I didn't even realize enough time had passed for her to finish filling out all my paperwork.

Get it the fuck together, Logan.

When Elise returns, I somehow manage to give her a small smile. "Thank you for doing that."

"Of course."

The smile she gives me in return is similar as before. The one that glows brilliantly on her face, makes her shine brighter. I used to love to see her frown when I hurt her or her brows drawn tight when I pissed her off. Now, all I want to see is this—the pure happiness that's in her eyes when she looks at me like this, those halos glimmering gold. When she's not hurt or disappointed or angry because of me.

"I told you I want to help," she adds. "Whether you need it or not. If it makes your life easier, then I want to do it."

"You just worked a twelve-hour shift," I point out. "How are you still so perfect even when you're sleep deprived?"

Her lips part, probably a reaction to the word *perfect*.

I grin as I watch a rosy hue bloom across her cheeks. "I just meant you didn't have to come with me. I know you don't get much sleep as it is."

"I can sleep after. I wanted to come with you."

I wanted her to come with me too.

The door in front of us opens, and the nurse calls my name. Elise and I both stand, and she matches my slower pace as we walk across the lobby and through the door.

On the other side is a bunch of cubicles that all have a large, cushioned chair inside them. This is the same place where oncology patients receive their chemotherapy, so it's a little depressing. But at least it looks comfortable.

The nurse leads us to one of the cubicles and directs me to the chair. I sit, trying to relax. Elise takes a seat in the other chair that's the same as the ones out in the waiting room.

After the nurse leaves, telling us another one will be here soon to start the infusion, I give Elise a smirk. "At least I get the comfy chair."

She takes my playful teasing with a grin. "You're going to be sitting here with a needle in your arm for an hour. I'd say you deserve it."

A nice, comfortable recliner is probably about the extent of good things I deserve, but I don't really need to go back to that train of thought right now.

Another nurse shows up and gets the IV drip of steroids started. Her name is Joy, which turns out to be quite fitting. She's all smiles, despite the place she's working. She and Elise unsurprisingly hit it off while I sit there mostly quiet. However, having two of them around offers some comfort I wouldn't otherwise admit I need.

Joy leaves, and Elise pulls a book out of her oversized purse, the one I had been reading in her apartment.

"Do you want this?" she asks as she offers it to me.

"We could talk," I suggest instead.

The corner of her mouth twitches like she's trying to disguise how happy that idea makes her. She places the book back in her purse and asks, "What do you want to talk about?"

"What's your favorite color?"

She laughs quietly but answers with yellow, baby blue being a close second.

I'm not surprised.

Deep conversation is out of the realm of my current capabilities. However, as we spend the next half hour asking questions and getting to know more about each other, it feels like anything but a trivial game of twenty questions. The unspoken meaning behind it all is just as deep as if I were to tell her I want her to be mine.

Joy returns, appearing from around the corner of the cubicle. "How are you doing, Logan?"

"I'm okay," I answer, and it at least doesn't feel like a lie. "But, umm…is it supposed to taste like I've been sucking on pennies?"

The nurse grins and nods. "Yes, a metallic taste in your mouth is normal."

Elise pulls out a bag of mints from her purse, handing them to me. "You should've said something. I thought you might need these."

With my gaze locked on her, I take them and pop one in my mouth.

Fucking perfect.

I can't seem to take my eyes off Elise as I start sucking on the candy, satisfied as it helps to dull the taste of pennies.

"Someone came prepared," Joy comments as she starts walking away. Before she disappears, she mouths behind Elise's back, "She's a keeper."

Okay, so I was definitely not subtle with the way I was staring at the woman I brought with me. But Joy isn't wrong.

I want to keep her.

Once the hour is up and the IV bag is empty, Joy comes back around to disconnect me from the drip, removing the needle from my arm and bandaging me up. I'm still walking with one foot made of lead as we leave, but it's not like I was expecting the steroids to do their job immediately.

Elise drives us back to her apartment, and when she parks, I stare at my car beside hers.

I don't want to go home.

"This is around the time you usually sleep, isn't it?" she asks.

"Yeah, my schedule isn't too different from yours."

When she's silent for several seconds, I turn my head to look at her. She's biting her lip, hesitating.

"Would you want to sleep here?" she asks. Then she quickly adds, "You can say no."

She has no idea what she does to me.

"Why would I say no?"

She beams at me and then shuts off her car. We head up to her apartment, and she drags me into her bathroom where we enjoy a slow, sensual exploration of each other's bodies beneath the warm spray of the shower.

With the midday sun veiled by the blackout curtains in her bedroom, I pull her into the bed and into my arms, and we fall asleep in the dark to our makeshift night.

When Elise's alarm goes off that night, we kiss good morning, slow and deep and not as long as I'd like. She attempts to scramble away, complaining about her own morning breath, but I pull her back for just a little more.

While she gets up to get ready for work, I throw on a pair of underwear and a tank top before heading into the kitchen. I start a pot of coffee so she can take some with her to work. It's not until I cross the small kitchen to the fridge to get the creamer to drown my own coffee that I notice a change.

It's quiet.

My bare foot isn't smacking the hardwood floor.

There's no slap echoing off the walls.

There's nothing but the soft padding of my normal steps as I walk back across the kitchen. And again. Pacing to test my control over my movements. I feel more balanced than I have in weeks. That weak feeling still lingers, but…

I can fucking walk.

"Elise!"

Fuck, I could cry. My eyes sting, but I hold back the tears of the immense joy I feel.

Elise comes rushing down the hall and into the kitchen, her brow furrowed with worry. "What's wrong?"

"Nothing," I tell her as my face breaks out into a smile.

That crease between her brows deepens, this time with confusion. "What—"

I cross the kitchen one last time, take her face between my hands, and kiss her. We both end up falling into it, a hard press of lips, tongues tangling passionately, until Elise does that thing where she insists we come up for air.

It takes her a few seconds to catch her breath and for her to register what I called her in here for.

She glances down at my feet and back up to my face, her mouth slowly curling upward. "Your foot drop is gone."

I nod, still unable to stop smiling. "I didn't think the steroids would work that fast."

"Well, I'm happy they did."

I believe her. She looks as ecstatic and relieved as I feel.

"Do you think I have to—"

"Yes. You have to finish the entire round of steroids your neurologist prescribed, Logan."

I'm slightly surprised she knows me that well already. I guess I shouldn't be though, not with how little I try to hide my innate stubbornness, especially around her.

The strict expression on her face is adorable, with the determined set of her jaw and her eyes attempting a hard stare but failing miserably because they're just too perpetually bright.

I almost want to fight her on it just to rile her up some.

Instead, I lean forward and place a soft, chaste kiss to her lips. "Okay."

Her eyes narrow. "Really?"

"Yes, really, Dr. Elise," I say, grinning.

"Good." She nods like she just won some imaginary victory. "Because I'll kick your ass if you don't."

My mouth stretches wider until it almost hurts. "I'd like to find out how that would end."

She shoves me playfully and laughs. "Knowing you, back in my bed, and I'd be late for work."

"Well, we can't have that."

I move back over to the coffee pot, trying not to skip just because I can. I fill a thermos before opening the fridge to grab the creamer. I slide both across the counter toward Elise. She opens the creamer and pours a fucking *splash* into her coffee.

"That's it?" I ask, disgusted.

She shrugs.

"That's still practically black," I point out as I peer into the thermos. "Only psychopaths drink their coffee black."

"Then I guess we'll both be psychopaths tomorrow." Then she actually sticks her tongue out at me.

"Unless you want that to get bit, you better keep it in your mouth."

She wiggles her brows at me suggestively.

I shake my head, hating her a little at the reminder that my spinal tap is scheduled for tomorrow.

One of the risks of the procedure is something called a spinal headache, which sounds just about as unpleasant as I suspect it is. Apparently, drinking black coffee is one of the things that can help avoid it.

"Are you going to be here when I get home in the morning?" she asks, focusing a little harder than necessary on the lid of her thermos as she screws it on.

"I was thinking of going home to see if I can maybe do some painting."

She meets my gaze with a genuine smile. "Oh, okay. I imagine you've been missing it."

"I have. Do you want me to come over in the morning?"

"You don't have to…"

"Elise." I take a step forward, placing my hand on the side of her neck, staring into her eyes until I'm certain I have her undivided attention. "Tell me what you want."

She licks her lip, and my eyes track the movement of her tongue, the one seriously at risk of feeling my teeth's wrath. "I'd love to see you in the morning."

"Then I'll be here."

After another kiss that nearly lures us back into her bedroom, she lets me take a thermos of coffee, and we leave her apartment together, both of us heading our separate ways into the early night.

Instead of going straight home, I decide to stop by the studio first to see if Jacklyn's there. I want to give her an update. She had texted me yesterday to give me the news that Tate's successfully done a few tattoos, so at least she's had some help. But I'd like to give her some hope that I'll be returning soon so she doesn't replace me.

However, the moment I step inside the lobby, my great mood vanishes.

"What the fuck is with you Novaks showing up places you're not wanted?" I snap at the man standing at the counter as I stop a few feet behind him.

Declan Novak turns, a sneer already marring his face.

"Easy, tiger," Tate says from behind the desk. "I had to get some work done on my car, and I offered Declan a trade for a tattoo."

"He also said you weren't working here anymore," Declan grumbles, still scowling at me.

Tate holds his hands up in defense. "I did not. I just said you've been out for the past week."

If I'm going to believe either of them, it's going to be Tate.

Declan's narrowed eyes linger on me a few seconds longer before he turns back to Tate. "We all good for the appointment this weekend?"

I don't miss the way he says *weekend* like he doesn't want me to know the exact day.

"Sure thing. See ya then."

As Declan heads across the lobby toward the door, he stops in front of me. "Wanna get out of the way?"

If he looked at Elise the way he's looking at me, I'm going to cave his face in.

I hold my arms out to my sides. "There's plenty of space, douche."

"I'll tell you what," he says, his eyes turning darker, the sight strange on his boyish face. "I'll move around you if you agree to leave my fucking sister alone."

"I'm not the one who's hurt her most recently."

"You don't know what the fuck you're talking about. I'm trying to protect her from *you*, dyke."

Don't hit him. Don't hit him. Don't hit him.

Fuck, I really want to.

But Elise begged me not to make things worse. As much as I should attempt to play nice, I quite physically can't. But I can at least not send him to the hospital where Elise would have to treat all the injuries I'd give him.

Not to mention I don't need to add assault charges to everything else right now.

"And that's the exact reason why she needs protection from *you*."

With that, I take one step to the side, giving him space to walk past me. Because there's no way in hell I'm leaving Elise alone.

He gives me one last scowl before he moves, bumping into my shoulder purposefully on his way to the door.

The moment it closes behind him, I try to relax the taut muscles in my body, unclenching my jaw. There's still so much tension coiled tight as I step up to the desk and glare at my supposed best friend.

"What the fuck, Tate? How could you let that prick in here?"

"Sorry," he says, not sounding sorry at all. "I didn't want to pay to get my car fixed. Besides," he adds with that mischievous grin of his that's particularly annoying this time, "he's kind of hot."

"Ew. Gross. Don't forget homophobic."

"I don't know." He shrugs. "Seemed kind of interested to me."

"Yeah, well, I think you're gaydar is off, buddy."

"Maybe we'll find out."

I shake my head. "Make sure he gets tested first." Of course, the thought of Tate getting involved with an asshole like that has my insides squirming. "Is Jacklyn here?"

"Yeah, she's in the back."

I start heading around the desk, my feet stomping on the floor out of anger instead of disease.

"Hey," Tate says, stopping me in my tracks. "You feeling better?"

I glance down at my feet, then nod. "Getting there."

"Good. I'm glad."

I share a smile with him. "Me too."

Leaving the lobby, I walk down the hall to Jacklyn's office to share the good news with her. Unfortunately, it's slightly tainted now after my run-in with dipshit Declan. I'd been considering having that talk with Jacklyn about the studio, but I've changed my mind. I couldn't handle it right now if that news ends up to be the bad kind.

After I talk with Jacklyn and tell her I'll keep her updated on when I can come back to work, I make the drive home. I don't know if my hand will function well enough to paint yet, but I already have an idea of the next one I'll be doing for Elise.

20

ELISE

Logan's changed so much since I saw her for the first time in eight years when I returned to town. She went from hating me with the heat of a thousand lightning strikes to being consumed by anger because of this illness. I can't say I blame her for either of those things.

But now, I can see hope making its way through, clawing past all her defenses. I've seen a side of her I never thought I would.

She still likes to hurt me in bed a little, but it's always in ways that blend with the pleasure, heightening it. I get the feeling she doesn't want to hurt me in other ways anymore.

Those hard walls of hers crumble a little at a time when I'm with her. I'm chipping away at them, getting to see more of her soft and sweet with each one I take down. Sometimes she tries to build them back up, but I refuse to let her hide away in her fortress again.

Which is exactly why I have the radio in my car turned up to an obnoxious volume, blaring "Fight Song" by Rachel Platten as I drive Logan to her spinal tap. It felt fitting for what Logan's about to have to endure.

However, I can feel the heat of her glare on the side of my face as I keep my eyes on the road.

"I hate you!" she shouts over the music.

"You said you can't!" I stick my tongue out at her.

"What did I say would happen to that tongue, Elise?"

A shiver runs up my spine.

I wish she would.

"I'm driving. Maybe later."

I glance over in time to see her roll her eyes, and I laugh quietly under the noise from the speakers. When I start singing along, Logan slumps in her seat and groans.

"You can't sing for shit."

I start singing louder.

Logan laughs.

Mission accomplished.

We pull up outside the hospital, and I turn the volume down. We sit there for a few moments while I give her the time she needs to be able to brave the walk inside.

"I'm so sick of doctors," she mutters.

She swings her head around to look at me, and I raise a brow. But I can't even pretend to be offended with the way the corner of my mouth rises too.

"I mean *these* doctors," she says, waving a hand at the building in front of us. "These hospitals and all the tests. I'm tired."

"I know." I can only imagine how exhausting it is to be poked and prodded like she's been these past couple weeks. "They just have to rule out other things. It's part of the process."

She nods reluctantly, takes another few seconds, then opens the door. "Let's get this over with."

We head inside the hospital, and we don't have to wait long before we're taken back to pre-op. They have Logan change into a gown and sit on a bed. I take a seat in the chair in the corner while we wait again.

I can't help but check her out. Even dressed in a less than flattering hospital gown, she's breathtakingly stunning. My eyes roam down her body to her tattooed legs, a drastic contrast against the white gown and white sheets of the bed.

"You really need to stop that."

Her voice pulls me back, and my cheeks heat. "I can't help it. Somehow, you look sexy even in that thing."

"That's because it's *all* I'm wearing," she says with a wink.

"Now who's being bad?"

"I'll be *very* bad for you when this is all over."

I shift in my seat, rubbing my thighs together. This woman is a witch who could make me wet no matter where we are.

Fortunately, a nurse comes in before I can completely soak through my panties.

Logan's wheeled back to an operating room while I'm left to wait as they do the procedure.

I've never had a lumbar puncture, nor have I performed one outside of simulation-based training. I'm sure that's one thing I'll eventually have to do at some point during my residency. I've heard the worst part is the anesthetic injection, which shouldn't feel like more than a bee sting. After that, it's mostly just pressure.

It'll be my job for the rest of the day to make sure she takes it easy to avoid any of the nasty side effects.

With how stubborn she is, I'll have my work cut out for me.

It's not even thirty minutes later that Logan is wheeled back into the pre-op room. They have her lying on her back, and she's glaring up at the ceiling.

"How was it?" I ask a little cautiously.

"That sucked," she mutters.

The way she pouts is kind of cute, so I can guess which part sucked for her most. She had to lie on her stomach while at least two or three doctors stood over her. She probably felt exposed and vulnerable.

"Well, you can get dressed now, and you'll be on your way," the nurse says before she leaves so Logan can change.

When it's time to leave, Logan bitches about having to be taken to my car in a wheelchair. She argues and tries to convince the nurse to let her walk out. After I give her my best stern doctor stare, she rolls her eyes and shuts up.

I bring my car up to the entrance and lean the passenger seat as far down as it goes when Logan gets inside. She complains almost non-stop about having to lie back the entire drive to my apartment. I let her.

When we get to my place, I resist the urge to help her up the stairs, only because I'm somewhat concerned about her suddenly feeling dizzy. But I don't want to give her a reason to act like she needs to tough it out, so I just keep an eye on her as we go up to the second floor.

As soon as we get inside, I order her to lie down on the couch.

She *sits*.

"I don't think so." I move over to the sofa and rearrange the pillows at one end so her head can rest comfortably. "On your back."

Her gaze darkens as it lands on me. "Only if it's so you can sit on my face."

I pick up one of the pillows and lightly hit her shoulder with it. She laughs, and the noise is contagious.

"I mean it, Logan. You need to lie on your back for at least a few hours."

"Fiiiine," she says as she kicks off her boots and finally lies down. She laces her long, enticing fingers together and rests her hands on her stomach. "But, you know, I might need some motivation to stay here."

"You really are insatiable."

"Says the woman who was checking me out in a hospital gown."

Touché.

"I'll tell you what." I tilt my head and let my eyes roam down her supine body. "You have to lie here for a while, but I don't see why I can't be the one to have some fun with *you*."

Her wicked grin slowly morphs into a sad smile. "You'll probably be the only one coming for a while."

"What do you mean?" I ask, my brow knitting.

She clears her throat and glances away. "I'm a little numb down there."

I frown. "I thought the steroids were helping?"

"Oh, they are," she says with more optimism than I'd expect. "I still have some numbness though. And this goddamn itch that won't fucking go away," she adds as she scratches at her right forearm.

She gets lost in the act, scratching so violently I fear she might make herself bleed.

"Okay, stop that." I lean over to place my hand on hers until it stills. "I'll get you some ice. That should help at least a little. And I'm making you some coffee."

Logan groans, then quickly covers it up with an uncharacteristically sweet smile as she blinks up at me. "With creamer please?"

"*Black.* You're really determined to get that spinal headache, aren't you?"

With a heavy sigh, she shrugs. "Fine. But just remember, if I puke, I'm not allowed to move. So you'll be the one cleaning it up."

"Are you sure you don't still hate me?"

Something in her expression changes. Her eyes soften. Her smile is relaxed and makes her glow.

"I'm sure."

There's a twisting and writhing in my chest and in my stomach, and it's not at all unpleasant. I'd say it's butterflies, but I don't think even a hundred of them would be able to flutter their wings strong enough to give me this feeling.

Leaning over, I place a quick kiss against her lips. "I'll be right back."

I go into the kitchen and start a pot of coffee. While that's brewing, I put some ice into a bag and wrap it in a dishcloth.

With the ice on her arm, Logan takes the steaming mug from me with her free hand, sitting up just enough to take her first sip. Her lips purse, and she looks like she wants to spit it out. But somehow, she manages to get the whole cup down, making faces with each drink she takes. She sips on the second cup with less complaining. By the fourth, she's drinking it like it's water. I don't know if it's because she's getting used to the taste or if she's distracted.

I turned on the TV, but the volume ended up low enough for background noise as we fell into conversation instead. At first, we avoided the too difficult topics, the ones that have only ever stoked the flames of animosity between us.

Somehow, we ended up there anyway.

I think Logan made a joke about her "daddy issues" before the subject evolved from there. She doesn't exactly open up like I hope she might, but she talks a little about her mom, about how she's never been sure if she hated or loved her before she died. I tell her it's okay to feel both.

Liam comes up after that, and we each share stories from our memories about him that have us both laughing.

I tell her the meaning of my other tattoo, the turtle inked into my hip. Liam and I were down at the river one day and found one. We decided to take it home and trade off taking care of it, joking that it was our child and we were sharing custody. It was with me when Liam died, and my mom took care of it after I went off to school. When it died, I mourned it like it wasn't just a turtle. Because it wasn't.

While I still feel the tiniest bit of tension while talking to her about her brother, I can't help but wonder if it's one-sided now. She seems more at ease than I would've expected, at least a little more than I feel.

"Just tell me one thing," she says as she sets the empty mug from her fifth cup of coffee on the table. "You and my brother never…"

"No." I press my mouth into a line in an attempt at stamping out my grin, but I know it still shows. "If you really want to know, we never did much of anything. Liam was always more of a friend than anything else. He was my best friend. We thought with how close we were, we should see if we could be more, but it was difficult getting past that stage."

Logan sighs, lays her head back, and closes her eyes. "That's good to know. I was hoping I wouldn't have more reason to feel guilty."

She doesn't have to explain. If Liam and I had been more than what we were, I might've felt guilty too.

"I don't think he would've minded. Not if…"

Peeking one eye open, she gives me that same small, soft smile as before. "Not if it's what makes us happy."

I nod and whisper a quiet, "Yeah."

Happy.

I never would've thought Logan Delaney would be who'd make me happy.

But she does.

Logan's eyes fall closed again, and after a minute or so, her breathing is slow and steady, her lips slightly parted. Even after five cups of liquid caffeine, she's managed to fall fast asleep.

In her defense, caffeine doesn't work the same on everyone. Also, it's well past noon, which is past both our usual bedtime.

Fortunately, tonight is one of my rare nights off from the hospital, so I don't mind having had a busy morning or staying up later than normal. I probably wouldn't have minded anyway.

While Logan sleeps, I get up to wash our coffee mugs and change into more comfortable clothes. I check my phone and see a couple new texts. One's from Declan, and I do little more than glance at it before checking the next. When I see it's from Darcy, I smile and quickly text her back.

"Who's making you smile like that?"

I startle at Logan's sleepy voice and nearly drop my phone before sending the text to Darcy. When I peer up at Logan standing on the other side of the kitchen bar, I almost jump again at the hard, possessive glare she's giving me.

"Just a friend from university," I tell her as I set my phone on the counter.

"And what's this friend's name?"

I find myself tongue-tied as she starts to round the bar, stalking me, the look in her eyes turning more feral. I'm only able to answer seconds before she's right on top of me.

"Darcy."

Logan's hand wraps around my throat, hauling me closer so her lips can brush against mine. "Does Darcy know you're mine?"

I'm quickly turning into a puddle from her possessive hold on me, her warm breath kissing my lips. I never thought such a dominating and territorial display would make me weak in the knees like this. And maybe if it were a man in front of me instead of Logan, I'd be stomping on his foot and hitting him in the solar plexus. I guess I'll never know.

Never.

Because Logan's it for me.

If she'll have me.

"She's just a friend," I say, my voice already breathless. "I didn't realize I was bi until you, remember?"

"I *guess* you can have friends." Despite her reluctant tone, her eyes soften, and her mouth lifts at the corner. Her hand moves from my throat into my hair. She tugs at the strands, tilting my head back until she's licking a hot path up the column of my neck. She nips at my ear before whispering, "But I suddenly have the desire to make sure you know you're mine, that I'm keeping you. To fuck you so good until I've claimed you completely."

An involuntary shudder racks my body.

I should be careful, I know that. She says she's keeping me, but maybe it's the heat of the moment that has her speaking those words.

But, damn, do I want them to be true.

That brief moment of doubt has me able to fight past this lust haze *just* enough to gently push her back a step. "You're supposed to be lying down."

"So take me to bed," she says, smirking.

"To *sleep*."

"Yes, Dr. Elise." She leans forward, her lips an inch from mine again. "But you and I have a date with my cock soon."

While I'm left frozen in place, Logan places the softest touch against my lips with hers before slowly backing away, that smirk even more wicked than before. She turns, and as she heads down the hallway to my bedroom with a lethal grace, she shimmies out of her tight black jeans, giving me a view of her ass in those boy shorts.

If this woman wanted to be the death of me before, she could've just done all this from the start.

21

LOGAN

I had another appointment with my neurologist this morning. I didn't tell Elise because she's been doing enough as it is with coming to most of my steroid infusions and my spinal tap.

But I did find out my suspicion had been correct. My vitamin D levels were dangerously low, so I'll need to start taking supplements. All my time avoiding the sun has caught up with me. It's just one possible cause, but it's the only one that makes sense to me.

We also talked about treatment options, which I had been doing plenty of research on over the past few weeks. The choices are pretty fucking shitty. If it's not immune-suppressing drugs, it's ones that come with the risk of a fatal brain infection.

Joy.

I chose the lesser of all the evils—not that I should be thinking of any treatment for such a merciless disease as evil. MS is fucking evil. But my drug of choice is a shot I'll have to give myself three times a week. I'm aware it's not as strong a therapy as the others, so I may have to switch one day. However, at least for now, I'll have to worry about the least amount of side effects.

Instead of going to Elise's place after my appointment, I head home. It's late morning, and I don't want to risk waking her. It's something I wouldn't have worried about before.

Funny how so much has changed.

After I get home, I take a shower and crash for most of the day. When I wake up, I make an entire pot of coffee. I'm so fucking exhausted after the nightmare that's been my life these last couple months.

It would've been even worse if I had had to go it alone…

I pour some coffee into a mug and grab the creamer from the fridge. I pop the top open but pause as I stare down into the steaming black liquid.

Fuck my life.

I return the creamer to the fridge and take the mug with me into the living room.

The worst thing to come from that spinal tap?

I developed a taste for fucking black coffee.

I'm officially a psychopath.

While I sip on the rich, nutty drink, I stare at the painting I started the other day. My hand has been working a little better, well enough to paint at least. I don't think it's quite ready to tattoo again, but hopefully it will be soon.

I've already painted the base for the mountains of the Gore and Sawatch Ranges that dominate Vail. I've always loved painting mountains. No matter how fierce the storms that

I brush onto these canvases are, the mountains will always remain strong, steadfast. Unmovable.

A symbol of resilience, of solidity. Of refuge.

I finish my coffee, set the empty cup on the table, and pick up my brush.

And *that's* when my phone decides to ring.

I pick it up from the coffee table where I left it to see a familiar number on the screen, one that hasn't called me in months.

Answering the call, I answer yes when the automated voice asks me if I wish to accept.

"Hey, Lo."

Landon's voice comes over the line, unmistakable, low and deep. It's like coming home.

I push past the wave of emotion, the kind I hate, the kind I always try to stamp down. It clogs my throat until I have to clear it away.

"You said you'd call more often."

"Yeah, well, you left pretty upset with me. I didn't know if you'd want me to."

"You promised."

He sighs. "You're right. I'm sorry. I was just scared of losing the only family I have left."

At least I'm not alone in that.

"I forgave Elise. I can forgive you too."

"Thanks," he says, slowly like he's fixated on something else. "You forgave Elise?"

"It's kind of a long story." I settle onto the couch and prop my feet up on the table. "But, yeah. I believe *her* when she says she doesn't remember what happened. But, honestly, Lan...I'm just ready to let it the fuck go. I know you said to leave Elise alone, but...well, I didn't. I couldn't."

"What does that mean?"

I bite my lip to keep from telling him exactly what that means, but I settle on the closest thing. "I might kind of be crazy about her."

Landon is silent for a long while, a lot longer than I would've expected. I don't understand why because he knows I'm gay. He's never had a problem with it, not in the same way Declan clearly does.

"You two are together?" he eventually asks, as though he's still working through the information.

"I don't know about officially, but...yeah. I think so."

"You haven't been around Declan, have you?"

I feel my brow scrunch, the question echoing in my mind.

This is the first time Landon's mentioned the other Novak sibling himself. Either one actually. He usually avoids the subject of them and that night completely. Him asking about Declan feels like him bringing it *all* up.

"Logan?" he presses when I still haven't answered.

"Why?"

"Why what?"

"Why are you asking about Declan?"

He sighs again, heavier than before. "I'd just rather you not be around him."

"Why, Landon?"

"I have my reasons," he says, his tone hard and final, reminiscent of our father.

It's those reasons I want to know, but I have no doubt that no matter how hard I press for an explanation, he won't give it to me. But it's clearer to me now more than ever before that there's something he's not telling me. There's something about that night that he's hiding.

"Let's forget it. Please," he says, his voice back to that of my brother. "That's not why I called."

"Then why did you call?" I ask, frustrated. But I can't bring myself to hang up on him like I did during our last visit.

"I have some bad news."

My heart sinks.

"Yeah, I do too." Since he hasn't called like he promised to, I haven't had the chance to tell him about my diagnosis. Since he's the last blood family I have, I guess I should. "You go first."

"They moved my parole hearing from the beginning to the end of next year."

"What?!" My feet drop from the coffee table as I lean forward, feeling as though I might throw up. "Why?"

"It happens, Logan."

I want to ask *why* it happened, suspecting he got into another fight or something. But I'm already too agitated with him for not answering any of my questions, so I don't even try.

"Since we're sharing bad news," he says, "what's yours?"

I'm tempted to be petty and not tell him since he doesn't want to tell me shit. But the hard truth is that I need to get it off my chest.

I need my big brother to know that I'm sick.

It's a selfish thought, but I need to give him a reason to try harder to get the fuck out of there.

He doesn't take it easy at first. He asks me in a hundred different ways how I'm doing, what the doctors have been saying, and what they're doing to help me. I almost feel guilty when he nearly breaks down because he's not out here with me. I can't remember the last time I heard him like that, and the reason usually would've made my skin crawl. When I tell him I've had Elise as support, he at least sounds a little more on board about our relationship.

I don't tell him this, but he also has her to thank for me not hanging up in his face for getting overly worried about me.

After we talk a few more minutes, we end the call on better terms than last time.

Even though I'm still a little pissed at him for hiding things—because now I'm *certain* he is—I'm hopeful he'll make more of an effort to come home now.

Maybe when he does, I'll be able to beat all his secrets out of him.

That thought almost gives me a renewed sense of energy. Or maybe it's just the caffeine. Either way, I force myself off the couch and once more pick up my brush.

I work all throughout the night. My hands, arms, and clothes are all stained with splotches of gray, green, and yellow shades of paint.

It's not until I hear a knock at the front door that I realize the sun has risen.

Which is fitting because when I open the door, it's my sunshine waiting on the other side.

The sunbursts in her eyes look even brighter as the sun behind her casts a halo around her head, painting her blonde hair with streaks of gold.

My mouth lifts into a full smile the moment I see her. I lean out the doorway to wrap my hand around her wrist and yank her inside, her chest crashing against mine. The squeak she lets out is damn adorable, and I swallow it up in my mouth with a searing kiss. My tongue slips past her lips, demanding entrance and taking it to swirl around hers. It's only when her whimpers reach my ears do I show her a little mercy and let her breathe.

"I missed you too," she says with breathless giggles. She peers at me beneath her lashes, her eyes roaming down my body. "You're covered in paint."

"Oh, shit."

Placing my hands on her shoulders, I spin her around until she's staring back out the door.

"Stay right here," I whisper in her ear. "I'd say I'd punish you if you don't, but you'd like that too much." I feel the shiver that races through her in my hands, making me grin. "So let's just say I'll give you whatever you want if you don't turn around. Understand?"

She nods and whispers a near silent, "Yes."

I brush her hair over her shoulder and place a kiss to her neck below her ear, eliciting another shiver. "Good girl."

She groans and rolls her head back. "I think you're trying to kill me."

A low laugh rumbles in my throat. "Don't die on me now, sunshine."

The little whimper that escapes her makes me not want to leave her for a second. When she breathes my name, the single word is laced with emotion I don't dare try to translate right now.

I eventually move away, back into the living room and over to the painting I've been working on all night. Grabbing onto the easel, I twist it around so the canvas is facing the corner of the room.

I'm not ready to let her see it. I don't want her to until it's finished.

Walking back to the front door, I stop a few feet away and let my eyes rake down Elise's backside, lingering on her ass. I suddenly have the urge to bite it.

Lowering my voice into that husky, demanding one I know she has a thing for, I tell her, "Walk backwards and close the door."

Her shoulders rise with a deep breath as she does as I say.

The moment the door is closed, I advance. I grab her and spin her around again before shoving her back against the door. Once more, I take her mouth with mine in a kiss even more intense and vicious than before. She melts against me, a moan slipping past her lips and then mine. I roughly paw at her right breast, and she moans louder.

When I break the kiss only to let my mouth travel down her throat, she pants as she tries to catch her breath.

"This isn't why I came over."

"You sure about that?" I ask as I roll my hips and grind against her.

"Fuck."

I grin and nip at the soft skin of the side of her neck. "I love it when you curse."

I noticed early on that she almost never does. She does it more when I have her in compromising positions. Those words seem to slip out of her despite herself, so full of lust and desire and raw need that she loses control. They're the only words her brain can form in those moments.

"I really did corrupt you, didn't I?" I whisper against the shell of her ear.

"Yes," she breathes as she moves her own hips in time with mine. "Never fucking stop."

The rumbling noise that comes from deep in my chest is feral. "You got it, baby."

She moans, but when I take a step back, putting distance between us, it turns into a groan of disappointment.

"What?" I tilt my head with an air of innocence that I know she can see right through. "You said that's not why you came over."

"Logan," she whines.

I chuckle. "Words, Elise. The quicker you tell me, the sooner we can get back to our regularly scheduled programming."

She laughs at that and shakes her head. "I missed you and wanted to make sure you're doing okay. I did text, but you didn't answer."

"Oh." I glance over my shoulder at my phone still lying on the coffee table among all my bottles of paint. I never heard it. Maybe it died. "Yeah, I've been busy painting. But I'm fine. Doing a little better."

"Good," she says with a slow nod.

Then it's her turn to pounce.

She closes the distance between us that I had created, places one hand on the side of my neck, and presses those full, soft lips to mine.

I spin her around and start backing her up without breaking the kiss. I continue guiding her backward into the living room, our tongues dancing together between the heat of our mouths, and my hands all over her. I never want to stop touching her. I wish I could fuse myself to her.

My hands slip beneath the hem of her shirt, and I lift it up and over her head, tossing it away while being careful not to land it on anything that's wet with paint. I move my fingers to the button of her jeans and pop them open. She lets me slide them down her legs, leaning over until she can't anymore, our lips only breaking apart at the last second as she steps out of her pants.

"Stay right there," I tell her as I take a step back, leaving her standing in the middle of the living room in only her matching pale purple underwear.

I can feel her eyes on me as I pour paint from a couple of the bottles onto my palette, then pick it up along with a brush.

"What are you doing?" she asks as I return to her, a grin playing at her lips.

I give her a smirk in return as I dip the brush in yellow paint. "I thought you might be jealous that I'm covered in paint and you aren't."

"So, you're...what? Going to use me as your canvas?"

"Why not? Look at all this smooth, creamy skin." I sweep my brush up from her navel over her stomach, a light, teasing stroke that leaves a line of yellow behind and has her arching her back the smallest bit, leaning into the touch. "It's so perfect. *You're* perfect."

Her lips part on a soft gasp. I don't know if it's the feel of the brush or my words that affect her, but I'm guessing both.

"What are you going to paint?" she asks, already breathless again.

"You'll just have to wait and see."

I spend the next ten or so minutes painting over Elise's abdomen, covering as much of her bare skin as I can with light brushstrokes so the paint dries quicker. I coat the entire area between her panties and bra with lines of yellow, highlighting the rays with white and bits of orange. Switching out brushes, I dip the clean one in a different color and start painting my version of a baby blue lily.

The entire time, Elise is biting her lip, trying and failing to stifle the beautiful noises falling from her with each graze of my brush. Her breathing picks up, and her purple panties become darker, wet with her arousal.

When I'm finished, I place the brush and palette on the table and take a step back to admire my masterpiece.

The petals of the lily take up most of the space of her stomach, beams of sunlight surrounding it. She peers down to look at it with me, her breath hitching.

"It's beautiful."

I take a step forward and place my paint-stained hand beneath her chin, lifting her gaze back to me. *"You're* beautiful."

I kiss her, just another light, playful touch of my lips against hers before my mouth moves to her ear.

"And now that I've marked you..." My hand slips into her panties, my fingers gliding through her arousal and swirling around her clit until her hips buck into my touch. "It's time to claim you."

22

ELISE

"*It's time to claim you.*"

Between the filthy words that come out of this woman's mouth and the way she touches me, expertly playing with my body and rubbing at my most sensitive spot, I'm already so close to the edge that I'm teetering.

"Don't you dare fucking come, Elise," she whispers in my ear, even as her fingers continue circling my clit, bringing me closer and closer. And closer. "You're only allowed to come when I give you permission. And that'll be when you're stuffed full of my cock."

The noise that comes out of me is obscene, a moan so deep that it rattles my bones.

It ends on a whine when she removes her fingers and steps back, taking my hand instead and tugging me through the house.

As we move down the hall, I try not to think about the times I was here almost a decade ago, about everything that's happened since, even as we pass the closed door to Liam's old room. I just want to be here *now*. With *her*.

She leads me into her bedroom. I know it's hers because it's the same one that belonged to her ten years ago. I've never been inside before now, but Liam had pointed it out to me several times when I used to come over to hang out. That means she never took her parents' old room after her mom died.

All thoughts as to why fly out of my head the moment she shoves me down onto her bed. I don't get the chance to take a long look around her room, but I see lots of black and dark colors. My back rests on top of a black comforter, the sheets underneath a deep teal. There are blackout curtains over the window just like in my own bedroom, and there are painted canvases of all different sizes hung on the black walls.

Before I can take in any more details, like the photos in the frames lining her dresser, she covers my body with hers. Her mouth comes down on mine as she slides an arm beneath me and undoes my bra clasp with a practiced hand. She tosses it away without ever breaking the kiss.

I wrap my legs around her waist, and she grinds against me. I briefly worry that the artwork she painted on my body is getting ruined, but as she moves one hand between us and runs it down my stomach, the paint feels like it's pretty much hardened and dried already.

"Fuck, Elise," she says, her voice husky as she trails her lips down my chin to my throat. "I can't wait to watch you come apart for me again."

I lie there, panting, little noises pouring past my lips, as her own lips continue moving south.

Her mouth closes around my left nipple, sucking and nipping the hard bud, and I find myself grinding up against her stomach, mourning the layers of my panties and her shirt between us.

Lacing my fingers in her hair, I hold her close, barely letting up as she starts to move again.

Slipping her fingers into my underwear on either side of my waist, she slides them down my legs until she tosses them away like she did my bra.

When I feel the warmth of her breath at my center, I have to drop my hands to grip the sheets tight to keep myself from bucking up into her mouth. But when it's her tongue licking a hot path through my arousal and flicking at my clit, all resolve flies out the window and I end up doing it anyway.

Her low chuckle rumbles through me. "Fuck, I love the taste of you. If I could eat one thing for the rest of my life…"

Her words trail off as she returns to me, her lips closing around my clit and sucking on it until I cry out.

"Logan, I'm—"

She pulls away and glares up at me. "Don't disobey me, Elise."

Another shiver races through me. I'm panting so heavily I can barely catch my breath. "It would've been your fault."

Her eyes sparkle with wicked mischievousness. "Seems like I'm going to have to fuck that attitude out of you."

I groan. "Yes, please."

Laughing again, she leans over me and brushes her lips against mine. "Stay right here. And make sure you stay nice and wet for me."

With one last lingering kiss, she exits the room, leaving me naked in her bed.

I don't let myself look around her room to study more than the little I've already seen, not wanting to distract myself from the task she gave me. Instead, I settle further back on the bed, nestling into her pillows. I let my legs drop open and my hand travel over the dried paint on my stomach. I move it down, down, until I feel my own wetness on my fingers.

Rubbing against my clit, I whimper, desperate to come. She's only teased me, and I already feel like I've been edged for hours.

But the promise of when and how I'll be awarded my next orgasm is too great to disobey her.

So I only touch myself lightly, denying myself the amount of friction that would get me off. My eyes drift closed as I soak up the pleasure while at the same time keeping myself from chasing the release I'm not supposed to have yet.

"Fuck, you're a vision."

My eyes flutter open, and I swear my heart stops.

If I'm a vision, what does that make her?

A goddess.

I'm not sure what kind of goddess stands naked with black straps around her waist that are connected to the black dildo that hangs heavy at her front. But if someone hasn't written that myth, then they should.

Logan tilts her head, and I feel at risk of catching on fire from her searing gaze, her eyes dragging down my body until my skin is burning. She brings one hand up and gently wraps her fingers around the dildo so that I get a good idea of its girth. It's bigger than anything I've had inside me recently.

Hell, maybe ever.

Not that I ever complained about the size of my partners' dicks, but I can already imagine the stretch of taking Logan's.

With that thought, a heat settles low in my belly, tight with anticipation.

"What about you?" Because I don't want to be the only one to feel pleasure. "Are you still…"

"Numb?" She gives me a small smile, then her hand moves to a button connected to the strap beside the dildo. My eyes had been drawn to other places that I hadn't noticed it before. "A little. But I can at least feel this."

She presses the button, and a low hum fills the room. A shudder visibly travels through Logan's body. Her lips part, and her back arches gracefully.

I'm so transfixed by her overwhelming beauty, her vulnerable pleasure, that I hardly notice when she turns off the vibration. But when I do, I only want her more.

"Logan, please."

She smirks as she gives the silicone cock a stroke. "You know how much I love it when you beg. Do it a little more, and maybe I'll show you some mercy."

I groan. "Haven't you teased me enough today?"

With my hand that's not still currently teasing myself, I brush my palm over the dried paint on my stomach in a gesture that says, *Exhibit A*.

"Oh, I don't think you've been teased nearly enough."

"Fine. Maybe I'll just do it myself."

I dip my fingers lower, pressing two inside of me until I let out a low moan.

As expected, Logan advances, wrapping her hand around my wrist in a tight grip. She doesn't pull my fingers out of me, but keeps my hand still. Her gaze darkens.

"You want to do it yourself?"

The question is a taunt, a dare.

Her hand moves mine, immediately setting a brutal, relentless pace, my fingers plunging in and out of my own wet heat. My eyes roll into the back of my head. My chest heaves, noises spilling out of me, as I once again come close to the edge.

Before I can tumble all the way over, Logan stops and yanks my hand away.

"I told you you'll only be doing that on my cock," she says, her voice hard.

"Then please," I plead again through heavy, erratic breaths. "Please fuck me."

She crawls up on the bed, her hands moving to my thighs, widening them to make room for her. She digs her fingers in until I whimper.

"Keep making all those noises for me, and I'll fuck you any way you want me to."

Grabbing the base of the dildo, she lines the head up with my entrance, gliding it through the copious amount of arousal gathered there. Her eyes watch it as she moves it up and down, teasing me further as she coats the silicone with my wetness.

"Is this what you want?" she asks as her eyes snap up to mine.

I nod as I lift my hips, trying to get her inside me. I barely manage a quiet, "Yes."

As she starts to push inside, I hold my breath, my gaze locked with hers. She slides it in slowly, letting me adjust, letting me feel every single inch of her cock as she fills me with it.

I wince when a slight burn joins the stretch.

"Relax," Logan whispers tenderly, her fingers coming up to tangle in my hair, tugging gently, offering both a comforting and distracting touch. "I know you can take me. Just relax."

I do what she says, or at least I try, easing the tension in my muscles the best I can.

"Good girl."

My resulting moan is like the cue for her to finish the drive forward. The moment she's fully seated inside, her weight comes down on top of me, her grip in my hair tightening as she crashes her mouth to mine. My legs come up to wrap around her waist, and the low growl she makes rumbles between our breasts that are pushed together.

She breaks our kiss, rises up just enough to peer down at where we're joined, and rolls her hips, pulling out just to thrust back in. Again, slowly. The move is so sensual and unbelievably sexy that all I want to do is watch her while she watches us.

Her gaze comes back to mine, and she leans down once more. My mouth attempts to chase hers, but instead, she licks across my lips.

"I should've warned you before." One corner of her mouth quirks while her eyes turn darker. "I like to fuck hard, baby."

That's all the notice I get before she rocks her hips back only to pound into me, causing my back to slide up the bed. I cry out and throw my hands out to grip her upper arms. Like she can be my anchor while simultaneously ruining me.

"That's it," she says, both corners of her mouth now curled up in that wicked, beautiful smirk. "Hold on."

I do. For dear life.

She pounds into me again and again. And again. Until there's no air left in my lungs, and I fear I'll never be able to suck in another breath.

Then she kisses me, breathing life back into me.

Only to take it away once more when she reaches between us and presses that button again.

"Oh, fuck!"

I cling to her as the vibrations send jolts of heat and pleasure rippling through me, igniting me from the inside out. Our moans join and mingle in the air as her lips travel over my jaw to my throat where her tongue and teeth and warm breath caress my skin.

"God, I love fucking you." Her breathless voice ghosts across the side of my neck. "You feel so perfect beneath me."

She never stops the thrusting of her hips, never faltering in her ruthless fucking.

"Logan."

Her name sounds like an invocation, gasping and pleading. The only word I'm capable of speaking to let her know I'm close.

Everything is tight, the pressure building and building until there's no way I can hold it back. How I've held it back this long is a mystery to me. She told me I was only allowed to come when she gave me permission. She hasn't granted it yet.

Then, mercifully…

"Come with me, Elise."

Her movements stutter.

Her teeth sink into my throat.

I erupt as the pain of her bite adds another layer to the pleasure. I cry out an ungodly noise, somewhere between a moan and a scream as waves crash into me. It's one after another, great big tidal waves of euphoria so intense that I'm drowning in their waters as they roll over me. It's like they're flooding my lungs. But I'm not afraid. I'm not suffocating. I'm floating on a sea of bliss.

It's not until the waves recede that I realize the vibrations have stopped. My heavy eyes flutter open to see Logan staring down at me, her bare chest heaving and glistening with sweat. Her brows furrow.

"Are you okay?"

I smile. Or I think I do. My entire face feels weighed down. When I speak, it comes out dry and scratchy like my throat. "Never fucking better."

She laughs lightly. "I was planning on making you lick my cock clean, but you look like you're about to pass out."

Fighting past the weight and grogginess, I shake my head. "Let me."

She makes that growly noise again before slowly pulling out of me. I whimper, already knowing I'm going to be sore as hell for days. But I think it's the loss of her, the empty feeling I'm left with, that has me the saddest.

Logan crawls up my body, straddling my chest and steadying herself on the headboard as she sways, apparently just as off balance as I am. She takes the dildo in her other hand and brushes the tip of it across my lips, her eyes locked on mine as I open my mouth. She rolls her hips, gliding the silicone dick over my tongue so that I get a burst of my own flavor.

"You know," she says as she gently slides in and out of my mouth, "I think I get the appeal. I might not be able to feel it, but your lips sure do look good stretched around this thing."

A weak moan reaches my ears, and I'm almost surprised it came from me, not entirely sure how I'm still capable of making noise.

"Maybe I'll have to get a double-ended one so I can fuck your mouth while the other end fucks me."

My pussy throbs, reminding me of the ache that's still there even though it seems to want more already.

There's no way I could survive more right now.

As though reading my mind, Logan pulls the dildo out of my mouth and moves to kneel beside me. She removes the strap around her waist, and I get a glimpse of a small black bullet on the opposite side of the dildo, the vibrator that's glistening with her own release. I'm tempted to ask if I can clean that too, but I already feel my eyes drifting closed.

"I'll be right back." Her voice reaches me from a great distance as though I'm still out at sea.

My eyes close for two seconds—or at least it feels like two seconds—before Logan returns. Her arm slips beneath me as she helps me sit up just enough to take a sip of water from the glass she raises to my lips. I take three big gulps, then move my head away.

She lets me lie back down, places the glass on her nightstand, and curls up at my side, her naked body pressing against mine as she lifts the sheets to cover us.

"This is going to be a nasty mark," she says as her fingertips brush over my neck where she bit me.

I shiver at the contact as my eyes close once more. "You're lucky I'm good at covering up your marks."

She hums. "I wish you didn't have to. I like seeing them on you."

I think I'm already halfway to sleep when I whisper, "I do too."

I wake up earlier than usual, even without the assistance of my alarm. I was too damn exhausted to even remember where my phone was, let alone to grab it. After I place a featherlight kiss to Logan's cheek so as not to wake her, I slip out of her room and find it among the pile of my clothes that Logan stripped off me this morning.

Not bothering to put on my panties that I had soaked through around that time, I step right into my jeans without them. I go ahead and put on my bra too, but I'm not sure what to do about my shirt. The painting that Logan did on my stomach is already pretty badly faded and smeared, which I'm a little sad about—though I don't regret the savage way she fucked me for even a moment.

It probably wouldn't hurt to put my shirt on, but I leave it off for now anyway.

I have a thing for *all* the marks she gives me, even if some are more temporary than others.

Since I have to leave for work in about an hour so I can stop by my place to change, I decide not to wake Logan. I start a pot of coffee for her for whenever she does wake up. While it's brewing, I look around. I have no interest in snooping. I'm more curious to see if anything of this home I remember is the same.

There are no family photographs in the living room. I saw some of Logan and her brothers in her bedroom before I walked out, but it's as if she doesn't want the reminders in the space she spends most of her time in.

I move down the hallway, seeing only empty nails on the walls where photographs once hung. I imagine she has them all tucked away somewhere, but I can't blame her for not wanting to see either of her parents every day. Her father abandoned her and her mother, and her mother checked out long before she died.

Despite knowing that none of it is *technically* my fault, I still feel a pang of something similar to guilt.

I was on that bridge.

I was drunk.

And Liam died.

I was there the night of the tragic event that led to the collapsing of Logan's family.

When I find myself standing in front of the door to Liam's old room, I feel the weight of his loss. I never did condemn Logan for the way she treated me. Standing here now, I actually feel a little surprised she doesn't still hate me.

It's not that I think myself a martyr who should be punished for something that all three of us who were there with Liam that night should've prevented. But the fact that it didn't lead to Logan having some kind of villain origin story is a miracle in and of itself.

She lost so much.

I could spend the rest of my life giving her everything that I possibly can.

I *want* to.

As though seeking permission from the other side, I push open the door.

The room appears to be untouched, like no one has even stepped inside in a decade. It's like walking into a memory from ten years ago.

Except Liam isn't here.

I don't see his bright, charming smile or hear his infectious laughter. I don't see him playing his video games on the TV that's still in here. I don't see him studying with me, both of us surrounded by books laid out on his floor.

But all of his things are here, in almost the exact spots where they were last time I was in his room. No one packed anything up. No one disturbed any of it. Like someone was expecting him to return one day. The dark blue sheets are even carefully arranged and smoothed like the bed was just made up.

I move over to the dresser to look at the photos trapped in their dusty frames.

A smile breaks out on my face as I pick up a picture of Liam, Declan, and me. We all look so young, crammed into one side of a booth at Liam's favorite restaurant. We were there for his eighteenth birthday. Moments after this photo was taken, Declan smashed Liam's face in the chocolate lava cake that was on the table in front of him. Fortunately, he got as much of a laugh out of it as Declan did.

Liam and I were friends first. We got paired together for an art project when I was a freshman and he was a sophomore. We hit it off and spent a lot of time at each other's houses and hanging out around town. Sometime around my junior year, when Declan was a sophomore, a few months before Liam and I officially started dating, Declan wormed his way in, and our little group became a trio. I didn't mind. While Declan and I have had sibling squabbles like any other, we've always been pretty close.

Landon didn't hang out with us much considering he was about four years older than Liam. But Liam and Landon were pretty close too, and Liam had convinced him to buy us all beer and hang out that night on the bridge.

As I stare down at the photo in my hands, I wonder what life would've been like had Logan not been the black sheep of her family. If she had been a part of our group.

Would we have all been on the bridge that night together?

Would we never have been there to begin with?

Would I have fallen in love with her all those years ago too?

The frame slips out of my hand and crashes on the floor at my feet.

"Fuck."

Well, Logan wanted to corrupt me, and it would seem she succeeded.

But the most surprising revelation of the past ten seconds is that I'm in love with Logan.

It *shouldn't* be that much of a shock—a deep part of me already knew that—but for some reason, it kind of is.

I take a deep breath and lean over to pick up the frame. Fortunately, the floor is carpeted, so the glass didn't shatter. However, the back did pop off. The corner of what I assume to be the photograph I was just looking at is poking out, so I go to tuck it in. But it doesn't seem to want to budge.

I pull it out instead.

It's not the same photo. When I flip over the long, narrow strip, I see four different images on the page, one printed from one of those photo booths. I grin as I look down at the pictures of Liam and my brother.

But the longer I look…

My face falls.

In the top photo, they're smiling at the camera. In the next ones, they're facing each other. Liam's arms are around Declan, and the way they're staring at each other…

I've seen that look in Liam's eyes before.

I've seen it in Logan's when she looks at me.

I've never realized how similar their eyes are—both a stormy gray. But it's not the color that's so familiar. It's what's behind it.

Intimacy.

Passion.

Love.

My heart throbs in my chest, pounding like a drum against my ribs. Blood rushes in my ears as my brain catches up with what my eyes are seeing. It's right in front of me, yet I can't believe it.

I hear the shifting of sheets from the other room, and I quickly put the frame back together and return it to the dresser. Folding the strip of photos, I place it in the pocket of my jeans and exit Liam's room, closing the door softly behind me.

Back in the living room, I throw my shirt on and walk to the front door, peering over my shoulder into the hallway.

I'm not ready to share this discovery, and I don't trust myself enough to think Logan wouldn't notice that something's wrong. The thumping of my own heart is deafening. My mind is all twisted up trying to make sense of things.

Before Logan can wake up and come out of her room, I leave the house, those photos weighing heavy in my pocket and on my mind.

23

LOGAN

My fucking foot drop came back.
Well, it started to. My leg started feeling weak again like it did before. I called my neurologist, and he prescribed three more fucking days of steroid infusions.

This is seriously fucking bullshit.

I thought I was better.

I thought I wouldn't have to deal with this again for years at least, until my next relapse. Not the same fucking one resisting steroids.

This isn't self-pity this time.

This is rage.

As I sit in this familiar chair in the quiet, secluded cubicle, I'm tempted to rip the needle out of my arm and storm out.

I'm so tired of tasting pennies.

I'm tired of hospitals and doctors and these drab, depressing rooms. Of tests and drugs and needles.

But I stay. I deal with it. Because it's the only treatment that's available to me, and if I want to continue to have the ability to walk, I need to stick it out.

And I do. I want to walk. I want to walk out of here for the last time for what I hope is longer than a few weeks.

What I *really* want is to walk out of here and make my way to Elise.

But…I can't.

Not anymore.

If five rounds of steroid infusions wasn't enough to fix me the first time, what's the rest of my life going to look like?

Elise isn't here because I didn't tell her I needed more infusions. Fortunately, I have a pocket full of those mints she brought with her the first time. I take one out, unwrap it, and pop it in my mouth before the pennies can hit.

When all of this first started, I tried to talk myself out of wanting Elise, out of letting myself have her. It was to save her from my darkness, my storm.

Now?

There's even more I need to save her from.

I didn't hear from her for a couple of days after we fucked in my bed. I know she gets busy and worn out from work, but I was beginning to feel slightly concerned.

That was around the time my symptoms started returning.

That concern turned to relief.

If for whatever reason she decided she was done with me, realized I was too much or not enough for her, then it was good fucking timing.

But then she texted saying she needed to talk to me.

I ignored it.

Nothing felt as important as protecting her from me, from *this*.

If she was wanting to break things off, then I'd save us both the messy breakup scene. If it was something else, well… it didn't matter anymore.

But she won't stop texting.

In an ideal world, she'd take the hint and stop trying to contact me.

I want Elise. More than I've ever wanted anyone or anything in my life. It wasn't a lie when I told her I wanted her to be mine. If I could, I'd make her mine forever.

But this isn't about what I want.

For quite possibly the first time, I'm putting someone else first.

One of the most terrifying things about MS is that it's so unpredictable. It affects everyone differently. I don't know what to expect. I don't know what my life will be like in a year, let alone five or ten.

I won't make her take care of me if and when I can't take care of myself.

I don't know if it's the right decision, but I do know the right ones are sometimes the most difficult to make.

If that's the case in this situation, then it's the right one.

Doesn't mean it doesn't hurt like hell.

After I leave the hospital and get in my car, I get yet another text from Elise.

Elise: I'm coming over before work tonight.

Of course she'd let me know because she has more manners than I do.

But...*great*.

Looks like we get that messy breakup scene I didn't want.

It's late morning, so she's most likely getting ready for bed. Which is exactly what I plan on doing when I get home too. I'm going to need my rest before I break this perfect woman's heart.

But I know in *my* heart that I'm saving her.

I'm awakened by a heavy knock on my front door. I didn't set an alarm because I might've been hoping she wouldn't show up. And if she did...well, at least I'd wake up nice and cranky.

Throwing the covers off, I climb off the bed and head down the hallway. I glance over in the corner of the living room at my latest painting that I still haven't finished. There's a sheet draped over it because I haven't been able to bring myself to work on it these last few days, let alone even look at it.

It hurts too fucking badly.

In nothing but my underwear and a tank top, I open the door. I'm not worried about who's on the other side because I already know it's her, and not just because she texted me this morning.

I sense her.

I sense the dread of what's coming.

"Why haven't you been answering my texts?"

She spits the question out before the door is even fully open. Her arms are crossed, and there's a mix of anger and concern swirling around those halos in her eyes.

She's already on the verge of pissed.

Good.

It would make this easier if she stayed that way.

I rub at my tired eyes. "I'm surprised you haven't invited yourself over before now with how fucking clingy you are."

"Excuse me?" she snaps.

When her eyes finally take in what I'm wearing—or the lack of what I'm wearing—she huffs before pushing her way inside and closing the door.

"What the hell is going on?" she asks as she rounds on me again.

"What do you think, Elise?" I force one corner of my mouth to curl, but it physically hurts. "I got what I wanted."

And just like that, what little anger had been brewing inside her vanishes. Her lips part on an exhale, a small puff of air that swirls around in the space between us and turns rotten, poisoned by my toxic lies that linger there.

She shakes her head, refusing to believe them. "That's not what this is about."

"Oh?" I tilt my head, taunting her, daring her like I used to. It wasn't a mask back then, but it is now. "Then, please, tell me since you're so clever. What other reason could there possibly be for me finally being able to say I don't give a fuck about you?"

"You were playing a game," she says, her voice rising again. "I knew that from the beginning. You wanted to hurt me. But things have changed since then, haven't they?"

Yes.

God fucking yes.

I clench my jaw, holding those words back behind a steel wall. "Nothing changed, Elise. Looks like I won."

Again, she shakes her head.

Believe it. Run away.

She swallows, takes a breath, and asks, "Do you know?"

Okay, that catches me off guard.

My brows dip in genuine confusion. "Know what?"

"Nothing," she answers quickly. Too quickly.

"No. What the fuck are you talking about?" Of course, my first thought is the thing that started this all. My assumption makes my blood boil in two seconds flat. "Have you been lying to me this whole fucking time?"

When I take a step forward, Elise mirrors it, stumbling back a step. It could be either shock or fear that flashes in her eyes. For a moment, I'm stumped if I even care.

Before, I *wanted* to scare her. I wanted to hurt her.

But now? I don't know.

If she's been lying to me about everything, then maybe we're right back to where we started.

"No." She shakes her head. "It's not like that. I swear."

I take another step, and this time, she holds her ground. For several long seconds, I keep my gaze locked on hers, staring into her eyes like I can find the truth in their depths. Instead, all I find is uncertainty and anguish.

"What the fuck aren't you telling me, Elise?"

"I can't. Not now." Her voice is quiet but steady. There's so much behind her unwavering gaze that haunts me—rage, betrayal, confusion. Heartache. "I swear it's not what you think. But if you're going to do this to us for whatever stupid reason, then I can't talk to you like I thought I could."

She's confusing the hell out of me. I know she wanted to talk to me about something, and I truly thought it wouldn't matter in the wake of what I needed to do. But that look in her eyes has me second guessing.

I want to know what the fuck it is, but I know I can't make her tell me.

Not now.

The woman who was once the poster girl for healthy communication can't tell me whatever significant information she came over here to share.

Breaking her trust hurts as much as breaking her heart.

For a moment, I doubt what it is I'm doing. Losing her hurts worse than I expected it would, and I had already been preparing myself. Or, at least, I thought I had. It turns out I couldn't even fathom what this would do to me.

I'm ripping apart my insides, clawing my own heart to shreds that I would've willingly laid at her feet had life dealt me a different hand.

But saving her from me, from the kind of life I'd give her, is more important.

"Fine." My jaw ticks with the pressure it takes to hold in the emotions I'm feeling, to maintain this mask. "Then we have nothing left to talk about."

"I guess we don't."

With that, she turns to the door, turning her back on me.

A sharp pang stabs through my chest.

I swear it's going to kill me.

I'm glad that she's not fighting this. I don't know how much longer I can bear witness to that hurt in her eyes, the one *I* caused. If she stayed, whether she cried or screamed, I don't know if I could've kept up the act, if I could've purposefully hurt her more than I already am.

If I could hurt *myself* more than I already am.

But at the same time…

Fuck. It's killing me that she's *not* fighting this.

She opens the door, the one that's going to save her from me. Before she leaves, she peers over her shoulder. The faint smile on her lips doesn't meet her eyes that glisten with unshed tears.

I'm not a stranger to self-loathing. I've felt it in those low moments of my life.

But right now?

I've never hated myself more.

"If you ever need me," she whispers, keeping her voice soft so it doesn't break. "I'll still be here for you."

She steps out, and the door clicks shut behind her.

Now I don't hate myself as much.

I hate everything else.

I hate how fucking perfect she is. How she can still be so kind to me after what I just did, when it's the last thing I deserve. I hate that I never deserved her at all. It's as though I was starting to forget that and the universe decided to remind me.

This curse is mine to bear.

And now she's free of it.

24

ELISE

I've always prided myself on being able to compartmentalize my thoughts and emotions. Not just while at school or at work, but whenever I need to. It's not that I don't feel things deeply. I do. But that's one reason why it's become more than just a means of making sure I can concentrate in a very demanding field. It's almost a defense mechanism.

For the past four days, that mechanism has been failing greatly.

I've been distracted at work, which might as well be a death sentence for my career. Fortunately, it's my own mother I've been working for, and she's been more lenient than anyone else would be. She's had to catch a couple of my mistakes before I could make them. Every time she's asked what's wrong, I've told her I'm just tired and that I'll try to get more sleep.

I hate lying to her.

But what am I supposed to tell her?

I fell in love with a girl and she broke my heart?

Okay, it doesn't sound that bad. I *could* tell her that. I *should*. But I didn't get to keep Logan to myself for nearly long enough, and I'm not ready to share even memories of her.

Tonight is my first night off from the hospital in a couple of weeks. It's actually my first night of two that I get off, which I hadn't expected to happen at all during my first year of residency. I should take advantage of it and try to clear my head. Clean the apartment. Read a book. Something. *Anything*.

Instead, I'm lying on my couch, staring at all the artwork hanging on my wall.

I could get rid of it. I spent a lot of money on each piece, but I could always try to sell them. Clearing them out of here would probably be the safest option, but I know I'd never be able to bring myself to part with them. Not only do I genuinely love each and every one, I don't want to simply erase Logan from my life.

No matter how badly she destroyed me.

I wanted to fight for her.

But if I've learned one thing about Logan, it's that she's stubborn as hell. When she sets her mind to something, it's damn near impossible to talk her out of it. Anytime I've been able to, I'm certain it's been by sheer luck.

The look in her eyes told me I wouldn't have that same luck with this.

Her mind was made up.

I just couldn't figure out *why*.

I don't believe her when she said nothing's changed. I don't believe she's been able to fake what I see in her eyes when she looks at me, or what I feel when she holds me as we fall asleep.

It stopped being a game a long time ago, and she'll never be able to convince me otherwise.

But then...*why?*

I thought maybe she somehow knew I had snuck into Liam's room and stole that picture, but I could tell she honestly had no idea what I was talking about. I have a feeling she never even knew about those photos. If she had, she probably would've confronted Declan a long time ago.

Which is something I should do myself, but...I don't have the kind of fearlessness that Logan does.

I should've told her sooner.

I shouldn't have hidden it.

I was just so worried about what she'd do, what she'd assume. By the time I had finally worked up the courage to share the discovery with her, she had already made the decision to end things.

Maybe it's for the best.

There's no telling what she would've done.

I don't even know what *I'm* supposed to do with this information. My curiosity is urging me to ask Declan about it, but with how he's acted toward me hanging out with Logan...I'm a little scared.

When my phone dings, I reach over and grab it off the end table, grateful for the distraction from my spiraling thoughts.

Darcy: Morning, sunshine!

My heart leaps into my throat, and I have to double-check the sender. I shouldn't have let it surprise me like that. Darcy's always had quite the bubbly personality, which is probably why we get along so well. Only she would send a good morning text this late at night.

Darcy: I miss your face.

Darcy: But I'll accept your voice instead if you're up for a call in the morning?

I consider it, but then I groan when I remember I have plans tomorrow.

Me: I have dinner with the family tomorrow night. Gonna need as much rest as I can get.

Darcy: Oof. Good luck with that. Let me know the next time you're free!

Me: Will do! Miss you too!

She sends back a string of heart eyes and kissing emojis that make my mouth pull up at the corners. Those muscles in my face move slowly, stiff from a lack of use.
Is that really the first time I've had a genuine smile in four days?
It falls all too soon as I sigh and set my phone back down.
As I go back to looking over at the artwork hanging on my wall, my chest constricts. There's a vise around everything behind my ribs, making it difficult to breathe. Logan's face

swims in my vision against the backdrop of the storms she's painted for me. Her hair whips around her beautiful face, and my heart aches.

I fucking miss her.

Rolling over onto the couch, I bury my face into the throw pillow, barely resisting the urge to scream into it.

Why did I have to go and fall in love?

When I get to my parents' house the following night, there's a vase of lilies on the kitchen island along with all the ingredients to make madeleines.

"I thought you could use a pick-me-up," my mom says as she gives my shoulder a comforting squeeze.

"I could," I admit.

Leaning forward, I smell the bouquet of flowers, my eyes fluttering closed. Their light, sweet fragrance hits me and settles in my lungs.

These flowers used to remind me of my parents, of a love so true, so unbreakable. Of something I could only hope to find one day. I wasn't desperate for it. I was always sure it'd come to me when it was meant to.

Now they just remind me of Logan.

And of everything I'm desperate to have back.

"Thanks, Mom."

I give her the best smile I can muster, but it must not be convincing judging by the small, sympathetic one she gives me in return.

My mom and I spend the time before dinner baking madeleines, which somewhat helps take my mind off things. It's not a cure, just a brief reprieve.

We get a break from having to cook dinner tonight since my dad is picking something up on his way home. My mom's been working almost as much as I have this past week—probably to keep an eye on me since I've been so out of it—so takeout was the obvious choice.

After the madeleines are done, my mom puts over half of them in a Tupperware container for me to take home. I have every intention of binge eating them later tonight.

When my dad gets home, the scent of Italian food follows him into the kitchen. He sets the food on the counter, then scoops me up for a tight hug. It's been a few weeks since I've seen him, and I've missed the warmth and weight of his embrace.

"Missed you, Ellie Bear," he says in a way that makes me guess my mom's told him things.

"Missed you too, Dad."

He moves over to my mom and places a soft kiss against her lips. It's quick, but it still makes my heart ache all over again.

He leaves to change out of his uniform while my mom and I set the table. We're just about finished when the front door opens and Declan walks into the dining room. He gives my mom a hug, but neither of us move to do the same with each other.

Instead, he nods and says a curt, "Hey."

"Hey."

My mom looks between us, and I expect she's more observant than she lets on. Fortunately, she says nothing.

Once my dad returns, we all sit down to dinner. It starts the same, everyone exchanging small talk. My mom asks Declan why he didn't bring anyone to dinner—because he usually does—and he responds that he's between girlfriends. Everyone but me laughs at that.

Conversation between them all becomes background noise as I pick at my food. After a few bites of pasta, my stomach is doing somersaults.

Between the empty void in my chest and sitting here across the table from Declan at family dinner, my fight or flight response is kicking in. I can't even make eye contact with my brother. If he knew what had happened with Logan, he'd think he was right all along.

If he knew I had found those photos of him and Liam?

That might be even worse.

I still don't know what to think about them.

Clearly, there was something between the two of them. As far as what that means for my brother's sexuality, how he reacted to me being with Logan, or if that changes the truth of what happened the night Liam died, all of that is still a mystery.

"You're awfully quiet, Elise." My dad's voice snaps me back to the present.

"Sorry," I say with another forced smile. "Just had a lot on my mind lately."

"What's been going on?" he asks.

I peer between him and my mom, still avoiding my brother's gaze. I get the feeling my dad's the one asking because my mom's asked enough as it is and hasn't gotten any answers.

It's probably about time I start giving them.

Sighing, I set my fork on my plate and lean back in my seat. "I was…kind of seeing someone."

"You were?" Surprise laces my mother's voice. "Why didn't you say anything?"

I stare down at my food, feeling the weight of Declan's gaze on me, heavy like a warning.

Braving whatever it is I'll find there, I look up at him.

Sure enough, there's a darkness in his eyes telling me not to speak the truth. His knuckles are white around the tight grip he has on his fork.

Fuck him.

I won't hide anymore.

I look at my mom and take a deep breath. "It was Logan."

"Oh." Her eyes go wide, but there's a faint smile on her lips that keeps me from running away. "Did you not tell us because it's Logan or because…she's a woman?"

"Both I guess," I answer quietly with a shrug.

My mom reaches across the table to place her hand on top of mine. "I'm sorry you felt like you couldn't tell us, sweetie."

I'm actively avoiding looking at my brother again because I can still feel the oppressive force of his stare on me. My eyes skip right over him as I look at my dad.

"You guys don't think differently of me?"

I barely manage to not choke on the words, though my voice is anything but steady.

"You'll always be my Ellie Bear." My dad gives me his brightest, warmest smile. "Our love never was or is conditional. We've always wanted you kids to just be yourselves."

I didn't realize just how much weight I had been carrying around with me until it lifts with my father's words.

While my bisexuality wasn't difficult for me to accept for myself, I was scared to come out to my parents. My dad has always been my rock, my mom my inspiration. If they couldn't accept me? If I suddenly lost all that, especially after losing Logan?

I'm not sure how I would've survived.

Declan's chair scrapes across the tile as he stands and storms out of the dining room.

Just like that, the air is heavy again.

My parents exchange looks of concern before turning them on me.

"He's been acting strange too," my mom says. "Do you know what's going on with him?"

I shake my head.

It's not the full truth, but I can't tell them anything when I don't know enough of it myself.

"I'll go talk to him," I offer as I stand too. Before leaving, I lean over and give my dad a kiss on the cheek. "Thanks, Dad."

Exiting the dining room, I peer into the living room, not really expecting to see him in there. I move to the stairs and climb up to the second floor. The door to his old bedroom is closed, but I hear noises coming from the other side.

I cross the hall and knock. Without waiting for a response, I open the door.

Declan is standing at his old desk, rummaging through the drawers. The moment I step inside the room, he slams one of them shut and spins around to face me. His eyes are rimmed red, his jaw clenched, nostrils flared.

"I told you to stay away from her, Elise," he snarls. "I told you she'd just fucking hurt you."

"Yeah, you did." I nod, keeping my voice quiet like he's a wild animal that could be set off at any second. "But it wasn't for some petty revenge."

He scoffs. "I have a hard time believing that."

"Believe whatever you want."

"Says the dyke."

I flinch like he just struck me.

He may as well have.

However, my parents' words give me the strength I need to face whatever my brother wants to throw at me.

"What the hell is wrong with you?" I snap. "You really hate yourself that much that you'd say that to your own sister?"

"I don't know what the fuck you're talking about."

Except there's already something creeping into his eyes, something on the verge of regret. Something that says there's so much more that's haunting him.

"Really? You don't?"

I point to the ground beside the desk where an old photo lies among a pile of other papers and knickknacks that he had thrown out of his drawers. It's a little faded, a prominent crease right down the middle as if he had folded and opened it many times. His and Liam's faces smile up at us.

Declan's jaw ticks as he faces me again. "What about it?"

Reaching into my back pocket, I take out the narrow strip of photos I found in Liam's room and hold it out toward him.

I didn't know if I was going to have the guts to confront him tonight, but I hoped I would. I knew he wouldn't admit to anything unless the proof was staring him in the face.

Declan appears to freeze as he peers down at the four pictures. I expect him to take them from me, but he doesn't move, paralyzed. I don't think he's even breathing.

"Where did you get that?" he asks in a tormented whisper.

"Liam's room."

His Adam's apple moves up and down with a hard swallow. When he tears his gaze away to meet mine again, his eyes are even redder than before.

"That was a long time ago." His voice is hard, a part of whatever shell he's built up around himself. "And none of your fucking business. You had no right going into his room."

"Is that why you didn't want me hanging out with Logan? Do you think she knew?"

I don't think Logan knew. Surely, it would've come up in the months we spent together, especially with her wanting so badly to know the truth of that night. I imagine it would've been an avenue she would have explored. Because it has even me questioning things.

Declan doesn't answer, just clenches his jaw even harder.

"I don't blame you for hiding it, Dec. I really don't. Just… tell me there's not more to it than that."

That was the wrong thing to say.

His eyes darken. "What the fuck is that supposed to mean?"

When he takes a step forward, my feet instinctively step back.

"That bitch really got to you, didn't she? You seriously think I fucking killed him?"

I've never been afraid of my brother. But, right now, there's something dark swimming in his eyes I've never seen there before. I've always trusted Declan, and questioning him isn't what I want to be doing. It has nothing to do with Logan. He clearly has his own *internal* reasons for hiding things, and if I thought that's all it was, I'd understand. But his reaction to his own secrets brings about a new level of uncertainty.

For the first time in nine years, I doubt my own brother.

"What? No, of course not. That's not what I meant." It's not that I believe Declan killed Liam. It's that I can't help but wonder how much more to the story there is, how many more secrets. "Forget I said anything."

I turn away, ready to get the hell out of here.

Before I can get far, Declan grabs onto my wrist to stop me.

"We're not fucking done, Elise."

I spin back around to face him, barely holding back a wince at how tight his grip is. His fingertips dig into my skin. After my experiences with Logan, I have no doubt there'll be bruises.

"Let me go, Declan."

"Whatever you think, you're wrong," he snarls in my face.

"I don't know what to think because you won't talk to me."

What is up with the people in my life, the ones I care most about, keeping secrets from me?

"Because it's none of your goddamn business."

And just like that, I'm *furious*.

"It *is*, actually. Considering he was *my* boyfriend."

It's a cheap shot. I don't care about that. Had they come to me back then, I wouldn't have thought twice about letting them be happy together.

But it seems to do the trick because he releases me and takes a step back, his face falling.

"I'm…"

I don't stick around to find out whatever it is he wants to say. I turn my back on him again and leave the room.

Back downstairs, I apologize to my parents and tell them I have to go. They each give me a hug, not prying but not hiding their worried looks either. I tell them good night and make sure to grab my madeleines on the way out.

I head home with no more answers than I had before. Only more questions.

25

LOGAN

I'm so fucking tired.

For the past few days, I've experienced a whole new level of tired. All my other symptoms have completely gone after my last round of steroid infusions, but that hell of a flare seems to have left me with one symptom that might just be the worst of all.

MS fatigue is a bitch.

It's not just a normal kind of tired. No matter how much sleep I get, I never have any energy. I've lost track of the hours I've spent lying on my couch and doing nothing else. I can barely bring myself to lift my phone in front of my face, let alone pick up a book or watch TV or even attempt to paint. I couldn't concentrate on any of it even if I tried. Some of that brain fog might be settling in as well.

It's payback for what I did to Elise.

Karma's a fucking bitch too.

Tate called me yesterday to check in and give me an update on the studio. I hardly managed to answer my phone. When I told him how tired I've been, he said he's been tired too.

I found myself glaring up at my ceiling from my horizontal position on the couch.

I'll forgive him since I didn't mention that it's the MS.

But MS tired is different than normal tired. Just like cancer tired is different than normal tired. Depression tired is different than normal tired.

PSA: If someone with a chronic or mental illness tells you how tired they are, don't say you're tired too.

It's not the same.

Not unless you're battling something together.

Maybe it's just the fatigue putting me in a cranky mood, but I still think it's valid.

When Tate told me that Jacklyn has been packing up her office, I knew I needed to try to get up there soon to talk to her. However, I feel like I need to sleep for a week straight before I can make that kind of journey. Just going to the kitchen for water or taking a trip to the bathroom wears me out. And don't even get me started on taking showers. With how long my hair is, I'm about to give up washing it completely.

I consider trying to drag myself to bed. It's about that time in the morning when I usually do. But I've found that when I *try* to sleep, I can't. When I want to stay awake, I don't.

So, instead, I remain on the couch and hope I drift off soon.

It takes me another three days before I finally get off that damn couch. After a shower and the immense effort it takes just to wash my hair, I want to crash again. But I'm going to take advantage of this minimal amount of energy I have because I'm fucking sick of lying around.

If I spend one more minute feeling sorry for myself, I'm going to throw up.

Not that I've been feeling sorry for myself. I've been too tired to feel pretty much anything else.

Even though caffeine hasn't done shit, I make a pot anyway and take a thermos with me. Once I'm outside, the fresh air helps more than the caffeine has.

By the time I make it to the studio, the coffee is gone, and I'm feeling better than I have in days. Getting some sunlight is probably contributing, though I've been taking vitamin D supplements since I found out just how deficient I was. Along with the shots I finally got.

Fighting my insurance company sure was fun…

The shots are nothing. Occasionally, they'll give me welts and leave my skin stinging. But compared to the flares I could be facing without them, I'll happily stab myself three times a week.

It's a good thing I don't have a fear of needles.

"Hey, stranger," Tate greets me as I step inside the studio.

"Is Jacklyn here?"

"Yeah. She's finishing up with a client."

I nod and walk the few steps over to one of the red leather couches in the lobby, falling onto it.

"You good?" Tate asks as he sets down his tablet and moves out from behind the front counter. He stops at the large square table in the middle of the room and leans down to rearrange the magazines and artwork portfolios.

It's quiet in here today, so it's either an attempt to be productive or an excuse to check on me with a closer eye.

"Shit's just kicking my ass, Tate."

He straightens back up and crosses his arms over his chest. "So kick its ass right back."

I scoff. "Easier said than done."

"I never said it'd be easy."

He circles the table and plops down on the couch beside me. I can feel his eyes on me, but I'm too busy staring at his sloppy organization job. I have a feeling I'm not going to want to make eye contact when he tells me whatever's on his mind.

"Look…" He releases a huff, and I can hear the frustration packed in that single breath of air. "You know how allergic I am to emotions and shit. So you should know I mean it when I say you're the strongest person I know, Lo."

Yeah, I was right.

I keep my gaze locked on the magazines on the table, my jaw clenched. I might be allergic too.

"I'd like to think I know you better by now than to think you'd let this ruin your life. I did my own research on MS and—"

"You did?" My eyes snap up to his.

He shrugs like it's not a big deal. Yet the simple gesture means more to me than I care to admit.

"I had to know what my bestie's going through." He gives me a playful smile that's still on brand for him. It helps keep those sentimental feelings that we rarely express with each other at bay. "The point is, I have all the confidence that no matter what this thing throws at you, you'll beat it. That's who you are. Life kicks you down, and you get right back up. You've been doing it your whole life. You'll do it with this too."

I wouldn't need all the fingers on one hand to count the number of times Tate has shown there's a deeper side to him than he lets show. I'm a little stunned, but I'm even more touched.

"Well, at the risk of giving you a severe allergic reaction…" I bump my shoulder against his and give him a smile that comes surprisingly easy. "I really appreciate that."

He nods once, clears his throat like he's clearing the air, and stands.

"You might be wrong though."

He turns back to look at me, and I let out a sigh.

"I ended things with Elise."

For several seconds, he stares down at me until I start to feel uncomfortable, anticipating the scolding I'm about to get.

Maybe that's what I need.

"I wasn't wrong," he finally says. "You *are* strong. But you're also a fucking moron."

A laugh bursts from between my lips. I've always loved Tate for how blunt he is.

"I thought you'd be proud. Wasn't this originally your plan?"

"My plan didn't include you falling in love with her."

I freeze.

My brain short circuits.

I think a part of me has known for a while that I'm in love with Elise Novak. But I didn't expect to hear it now. Or to need it pointed out to me before that fact truly sank in.

"I told you," Tate says. "I know you. I also know it takes you a few tries to get your head out of your ass, so you should probably start practicing now before you lose her forever."

He's right about that too.

How do I do a hard reset on my brain?

If I knew the answer to that, I wouldn't be in the situation I'm currently in.

"Like I said, you're *not* going to let this ruin your life. Don't prove me wrong."

Taking a deep breath, I slowly nod my head. "I'll do my best."

"Good." He clears his throat. "I gotta get back to work. I think my throat is closing up."

I laugh quietly as he turns and marches back to the counter where he picks up his tablet, getting back to whatever he was working on before I came in.

While I wait for Jacklyn to be finished with her client, I lean back on the couch and take out my phone. I open my gallery and find the one picture I have of Elise.

Why didn't I take more? Why don't I have any of the both of us?

I'd go to her social media instead, but it's all pretty inactive. Between dealing with her first year of residency and…

well, me, I'm not surprised she doesn't have the time for it. And I only know that because I've already stalked it a time or two.

Besides, I need a recent photo, one to remind me exactly what I had. What I gave up.

I took it the day I was forced to lie on Elise's couch on my back for hours after my spinal tap. She was sitting in her armchair, brilliantly beaming at something I had said. I don't remember what it was or what we had been talking about. But I remember the way I felt. The way my heart was damn near bursting out of my chest at the sight of her.

I don't know if she noticed me taking the picture, her gaze pointed away from my phone.

I'd give anything to see that smile on her face with her eyes on me again.

Tate was right.

I'm a fucking moron.

I saved Elise. I freed her from the dark unknown that my life will forever be. I didn't want her to suffer with me, to be tied down by someone who's...broken.

But as I stare at the picture on my phone, I don't remember feeling broken in that moment. My foot drop was pretty much gone, but I still had other symptoms. My hand wasn't yet at a hundred percent. I still had numbness and pins and needles and that neuropathic itch. How I managed to not scratch the skin off my arm, I'll never know.

Despite all that, I felt anything but broken.

And Elise looks nothing like a woman trapped, like being a prisoner to a disease that's not hers is a thought that never even crossed her mind.

That's not to say that it wouldn't come to that one day. But…

What if it didn't? What if I've already done what Tate said I wouldn't? What if I let this shit ruin my life? What if it's too late to fix it?

"Hey, Logan."

Jacklyn interrupts my thoughts before I can spiral head-first right into a panic.

I peer up from my phone, not having even noticed that her client was up at the front counter. Taking a deep breath in an attempt to calm the nerves rattling around inside me, I lock my phone and return it to the pocket of my jacket.

"How are you feeling?" Jacklyn asks as she sits on the couch next to me.

"Better. Thanks."

It's not a complete lie. I'm still feeling the effects of the fatigue, but I'm at least feeling better than I have been.

"I think I'm actually ready to come back to work. If I still have a job here."

I haven't been able to tattoo in weeks, so I wouldn't blame her if she'd already started looking for a replacement. Or a buyer.

"Of course you can come back," she says with a smile. "This place is going to need someone to run it."

My face falls. I blink at her.

Did I hear her right?

"What?"

"Did you really think I'd trust anyone else with this place?"

"I…" What the fuck do I say? "I was going to see if you'd let me buy it from you."

"Logan." She cocks her head to the side, looking at me as though I've been struck dumb.

Which is exactly what's happened.

"You've been here since you were eighteen. I've watched you pour your heart into this place as much as I have. You're one of the most talented artists I know. People like us, we make our own family. Sometimes we don't realize that's what we're doing."

Is that what happened with Jacklyn and Tate?

Jacklyn's someone I've always looked up to. She lost her family at a young age like I did, and she successfully made something of her life like I've been trying to do. We've spent time together in and out of this studio. There's been birthday parties and holidays and dinners.

Family is such a foreign concept to me.

And now I'm losing her before I even realized that's what she was.

My eyes sting. I throw my arms around her before I do something stupid like let myself cry.

"I'm going to miss you," I tell her, not even caring how choked up I sound.

"I'll visit."

Tate coughs, and Jacklyn and I break apart.

Jacklyn's last client has left, so it's just the three of us in the lobby. Tate stands behind the counter, his arms crossed, narrowed eyes on us.

"I'm going to need some EpiPens around here."

Jacklyn and I both laugh.

I'm definitely not broken.

26

ELISE

I ate all the madeleines I took home with me that night. In one sitting.

The relief I felt at my parents' reaction to me telling them about my sexuality was shrouded by the dread of my confrontation with Declan.

Two days later, and the bruises he left around my wrist are a deep, dark purple.

I've been wearing long sleeves beneath my scrubs to work, but I still cover the bruises with makeup just in case. However, just knowing they're there is enough to keep diverting my attention.

Between thoughts of Logan and my brother taking up so much space in my brain, it's impossible for me to compartmentalize.

My mom put that vase of lilies in her office that we've been sharing. I know she did it in the hopes they would cheer me up, but every time I look at them, it just intensifies that ache in my chest.

I haven't felt loss like this since Liam.

I've considered trying to see her, if just to tell her what's been happening with Declan. I need someone to talk to about it. I need to talk to *her* about it.

But I'm too afraid.

Not of her reaction.

If I see her and I'm not allowed to touch her? To hold her? To kiss her?

I'm already falling apart. I don't know how much more I can break before every piece of me is lost.

My mom walks into her office, and I peer up from the paperwork I'm supposed to be filling out. I'm horribly behind.

"We just had two patients come in," she says. "I need to run some tests on the older gentleman who came in with heart attack symptoms. There's a woman out there who might have broken her foot. Can you take care of her?"

"Of course."

I stand and leave the office with her.

A broken foot.

I can handle that.

I think.

I grab the woman's chart and look it over. She's in her mid-thirties, married with kids, and blind.

Knocking on the door, I slowly open it before entering the room. The woman lies on the small bed with her foot propped up on pillows, and her husband sits in the chair beside her.

"Hi. I'm Dr. Novak. How are you feeling, Mrs. Miller?"

"Better than my husband, I think," she says with a soft laugh.

Mr. Miller grimaces. "I left my toolbox out while I was putting the kids to bed."

"And I told you it wasn't your fault." She turns her face to me, smiling despite her situation and most likely the pain she's in. "I usually use my cane around the house. This just happened to be one of the rare times I wasn't."

I return her smile, making sure it comes through in my voice. "Well, we'll get you some X-rays so we can take care of that foot." I set her chart on the desk before walking over to the bed. "Let me just take a quick look."

"I need to use the restroom," Mr. Miller says as he stands. He leans over his wife and places a kiss on her forehead. "I'll be right back, baby."

"Okay," she replies with a nod.

Her husband leaves the room. It's none of my business if he has an ulterior reason. Maybe he doesn't want to see his wife in pain and add to his guilt. Maybe he doesn't want to leave her alone and saw an opportunity because he really does need to go.

I never used to dissect others' relationships before I had one of my own that I was constantly trying to understand.

Still am, if I'm being honest.

I wish I knew why she ended it.

But right now I have a possibly broken foot to attend to.

When I reach out to touch the woman's swollen ankle, she winces before I can apply barely any pressure, a hiss passing her lips.

"Do you have any numbness or tingling?" I ask as I inspect her ankle and foot.

She shakes her head. "No. Just the pain."

"It could be a sprain." I head back over to the desk and pick up her chart to jot down a few notes. "But we'll do those X-rays to be sure."

"Thank you." She sighs and shakes her head. "I really am usually more careful than this. Can't afford to be out of commission with three kids running around."

"It seems like you have a good husband to help hold down the fort."

She smiles wistfully. "He's amazing. I just…"

I peer up from the clipboard to see her face slowly falling, a frown turning down the corners of her mouth. I wait patiently for her to finish her thought, finding myself more invested than I might usually be.

"I just hate being a burden to all of them."

Something in my brain clicks into place.

Is that…

It couldn't be.

"I'm sorry," she says with another soft laugh, this one a little more self-deprecating than the last. "You're an ER doctor, not a therapist."

"No, it's fine."

My voice comes out thick, my throat clogged with this revelation. Maybe I'm wrong. But the more I turn it over in my mind, it doesn't feel like such a big leap to think I might be right.

"It may not be my place," I start, choosing my words carefully because this woman is still a patient. But if I can offer her any amount of solace, maybe I can find some myself. "And I may have only known you and your husband for five minutes, but he seems like a good man. He clearly cares about you. When you have a family who loves you, you can't be a burden. Even during times when you need a little extra help, you're not less deserving. We expect the people we love to lean on us when they need to. Sharing the weight is better than carrying it alone."

There might've been a part of me imagining Logan in this room, like I was talking to her. I wish she could've heard it.

My patient's smile returns. "Thank you, Dr. Novak. I think I needed to hear that."

I think Logan does too.

"Of course. I'll be back in after your X-rays."

Once I'm out of the room, I lean back against the closed door and take a deep breath.

I never expected a patient with a broken foot would be the one to give me some of the answers I've been searching for.

And maybe I really am wrong. Maybe that has nothing to do with why Logan decided to end things between us.

But if I'm right?

I have to see her. Even if it's the end of me, I don't want her to feel like the woman in that room did. Even if it changes nothing, I want her to know.

Whether she chooses to share the weight with me or not, I don't want her carrying it alone.

27

LOGAN

I spent all night working on Elise's painting.

I still haven't decided if I'm going to give it to her. Or what I'm going to do. I know what my heart wants, but it's so difficult to listen to it when my brain keeps telling me to save her.

My brush sweeps across the canvas, blending the yellow and orange and pink of the sunrise, the one chasing away the storm at the furthest edge.

I thought after ending things with Elise, that storm would've grown. That I would've given in to some innate urge to cover the canvas with its dark, dense clouds. Instead, it's still receding, like she's not completely gone.

I don't think she ever will be.

She lingers.

She's still inside me, taking up space. She carved out her own spot in one of my hollow cavities, dusting off the cobwebs and planting her flowers. Even though her physical presence is gone, they've left behind her scent. Refusing to whither.

Sunlight filters in through the blinds in the living room, dust particles dancing in its rays. It's not the first time that I haven't noticed the sun coming up while I've been consumed by my work. But as I step back, the painting complete, it feels more symbolic this time.

The light of the rising sun catches on its twin in the painting, making it glow brighter and turning the yellow to gold. It rises above the mountains that stand tall around Vail, shining down until no shadows exist. Until the only thing dark and cold in existence is the retreating storm, leaving everything bright, embraced in its warmth.

I want my sunshine back.

Without her, that storm promises to return.

Just as I feel those flowers in my hollow chest blooming like it's spring, their petals filling every void, there's a knock at the door. It's hard and urgent, causing my heart rate to spike.

I quickly cross the living room, throwing the door open wide.

The break of day has brought my sunshine back to me.

"You could never be a burden."

Elise blurts the words out like she had been holding them in, like they were her very breath and she was finally granted the ability to exhale. Her shoulders even slump, relieved of the weight.

As her words settle over me, I find myself frozen.

How…

"That's it," she says before I can find my voice. "I just wanted you to know that."

When she turns to leave, taking steps away from me, my heart kicks up again in a panic.

"Elise."

She turns back, her eyes searching mine. Cautious. Hoping.

"Are you sure about that?"

I have to ask because I *need* her to be sure. Because the fear of ruining her life is too great. Because she's the sun, and I'm the storm. No matter how bright she shines, dark enough clouds could shroud her light. I think that would break me more than watching her be happy without me.

I don't question how she knew the true reason I let her go. Of course she figured it out. Figured *me* out.

She moves forward again, stopping just on the other side of the threshold.

"A lot of things in our lives are out of our control. But then there are some things that we *choose*. I couldn't stop myself from falling in love with you, but I would *choose* to spend the rest of my life with you if you'd let me. I'd share the weight of everything with you."

My lips part, a heavy breath slipping past.

One step is all it takes for me to reach her, one hand on her back to pull her close and one hand threading through her hair to bring her face to mine. With our bodies pressed together, our mouths touch, open and hungry. Craving more of those words. Craving more of her.

We kiss right there in the open doorway, our tongues grazing, striking a match, igniting a flame. I feel the heat of it everywhere. In my skin, my belly, my bones. My fucking soul.

I continue holding her to me as I force myself to slow down, letting my lips slowly sweep against hers, breathing her in.

"I love you."

"You do?" she asks, and I almost grin at the surprise in her voice.

Instead of responding with words, I take her hand in mine and pull her inside. I close the door and lead her into the living room, moving behind her with my hands on her shoulders as I guide her to stand in front of the finished painting.

Her breath hitches.

Leaning forward, I brush my lips against the shell of her ear, feeling her shiver beneath my touch.

"You're the only thing that chases away the storm."

She spins around before she's on me, attacking me. With her mouth and tongue and teeth. Her body. Her heat.

I love it.

I want it.

For-fucking-ever.

She moans into my mouth, the sound and taste of her intoxicating. Her lips move feverishly against mine, swirling up a heatwave with her hands on my waist, squeezing me tight like she's afraid I'll slip through her fingers. My hands move to tangle in her hair, holding her just as close, refusing to ever let her go again.

Her panting breath fans my face as she creates a millimeter of space between our lips.

"It's beautiful. You're beautiful."

"And you steal my breath, sunshine."

She whimpers before her mouth is back on mine.

I turn her around and take a step, backing her toward the couch. My hands journey down, slipping beneath both her shirts, already too far gone to question the long-sleeve she wears under her scrubs. I slide them up, pulling them up and over her head before tossing them away. Her bra quickly joins them on the floor.

Tearing my mouth away from hers is worth it only so I can taste every other inch of her.

My lips travel down over her jaw, my teeth nipping along the column of her throat, my tongue licking across her collarbone. She arches into my touch, letting out a long, low moan when my mouth finds her right nipple, sucking hard as my hand gives attention to her other breast.

"Logan, please," she pants above me.

I slip my other hand into the waistband of her pants, dipping lower—over her panties because I feel like teasing her a little. My fingers slide lightly up and down over her soaked underwear, denying her much pressure.

She groans and throws her head back, pressing her breasts deeper into my mouth and hand. "Logan."

With a chuckle, I release her before pushing her backward where she crash-lands on the couch. I advance, and she lifts her hips for me to tug the rest of her clothes off.

Pushing her legs apart, I drop to my knees between them.

Her pussy glistens with her arousal.

Luring me.

Tempting me.

Who am I to resist?

When it comes to her, I'm helpless against her sweet seductions. I'd willingly and happily fall into whatever trap she sets for me.

Leaning forward, I sweep my tongue through her soft, slick folds.

Just a taste before I dive in to devour.

I eat at her like it's been years since I've feasted on her instead of days. Starved.

My tongue flicks over her clit as she starts bucking against my face, hips jerking when I increase the tempo, playing her body like an instrument. The noises that spill past her lips are the music. Low moans. Soft cries of pleasure. They grow louder and more frequent when I thrust two fingers inside her. Her breaths come quicker, and her hands find my hair, tangling in the strands and gripping tight as I fuck her with my fingers while worshipping her clit with my tongue.

Everything about this, about *her*, is wild. Erotic.

Perfect.

But, still…it's not quite enough.

"Fuck this."

Retreating from between her legs, I stand to my feet while Elise whines, peering up at me beneath heavy lids, full breasts rising and falling with equally heavy breaths.

I smirk down at her. "You're riding my face."

Suddenly, her eyelids aren't so heavy, going wide instead.

Reaching for her, I grab her arm and haul her to her feet. Her knees buckle, weak and unsteady, as she crashes into me. I hold her up until I'm confident she won't fall over, then start moving to the couch. Before I can get there, she stops me.

"Wait," she whispers breathlessly as she grabs the bottom of my tank top, practically ripping it off me.

I stand there, a little in shock, as she tears my basketball shorts and underwear off too until I'm as naked as she is.

"Corrupted is a pretty color on you." I grab her by the throat and drag her to me until she's close enough for me to lick across her lips, her whimper like flames dancing across my tongue. "So is needy. I love you all eager like this. Tell me what you want."

She blinks slowly. "I want to come."

"Where?"

She groans, then whispers, "On your face."

"Good girl."

I claim her mouth, kissing her hard, biting into her bottom lip until I sense I'm the only thing holding her upright. With her bottom lip still between my teeth, I step backward toward the couch, only releasing her once the back of my legs hit the cushions.

Crashing down, I tug her forward as I lie on my back. She sways on her feet beside me and the sofa.

"Looks like you're having a little trouble standing." I grin up at her as I lace my fingers with hers. "How about you take a seat?"

I yank her closer until she's forced to place a knee on the couch. She hesitates, but she eventually throws her other leg over me until she's straddling me, her wet pussy grinding against my stomach as she tries to subtly thrust her hips.

Running my hands over her thighs, I peer up at her as her eyelashes flutter and she lets out a shaky breath.

"Get the fuck up here, Elise."

She shifts forward until she's hovering above my head. I lick my lips as I stare up at hers, swollen and glistening and wet. I want to drink her down, quench my thirst with her nectar.

My own arousal coats my thighs, anticipation and heat swirling together in my belly.

My palms travel over her legs, around her hips, hot skin against skin. The moment my nails dig into her ass, she lets out a sharp cry, sinking down closer. Just enough for me to steal a taste, her arousal on the tip of my tongue.

It's not enough.

A low growl rumbles through my chest.

"Fucking smother me."

I dig my nails deeper into her flesh, giving her a little of that pain she loves to feel alongside the pleasure, forcing her lower, coaxing her where I need her to be. The weight of her on my face. The scent of her in my lungs. The taste of her exploding in my mouth as I thrust my tongue inside her.

"Oh, fuck!"

That's right. Scream for me.

I'd say that out loud, but I'm a little busy right now.

Elise rocks her hips, undulating above me, all hesitation and inhibition thrown out the proverbial window. Her heavy breaths and breathy moans fill my ears while the rest of her fills all my other senses. I keep my hands on her ass, skin soft and warm beneath my fingers. With my tongue, I alternate between fucking into her and flicking her clit. The trembling of her body intensifies. Vibrating. An earthquake ripping through her and into me.

"Fuck! Logan!"

It's a scream and a sob, a moan and a cry, all wrapped up in one. A present just for me.

She breaks.

Her movements stutter, grinding just a little harder against my mouth, her body a welcome weight.

I slowly ease my tight grip on her ass—no doubt my nails have left their mark. She starts to slide downward, and I shamelessly try to chase after her with my mouth as her slick pussy glides across my chin.

I don't even care if she can't hold herself up.

I'd let her suffocate me.

But she apparently has other plans.

She moves slowly, weakly, shimmying down my body. I widen my legs to give her room to settle between them. When her breasts are in front of my face, I lift my head to catch a nipple between my teeth, giving it a quick, sharp nip. Even the noise she makes is soft and feeble.

When it's her face finally hovering above mine, lashes fluttering against her flushed cheeks, I give her lips a more tender treatment. One light kiss. A delicate brushing of soft, rosy skin.

Her eyes open, gleaming, a twinkle within those halos.

Then she's moving again.

Her lips skim down my throat, joined by the wet warmth of her tongue. It journeys over the mounds of my breasts, swirling around each nipple before traveling lower.

Lower.

Lower.

I'm not numb down there anymore. I feel *everything*.

The warmth of her breaths. The touch of her lips. The exploration of her tongue.

Her mouth is on me, all over me. Kissing. Licking. Sucking. Not one molecule of my body or my soul goes untouched by her desire to give me pleasure like I gave her. I take it the same way she took hers.

"That's it, dirty girl." My voice sounds as wrecked as I feel. "Fuck, I love your mouth on me, baby."

Threading my fingers through her hair, I thrust my hips, encouraging the perfect rhythm of her tongue, laving at my clit. When I grip her hair a little rougher than I mean to, she moans, sending vibrations through my core.

I break for her the same as she broke for me.

She doesn't stop the flicking of her tongue as my body shudders beneath her, drawing out my orgasm. The pleasure and heat swirl around in my belly, igniting into one ball of fire. Like she's inside me. A sun going supernova.

By the time I'm coming down, cooling off, it's to feel her pressed against my side, one leg draped over mine, one arm hugging my waist. I slip my arm beneath her shoulders, holding her to me.

We're both breathing heavily, our bodies slick with sweat, sticky between our skin. But I couldn't give a fuck if I tried.

"You're getting fucking good at that," I say between panting breaths.

"We should go on a date."

I nearly choke on the laugh that bursts out of me. Pressing a kiss against her damp temple, I tell her, "I'll take you anywhere you want to go."

She smiles, sighing as she snuggles into my side. She absentmindedly starts skimming her fingertips over my stomach, her smile growing as her gaze moves to the other side of the room. I follow it, and my heart expands in my chest, blooming like the flowers that are thriving inside there too, when I see it's my painting she's staring at.

My life may be a storm.

But Elise is my sun.

And maybe together we can stand strong and tall like the mountains.

28

ELISE

When was the last time I went on a date? I can't even remember it's been so long. Years.

What do people do on dates? How do they act? What do they wear?

Half my wardrobe is scattered across my bed. Jeans, slacks, skirts, blouses. Nothing feels right. Logan told me to dress nice, but I'm so used to wearing scrubs that I'm not sure what that means anymore.

I go back to my closet, rifling through more of my clothes and trying to ignore the nerves that are making my heart beat wild in my chest.

I didn't get much sleep today, and I still have to work tonight. But when I told Logan yesterday that I wanted to go on a date, she asked if I'd be willing to do an early dinner—or breakfast for us—tonight. I said yes because I don't want to wait for my first date with her.

I might be nervous, but I can't remember ever being this happy either.

I've let everything with Declan sit on the back burner in my mind. Just for now.

I'll tell Logan soon. I will. Maybe tomorrow. I only just got her back, and I don't want anything to ruin our date. Which is why the bruises on my wrist have already been thoroughly covered with makeup.

A quiet rumble echoes in the distance.

Thunder.

This storm, one of those end of summer ones, is supposed to pass a little to the north, so hopefully it won't hit us. Even if it does, I refuse to let it ruin our date either.

Logan and I can deal with a little rain together if we have to.

There's a knock at my door, and I curse under my breath.

I'd wash my mouth out with soap if Logan didn't like it so much.

After throwing on one of my oversized T-shirts over my underwear, I stroll out of my room and down the hall. When I open the door, I freeze.

All the air has been sucked out of my apartment, right out the door, siphoned by whatever magic has conjured up the most stunning, jaw-droppingly beautiful woman I've ever seen in my life.

She's wearing a suit, clad in all black. It fits her frame perfectly, hugging her hips.

But the suit isn't the most shocking thing.

She cut her hair. *Short*.

It's buzzed on the sides, the top still a little longer. Loose, black waves hang over one side of her face. It's a strange thought to think she looks more *Logan* than she did yesterday. Her long hair was gorgeous, but this…

"Wow," I whisper with the last bit of breath left in my lungs.

Her lips slowly tilt up at the corners. It's an easy smile even while there's a flash of uncertainty in her eyes. "I hope that means you don't hate it."

I shake my head. It's all I can manage.

She seems to take that as a good sign as her body relaxes. Her gaze moves down, sweeping over me. "I feel a little overdressed."

Right. I'm only wearing a shirt.

It suddenly feels like it's scratching and burning my skin. Like I'd much rather have it off and have her hands on me instead.

Clearing my throat, I step back to let her come inside, closing the door behind her. "I just need to change real quick."

"I mean, you're welcome to go like that." She smirks, her eyes scorching as they linger on my bare legs.

"Stop it, or we're not going anywhere."

Her soft laughter follows me as I swiftly spin around and take my ass down the hall before I rip that damn suit off her.

Back in my bedroom, I take off my T-shirt and throw it onto the heap of clothes on my bed. I return to the closet and start combing through the rest of my wardrobe again, more flustered than before.

Another peal of thunder rolls outside.

Finally, I eye something I haven't worn in at least a couple years. I take out the baby blue sundress and hold it up. I don't wear dresses often, but it is the last day of summer.

I take it off the hanger and throw it on before checking it in the mirror by the bathroom. It has a cinched waist, short sleeves, and stops just above my knees.

I guess I could do worse.

After slipping into a pair of white flats, I exit my room and return to Logan.

I barely make it a few steps into the living room when her piercing gaze stops me dead in my tracks. It feels like a command, keeping me in place. She didn't even have to utter a word for me to feel the need to obey.

The longer she stares at me, the darker her eyes get.

"Fuck." That one husky word has me forcing myself to resist the urge to rub my thighs together. "I want to rip that thing off you."

"Does that mean you don't like it?" I ask in a small, unsure voice.

"No." She stalks forward, closing the distance between us. When she reaches up and brushes her knuckles across my jaw, it sends shivers down my spine. "It *makes* me want to rip it off you."

My lips part. Whether it's to say anything more than, "Oh," I can't be sure. Whatever was going to come out gets cut off when Logan's mouth comes down on mine, her tongue darting past my already parted lips. It twirls together with mine, a dance that already feels as natural as breathing.

I suddenly understand why she doesn't feel the need to breathe when we're like this.

Somehow, I find the willpower to break the kiss, being careful with her suit as I gently push her back because it looks too damn good to mess up.

"We better leave before we miss our date," I whisper, peering at her beneath my lashes, eyelids still heavy with lust.

She smiles. I swear that simple gesture makes my heart stop beating every time.

"We can't have that."

Outside, the sun is on its path toward the horizon, blanketing the downtown street in bright gold while dark storm clouds loom in the opposite direction. Petrichor lingers in the air as Logan opens the passenger door of her car for me, and I slip inside.

The restaurant she takes us to is the fanciest one in town. Not what I expected. I guess I shouldn't be surprised though considering she said to dress up. The Italian place opened up about a year ago, and I haven't had the chance to go.

Square tables are spaced out around the large room, covered in white tablecloths. The glow from the ornate chandeliers hanging from the ceiling is a dim, warm amber. My mouth waters at the aroma of fresh bread and herbs and wine.

Once we're seated at a table inside, the waiter takes our drink order and asks if we'd like to try any wine. Logan declines for the both of us since I have to be at work in a few hours.

I wish I didn't. I'm going to be sad having to leave Logan after this.

But I decide not to focus on that right now and turn my attention to the menu. My jaw drops at the prices.

"Get whatever you want," Logan says. "I'm taking *you* out."

I open my mouth, but she holds up a finger and points at me.

"Don't you dare."

I sigh, well aware that I have to pick my battles when it comes to her. "Are we celebrating something?"

She tilts her head to the side and hums in contemplation. "I suppose we could be."

"What?"

A slow smile pulls at her lips. The silent seconds that pass feel like they're for dramatic effect. Then she says, "Jacklyn's giving me the tattoo studio."

"Are you serious?" My own smile feels like it's about to break my face.

Logan nods. "She and her husband are moving to Oregon, and she wants me to take over. I just hope I don't run it into the ground."

I shake my head. "You have too much passion for that place to let that happen."

"I hope you're right." Her smile turns into an almost self-deprecating grin. "I used to never hope for anything. It's dangerous."

"Seems like things are turning out okay."

She stares at me, eyes full of so much more than words could say. It's that look that's the total opposite of the one she used to give me after the first time I stepped foot in her tattoo studio. The one that makes me feel all warm inside.

After several seconds, she nods. "I'd say so."

The waiter returns and takes our order. While we wait for our food, we continue talking quietly over the din of other patrons and the clinking of glasses and silverware. I notice a few times she clenches her right hand into a fist. It's not until we have our food in front of us that I give in and ask her about it.

"It's just tingling a little," she says as she picks up her silverware. "Not a big deal."

"You're still having symptoms?" I ask, frowning.

"Can we not talk about it right now?"

I understand why she wouldn't want to talk about it. We're having a nice date. But...

"Did you tell your neurologist?"

"Please don't do that." Despite her words, Logan gives me a small smile. "I let him know, yeah. But I don't want to feel like I have to let you know anytime I have a little symptom like this. The meds I'm on are supposed to take some time to build up in my system anyway. I'll tell you if it's ever important enough. Okay?"

I don't like it. Actually, I hate it. I hate that MS can have so many invisible symptoms. She could be dealing with something like this, and I'd never know it. But I have to respect her enough to let her decide how to handle it.

With a reluctant nod, I tell her, "Okay. But you don't have to fight everything alone."

"I know. But I promise I'm okay."

It's because she's strong. I may not know exactly what she's going through, but I don't know if I'd have the same strength as her if I was in her place.

We take a few bites of our food, eating in silence for a couple of minutes. It's long enough for me to come closer to a decision I've been trying to make for a while.

"I think I'm going to go into neurology."

"Really?" She arches a brow. After a moment, it falls, and she narrows her eyes instead. "Not for me, right?"

"Not exactly. I mean, being able to help, knowing more about it, would be a plus. But I never wanted to be an ER doctor like my mom, and family medicine never really called to me either. Besides, we need more specialty doctors in this town."

"I don't think I'd want you to be my doctor. I get enough of you trying to be that as it is."

I laugh at that, but I can't blame her.

We finish our meal with more comfortable conversation. When the check comes and Logan picks it up, I have to stop myself from arguing. But, again…I'm choosing my battles. I know her well enough by now to expect plenty of them in the future.

The future.

I've rarely thought about my future past becoming a doctor. That's always been the only sure thing.

But now I'm sure about Logan too.

When we make it outside, we discover that the storm didn't miss us. The rain comes down in sheets, obscuring the whole world and drowning it out with its leaden beat. The black sky opens up, pouring down its might as thunder roars overhead.

Neither one of us has an umbrella.

I peer at Logan where we stand beneath the awning just outside the front door of the restaurant. "Make a run for it?"

She grins and holds her hand out, palm up. I take it, threading my fingers through hers. She locks us together with a firm grip before we're bolting from beneath our shelter and out into the rain.

The sting of the wet, sharp drops is harsh against my face, and I raise my arm above me as a shield. The spray quickly soaks through my dress and drenches my hair.

We're a few feet from Logan's car, nearly close enough for me to reach out to throw my door open. Before I can, before I can get inside where it's warm and dry, Logan yanks me back, spinning me around so I crash against her chest.

Then her mouth is on mine.

And I forget all about my desire to get out of the rain.

My eyes flutter closed, raindrops dripping from my lashes, down my cheeks. Our kiss is wet, rain between our lips as she parts mine with her tongue before slipping inside. I get lost in the rhythm of the kiss and the downpour, her body keeping me warm, the steel bar in her tongue a contrast of hard and soft.

I've never kissed in the rain before. I thought it might be overrated.

It's not.

Logan's the first to pull back, beads of water cascading down her face as she beams at me. "I love you."

I don't care that we're standing out in the rain. I don't care that my entire body is shivering. There's a warmth in my heart, a fullness in my chest. Completeness. The world around us is dark and hazy, but everything in this moment, the two of us trapped in this bubble, is bright and clear.

"I love you too."

The chattering of my teeth must be what causes her to move so quickly, stepping around me to open the passenger door of her car and helping me inside. As soon as she's in the driver seat, she starts the engine and cranks up the heater.

"Your seats are getting soaked," I tell her, a tremor still in my voice.

She grins. "Worth it."

A moment later, her face falls as her gaze drifts down and lands on my arm. The one that was showered with rain, washing off the makeup, exposing the deep purple bruises around my wrist that are yellowing around the edges.

Fuck.

They're visible beneath the faint glow of the parking lot lights. Logan clicks on the overhead bulbs in the ceiling of her car and takes my hand again. I try to pull away, but she holds on tight. A darkness flashes in her eyes as she takes in the sight of the bruises, her jaw tense.

"What the fuck is this?"

Usually, I'd love that husky tone in her voice. Right now, it's downright scary.

I can't even make up a lie if I wanted to. The bruises are clearly the cause of a rough hand around my wrist.

Her dark gaze meets mine. "Who did this?"

I bite my lip in an attempt to calm the way it trembles worse than before. "Not now. Please."

"Yes, *now*, Elise."

She's not going to let it go. Even if this was one of the battles I chose to fight, I'd never win it. That's obvious by the intense scowl on her face that's directed more at the truth I haven't spoken than it is at me.

I take a breath. "Declan."

"Your brother?" Her grip on my hand eases slightly, but she still refuses to let go. "Why?"

"I was going to tell you, I swear."

"Tell me what?"

I hate the hard gaze she's pinning me with. I want to go back to the fun, easy mood of our date. The rain drums against the roof of the car, laughing at me.

"That day I spent at your house, I went into Liam's room while you were sleeping. I found pictures of him and Declan."

The crease between her brows deepens. "Okay? They were friends."

I shake my head. "Judging by those pictures and Declan's reaction to them, they were more than that."

"Woah."

"I'm so sorry I didn't tell you." The words rush out of me, desperate to not end this night with her angry at me. "I wasn't going to keep it from you, I swear. I just—"

"Hey, it's okay," she cuts me off. "It was my fault you didn't get the chance to tell me. It's not you I'm mad at."

I sigh, the breath full of relief.

But she *is* mad. I can see it in the hard set of her mouth, the tense tick of her jaw. Her gaze moves past me, far away, a little out of focus. Silence stretches between us while the hammering of the rain fills the space around us. Her eyes remain dark, mirroring the storm outside. The clouds within them swirl with thoughts I'm afraid to ask about.

"Logan, you can't do anything."

"The fuck I can't."

As though she's made up her mind, she lets go of my hand and puts her car in gear.

"What are you doing?"

"He fucking hurt you, Elise. I'm going to fucking hurt *him*."

I've never seen her this furious, not even when she hated me. It's a little scary, but there's a part of me that warms at how protective she is.

But, still, this is my *brother* she wants to hurt. Can I really just sit back and let her?

What if *she* gets hurt instead?

This tension and animosity between them was bound to reach a peak eventually. It was always inevitable.

At least with me there, I can keep them from killing each other.

Hopefully.

29

LOGAN

The rain is coming down so hard, so violently, that I can't drive as fast as I'd like. My vision out of the windshield is obscured, the wipers hardly able to keep up with the torrential downpour. Every time the tires skid through the rising water, I steer into it and slow down.

If Elise wasn't in the car right now, I'd be driving ten times more recklessly.

This red veil has been cloaked over my eyes since seeing those bruises on her wrist like a fucking bracelet. All the colors on each traffic light we pass are the same shade of red. Even the black sky has a crimson hue.

Declan has fucked with Elise for the last fucking time.

I know she doesn't want me to confront him. I can practically feel her vibrating with anxiety in the seat next to me. I'm well aware that she can stick up for herself, but it's different when it's her own brother. When it comes to family, it's more difficult to fight fire with fire. I couldn't always do what needed to be done when it came to my mother, but Declan isn't *my* family. I can face him for Elise.

We pull up out front of the auto shop where Declan works, and I park the car. I wasn't exactly sure where to find him, but when I see his Plymouth GTX out front, I know my first guess was correct.

"Logan, please…"

"You're welcome to stay in the car."

I don't mean to sound so curt toward her. This isn't her fault.

I'm just so fucking pissed.

Throwing my door open, I tear out into the rain. I don't even feel the sting of it on my face, like I'm so heated that the water simply evaporates as soon as it hits my skin.

Thunder rumbles.

Lightning strikes in the distance, illuminating the sky for a fraction of a second.

Instead of trying to escape the storm this time, I'm charging right into it.

The shop is closed this late in the evening, but one of the garage doors is open. I use that as my entrance, marching inside. The smell of gasoline and oil hits my nose and settles in my lungs, adding fuel to the fire raging inside me. There are a couple cars up on lifts but no one working on them. I don't see anyone.

"Declan!" My voice reverberates through the garage along with Elise's soft footsteps behind me. "Where are you, you piece of shit?"

Elise stops beside me, wringing her hands in front of her. But when I catch another glimpse of those bruises, her unease is the least of my concerns.

A commotion comes from the back of the garage, from behind a door that looks like it might be for a back office. The door opens, and we hear hushed voices before Declan steps out. His face is flushed, his hair a little wild. His mechanic shirt is stained with dirt and oil, and he's hastily buckling the belt looped through his jeans as he walks across the garage. He freezes halfway.

"What the fuck are you doing here?" he snaps the moment his eyes land on me.

I don't answer. I cross the rest of the distance, my hand already clenching into a tight ball. He has the sense to take a step back when I get close, but he's too late to avoid my fist when it comes flying at his face.

I put all the force I can muster behind the punch, beyond satisfied by the resulting crunch.

"Fuck!"

Declan stumbles back several steps, his hands coming up to cup his nose. I'm even more delighted by the blood gushing between his fingers.

I ignore the throbbing in my hand, instead focusing on the fact that Elise remains silent behind me. Even though it's her brother, she knows the prick deserved it.

"You fucking bitch!"

"*You're* the fucking bitch," I bite back. "Hurting your own sister because she found out your dirty little secret? Real fucking classy, Declan."

He drops his hands to his sides, bright red blood spilling out over his upper lip and dripping down his chin. "I don't know what the fuck you're talking about."

I sense Elise's presence next to me again. Glancing over, I see a frown etched so deep across her face that all I want to do in that moment is kiss it away.

"Why are you so ashamed?" she asks in a small, quiet voice. It's steady, despite the way she shivers, soaked in a fresh sheet of rain. "Why have you been spending all your life hiding?"

"I'm not hiding anything!" he snarls.

Except one thing he's hiding comes tripping out of the back office a moment later. Tate looks more mussed up than Declan, disheveled hair sticking up in all directions, shirt rumpled. Hickies purpling his neck.

Declan and I *both* glare at him.

"I told you to stay in there," Declan growls at him.

Tate's eyes bounce between him and me, like he's not sure which one of us he should be more afraid of. He hesitates before speaking. "I heard shouting. What the hell happened to your face?"

"*I* happened," I answer for Declan.

My friend nods, not looking the least bit surprised. "Oh. Okay." He turns to Declan. "You probably should've put a sock on the door."

"You really don't know when to shut the fuck up, do you?"

Don't do it, Tate.

But of course he does.

He shrugs, grinning. "Not without a cock in my mouth."

Declan's face twists into one of disgust. "Fucking faggot."

A rare flash of rage flickers across Tate's face. There's a total of one way to piss him off, and Declan just found it. How he hasn't witnessed for himself the man's homophobia, internalized or otherwise, I'll probably never know. If he had, I doubt he would've been in that room with him.

"Says the guy who just had his cock down this faggot's throat," Tate snaps back at him.

I see it coming before it happens, but I can't stop it.

Declan punches Tate in the jaw so hard that he goes crashing to the ground. He recovers quickly and starts scurrying backward across the dirty floor when Declan advances for another assault.

"Declan!"

Elise goes bounding forward. I almost stop her. I almost rush in with her. Instead, I make a decision to stay put, watching like a hawk as Elise grabs onto Declan's arm to stop him from attacking Tate again. I don't think he'll hurt his own sister worse than he already has, but I'm not going to take any chances.

When Declan rounds on Elise, that's when I make *my* attack.

"Touch either of them again," I say, my voice eerily calm even to me, "and I'll fucking kill you like you did my brother."

Everything falls silent. And still.

All eyes are on me.

Tate arches a brow, looking confused as hell.

Elise's eyes go wide, like she can't believe the words that just came out of my mouth.

It was a shot in the dark, one I had to take. Because it's Declan's reaction that matters most.

And judging by the immediate turmoil rolling off of him in waves, my words have hit their mark. His lips part, his eyes alert, pupils blown. He takes one step back, nearly stumbling over his own two feet, crumbling under the weight of the guilt filling his eyes.

Something in him has snapped. Just like that. The splintering of a branch, weak and weathered by its own secrets and lies. With just a few words, the mask he's been wearing all this time fractures and burns and turns to ash.

I didn't *want* it to be true.

But I have my answer.

The silence breaks with a clap of thunder.

I don't know if it comes from outside the shop or inside of me.

Declan shakes his head, his gaze faraway now as his chin trembles. "I didn't...I didn't..."

I can hear Elise's loud swallow from here as she stares at her brother in utter disbelief, like she doesn't recognize him. "Declan?"

Time moves too slowly. The noise of the rain finally creeps in, a deep staccato as it drums a beat against the roof. It joins the rushing of blood in my ears, all swirling together with anticipation of a moment that's nearly a decade fucking overdue.

His eyes are glistening with shallow pools by the time they come back into focus and land on Elise. "I didn't mean to."

"Oh my God."

Elise's haunted whisper cuts me nearly as much as the truth does. I recognize the pain. I've felt it myself.

"What else didn't you mean to do, Declan?" My voice is harder than before but somehow still steady. "Let my brother rot in prison for the past nine years?"

I can't feel the relief I thought I would if I ever discovered Landon was innocent, like I always believed deep down that he was. It's buried beneath a jumble of things that hurt. Anger. Resentment. Grief. The relief is there somewhere, but I don't know when or if I'll ever be able to grasp onto it.

"Dec, what happened?" Elise asks in that same tone, even quieter and more broken if possible.

I'm torn in two directions. One that leads to Declan and the urge to rip his throat out with my teeth. And the other that draws me to Elise and the desire to wrap her in my arms and tell her that everything will be okay.

However, I can't do either of those because my feet have grown roots.

Tate stands, swaying. There's already a deep, reddish purple bruise forming along his jaw. I consider telling him to get out of here, but I know he won't. I'm kind of grateful because I barely feel like I can hold myself up.

"He wanted to tell you." Declan sounds wrecked, gravel in his raw voice. He looks at Elise with a desperation for forgiveness or absolution that he certainly won't be getting from me. "He wanted to tell you about us for a long time. I wouldn't let him. Even when Landon caught us together that night, I couldn't bring myself to tell you. I was afraid. I hated myself for all of it. But mostly I just didn't want to hurt you."

Elise opens her mouth, but when no words come out, she closes it. She shuts her eyes for three seconds, swallows once more, and tries again. "It was you two who were fighting on the bridge?"

He nods, his eyes rimmed red. "We were arguing, shoving each other. I didn't...I didn't mean to push him over. We were both drunk, and I just...*Fuck.*"

Declan buries his head in his hands, fingers in his hair. He tugs hard at the roots and lets out a tragic sob that racks his entire body.

When he looks up again, tears are streaming thick and fast down his cheeks. They pick up a pinkish hue where they cross paths with the blood before dripping off his chin. The next words come tearing out of him, choked and broken, like he's ripping out his own heart with them.

"I fucking loved him!"

With that confession, I feel something I never would've expected to.

I think I feel a little...*sorry* for him.

Sympathy sucks being on this end of it too.

However, it's *not* enough for me to hate him any less.

Because I think I feel sorry for Liam all over again. He had even more torn away from him that night than just his life.

But I can't think about Liam right now.

"Why?" I ask, my voice no longer steady. I try to remain calm, but the more words come out of my mouth, the more I fucking break. "Why would you let Landon take the fall? It was *your* fault! Nine *fucking* years! He's been locked up for nine fucking years!"

Declan swallows hard, not even attempting to staunch the flow of his tears, to close that dam. "Because one of the last things Liam heard was his brother calling him a faggot with hatred and disgust in his eyes."

Everything in me goes numb.

It's not a literal numbness caused by my fucked up nervous system.

It's bone deep, a visceral denial.

"No." I feel myself shaking my head before I realize I'm doing it. "Landon wouldn't."

"Maybe sober Landon wouldn't."

Landon was one of the first people I came out to, the first one in my family I trusted with that truth. He was always supportive. He never looked at me with judgment or spoke with words of loathing or revulsion.

How could he do that to Liam?

Suddenly, something else becomes crystal clear.

That's why Landon didn't fight in court, why he so easily accepted his sentencing.

If those had been my last words to my brother before he died, I'd probably feel like I deserved it too.

But…

"Even if that's true, that doesn't justify sending him to prison." As I say it, the dam behind my own eyes breaks. The first tear hits my cheek, hot and wet.

I don't know if I'm crying for Landon or for Liam at this point.

Declan takes a few steps backward until his back collides with the wall. He slides down it as though his legs are no longer capable of holding him up. I have no idea how I'm still standing myself.

"Back then, it *did* feel like justice," he says, voice hollow as he stares off into the distance again. "We wouldn't have been arguing on that bridge that night if Landon hadn't caught us making out. Liam wouldn't have died heartbroken, believing his brother hated him. I was angry. I was *so fucking angry*. And it's never gone away."

"Then why—" Elise's voice cracks. "Why would you say the same things he did?"

"Because I've hated myself more." Declan peers up at his sister, wet tears and dried blood all over his face. "Because I was angry with myself more than anything. Because if I hadn't been with Liam, none of it would've happened in the first place."

It's as though once the truth started pouring out, he couldn't hold the rest of it back any longer. Just like the sky opened up tonight to dump its rain on us, something in Declan cracked open too, and he can't close it back up.

"You have to tell the truth."

I can hear the pain clearly when Elise speaks those words. Just uttering them out loud hurts her. If there was anything I could do to take that away, to make everything better, I would. But I can't. Because she's right.

Declan lowers his gaze to the floor, his shoulders slumped. Slowly, he nods. "I know."

Elise stares at him for several seconds longer before she turns to me. She looks like an angel standing out in the rain, her wet blonde hair dripping on her shoulders. The golden halos of her eyes glisten with tears.

"I'm so sorry, Logan," she whispers, her grief cutting into every corner of her face.

"Me too."

I mean it.

What I went through with *my* brother isn't something I would wish on my worst enemy.

I don't think I'd be happy even if I still hated her.

Declan sniffs loudly and pushes himself up, using the wall as leverage. "I'll go talk to Mom and Dad."

"I'll go with you," Elise says.

"I'm driving you."

She looks back at me, and I tell her with only my gaze that I still don't trust him enough to leave her alone with him. She eventually accepts with a nod.

Tate steps forward then. I'm actually proud of him for showing a little restraint and respect and letting us all work through things. He's never been the best at reading a room, but I appreciate he could tonight.

"I'll go with you two," he says, a solemn look on his face that's not much like him either. "I'll ride in the back."

"You don't have to, Tate."

"I know," is all he says.

I'm dropping Elise off at her parents' house. I won't go inside because it's not my place. This is between their family.

But…

I don't want to be alone.

Tate's a pain in my ass, but fuck if I don't love him.

We let Declan shut off all the lights in the shop and lock the place up. As we're leaving, he glances at Tate. I almost expect him to apologize when he opens his mouth, but he closes it instead and walks to his car without a word.

As we follow him to their parents' place, the inside of the car is filled with thick tension. The rain has died down, but I know the storm isn't over. I reach over and take Elise's hand while I drive, hoping I can somehow convey to her with just a touch that I'm here and that I'm not going anywhere.

Before I let her get out of the car, I pull her toward me, meeting her over the center console to press my lips to hers.

"I'll see you tomorrow?" she asks, and I don't miss the hope in her question.

"You better." I kiss her again, then whisper against her lips, "You're not getting rid of me."

All that pain still pervades her eyes, but for a brief moment, relief flashes within the sunbursts circling her irises.

While she and Declan go inside the house, I keep the car in park, staring after them.

"You okay?" Tate asks quietly from the backseat.

Am I?

For years, I've wanted to know the truth about what happened that night, and I finally do. I hoped, I *knew*, that Landon couldn't have been so careless as to cause our brother's death. But, in a way…did he? Knowing Landon's last words to Liam hurts almost as much as if he had. He still probably would've gone to prison for the part he played—providing alcohol to minors and reckless endangerment. But it wouldn't have been for a whole decade.

And then there's Elise. My heart aches for her more than it's relieved at knowing the truth. I continue staring at the closed front door where she disappeared through, knowing her life is about to change.

I can only hope it doesn't lead down a similar path as mine did.

I sigh and finally manage the only answer I can come up with. "I don't know, Tate."

30

ELISE

My mom's crying. Her quiet sobs are the only sounds that pierce the heavy silence that's descended over our home. My own tears fall freely and steadily down my face as I sit beside her on the couch in the living room, holding one of her hands in both of mine. It's the only small comfort I can give her right now.

Across from us, my dad sits in his chair, leaning forward with his head in his hands. In the other chair, Declan stares down at his lap.

I don't know how long the silence and stillness lasts. It could be minutes, but it feels like hours.

"I'm sorry," Declan says again. He's said it at least twenty times.

Each time, I swear I hear something breaking in all of us.

My dad finally lifts his head. His eyes are rimmed red as they focus on Declan. "I'm disappointed in you." His voice is all raw and gravelly and broken. "Letting that poor boy take the fall for his own brother's death. I'm glad you're finally telling the truth, but it shouldn't have taken you this long."

Declan nods. "I know. I'm sorry."

My dad sighs, and everything falls quiet again.

Every time the silence settles over us, there's no end in sight. I keep expecting it to last forever.

When Declan speaks again, it's so quiet I barely catch the words. "I know what you have to do, Dad. I'm sorry for making you do it."

Our dad shakes his head, the frown on his face deeper than I've ever seen it. "I never thought I'd have to arrest my own son."

My mom's next sob is loud and agonizing and heartbreaking. I give her hand a gentle squeeze.

"We'll go to the station in the morning," my dad says as he rises to his feet. "I'll make us all some coffee."

As soon as my mother has composed herself enough, she calls the hospital to get us both out of work, instructing them to get the on-call doctor to come in. I guess having one last night with my brother for who knows how long is enough of an emergency.

None of us get any sleep that night. It's not a cheerful time. There's no laughter or reminiscing, no jokes told or happy memories shared. My mom cries some more. Declan apologizes again and again until he's a weeping mess.

In the morning, my dad drives him to the station, and I go where I really want to be. With Logan.

Logan asked me to go with her to pick up Landon. I hesitated, only because I didn't want to intrude on their reunion. But as soon as I saw the desperate pleading in her eyes, I gave in.

If she needs me, I'll be there.

Forever.

It was a long drive to the prison, but much of the tension we've both been feeling melted away when we sank into easy conversation. After being worried I was going to lose her after she knew what my brother did, it felt good to see her smile and hear her laugh.

But now she's waiting for her brother to be released, leaning back against the front of the car while I wait inside. I climbed into the backseat so Landon could sit up front during the drive back. The least I can do is give them this moment together.

One of the guards opens the gate, and Landon steps out, blinking against the bright afternoon sun. The moment he sees Logan, he takes a breath and appears to hold it in his chest.

Logan doesn't move. I can only see her back, but I imagine her frowning as I take in the slight hunch of her shoulders.

I know she's happy that her brother is free, but I also know she's still angry with him.

Eventually, she makes a decision. Or maybe it's not much of a decision at all, more like the pull of the last family member she has in her life, drawing her in his direction. Her steps quicken until she's running and throwing herself into her brother's arms.

I avert my gaze, feeling like an intruder, but I can't look away for long.

Logan buries her face in Landon's shoulder, their embrace tight as her body shakes. Just imagining tears in her eyes brings tears to mine.

It lasts about twenty seconds before they're finally pulling apart and heading back to the car. Logan's wiping at her eyes, and by the time they're both opening their doors, their expressions have shifted. Their brows are drawn, tension written in the lines of their faces.

At least they were able to snag one moment of joyful reconnection, as brief as it was.

Now comes the inevitable clash.

"Hey, Elise," Landon mutters as he slides into the passenger seat.

"Hey."

As Logan pulls out of the lot, I shift uncomfortably in the backseat. Landon stares out his window, watching as the prison shrinks.

No one speaks for the first half hour. Pressure builds, the air swirling with unbearable tension, until I fear the car might literally explode with it. Logan's knuckles are white where she grips the steering wheel. Landon hasn't looked away from his view out of the window.

As badly as I want to break this oppressive silence, it's not my place.

After another ten minutes, Logan finally cuts through the quiet hum of the engine with one word.

"Why?"

Like it's all she can manage, the only noise she can force up her clogged throat.

Landon's shoulders rise and fall with a heavy sigh. With his gaze still fixed outside, he shakes his head. "I've been asking myself that question for nine years." Finally, he peers at Logan. "I was never like that with you. Why did I have to say that to *him*?"

Logan chews on her lip and shrugs. "Internalized homophobia seems to be popular these days."

I don't know if she meant it as a joke, but Landon responds with something between a scoff and a self-deprecating laugh. That's the only acknowledgment he gives to the accusation.

Another minute passes. A little of the pressure has been released. I start to think that's all the conversation they're going to have until they get home. I'd understand if they didn't feel completely comfortable having this entire discussion in front of me in the car.

But then Landon speaks again.

"I've spent nearly a decade wishing I could take that night back." His whispering voice sounds louder in the confines of the vehicle, his words lingering in the air. I catch Logan tense again. "I'll spend the rest of my life the same way. What I want most—what I'll never get—is to be able to tell Liam I'm sorry. Since I can't tell him…" He clears his throat and looks at Logan. "I'm sorry, Lo. I'm so fucking sorry."

I don't know where or what to focus on. My gaze stays mostly lowered, but I peer up at Logan now.

Her bottom lip trembles, and I wonder if I should offer to drive. But then I might feel even more like an intruder.

"I know you are," she eventually manages. "And you should be. But you still didn't deserve to be in there for a fucking decade."

The first hint of a smile crosses Landon's face, but it's a sad one and doesn't reach his eyes. "We'll agree to disagree."

The second half of the ride home is easier and more relaxed than the first. It's mostly quiet, but every now and then, some small talk passes between us. We stop at a fast food place, and Landon inhales an entire burger that's bigger than his head, plus what's left of Logan's chicken sandwich she didn't finish.

"I don't suppose I can get that jacket back?" he asks as we pull into town.

Logan peers down at the black leather jacket she wears so often it's like it's a part of her. I'm almost relieved when she answers with a simple, "Nope."

Landon grins. "Fair enough."

When we get to their house, we all climb out of the car, each of us stretching from the long drive. While Landon takes a moment to himself, standing on the sidewalk and staring wistfully at the façade of his old home, Logan approaches me.

She wraps an arm around my waist, pulling me close and placing a kiss on my cheek. "Thank you for coming with me."

"Of course." I turn into her, touching my forehead against hers. "Do you want me to leave? Give you some time together?"

"Please don't. I don't think I'm ready to be alone with him yet. I don't know what I'd end up doing. Crying for hours with tears of joy or…you know, killing him. Maybe both."

I laugh and take her hand, pulling her with me to follow Landon inside.

"I like what you've done with the place," he says with an amused grin as we enter the living room.

I offered to help Logan clean the place up for Landon's homecoming, but it's still littered with canvases and brushes and paint. She refused, saying her brother could deal with it.

"Yeah, well, I've been living alone for years."

Landon's face falls, wincing with the pain of an emotional wound.

"I didn't mean—"

"It's okay." He turns to Logan and gives her an understanding smile. "I have a lot to make up for. Are we going to be okay though?"

She peers at him, her mouth turned down like she's on the verge of crying again. "Of course we are."

"Good." He briefly glances over his shoulder down the hallway. "Do you mind if I take a few minutes? In Liam's room?"

Logan nods.

He turns and starts heading down the hall. Before he can get far, I open my mouth before I can stop myself.

"Landon."

He looks back.

It's going to burst out of me. I may as well get it over with now.

"I'm really sorry. For what Declan did."

The apology is sincere. I think I might always hate my brother a little because of the part he played in Liam's death, Landon's unjust incarceration, and the slow destruction of

Logan's life. But I also can't stand the thought of Landon hating me for it, not when I'm so madly in love with his sister.

"It's not your fault, Elise," he says. "He and I both made mistakes that night. And for a long time after."

How he can be so calm, almost closed off to the wrong that was done to *him*, surprises me. But it wouldn't take a therapist to see the remorse in his despondent eyes and the guilt weighing him down.

Landon walks off, disappearing down the hall and leaving me and Logan alone.

I slowly drift toward her, watching as she heaves a sigh, staring after her brother.

"It's going to be strange having him back."

Stopping in front of her, I drape my arms over her shoulders. Once her gaze meets mine, I smile. "Strange in a good way, right?"

She nods. "Yeah."

Wrapping her arms around my waist, she catches my mouth with hers in a slow, sweet kiss. It's not demanding or hurried. It's all about the touch of our lips and the air we share.

With a quiet, contempt hum, she pulls back. "I should warn you," she says as she brushes a strand of hair from my face. "You might end up getting sick of me."

"Why do you say that?"

"Landon and I would come first in a sibling squabble contest if that was a thing. I can only imagine how many times a day I'm going to have to resist the urge to choke the life out of him. It'll probably be best for his safety if I spend as much time over at your place as I can."

"Oh, really?" I arch a brow at her as I let my fingers rake through the short hair at the nape of her neck. "Is that the only reason?"

"Of course." She gives me that all too familiar look of mock innocence. "You think I have ulterior motives?"

"You know, if you're going to be spending all that time over there anyway, you should just *plan* on staying there."

"Dr. Novak." She beams at me as a wide smile breaks out across her face. "Are you asking me to move in with you?"

A heat rises into my cheeks when I realize that's exactly what I was asking.

"Maybe?" The one word comes out as a question because if she says no, then I was definitely *not* asking her that.

With another kiss, she whispers against my lips, "Okay."

"Really?"

I don't think I actually expected her to say yes.

"I want to be with you all the fucking time," she says as her hold around me tightens. "Living together would make that at least a little easier."

I'm moving before I can rein in my enthusiasm, crashing my lips to hers with maybe a little too much urgency considering the way the force of my eager kiss knocks her back a step.

Logan laughs. "If I thought that would make you this happy, I would've suggested it myself."

"*You* make me happy."

She smiles. "You make me happy too, sunshine."

I resist the desire to kiss her again to instead peer into her eyes, into the gray clouds swirling in their depths.

The sunshine to her storm.

EPILOGUE

LOGAN

Two years later.

We finally made it to Vail.

Elise and I talked about going last winter, but after only having Landon home for a few months, I wasn't ready to leave him all alone. We invited him to come along, but he said he didn't want to intrude on what would be our first vacation together.

Secretly, I was relieved.

But after two years, we're here.

I'm standing outside the lodge we're staying at, me and my snowboard both leaning against the wall. Morning sunlight is just starting to paint the sky, tracing the mountains with a golden lining. A fresh layer of snow blankets the ground from last night. It's well below freezing, but I'm pretty warm in all my snow gear.

Elise and I agreed to wake up early so we could catch the first lifts when they start spinning. I've told her how much I love fresh tracks.

Except…I'm still waiting on her.

She told me to wait in the lobby, but I was too eager.

She probably won't be too happy with me, but she's the one who's taking forever.

After two years, I've learned that extreme weather can bring on pseudo-flares. If I get overheated, my Lhermitte's comes back. In freezing temperatures like this, I get pins and needles in my hands. It doesn't always happen. When it does, it's more annoying than anything else.

It took a lot of convincing on my part to get Elise to agree on this trip. But when I told her I refuse to let this thing control every aspect of my life, she couldn't do anything but cave.

Fortunately, right now, I feel fine.

We'll see how I feel after the slopes.

I haven't had another real relapse in the last two years, of which I'm overwhelmingly grateful for. I'll take the pseudo-flares and fatigue that come in waves over another one of those any day.

Just as I'm about to go make sure Elise didn't get swallowed up by her ski jacket or something, she finally comes outside with her skis in tow.

"Why are you out here already?"

Despite her scolding, I can't help but smile at the adorable way her nose wrinkles with disapproval.

There are still times when I enjoy riling her up. But it's only to see her get a little flustered, maybe to feel the heat of that spark inside her that's brighter than ever. I think she likes to fight me just as much as I like to coax that side out of her. It's always worth the burn when she's so good at soothing it later.

I met her friend Darcy last year, and she didn't exactly love the way I couldn't keep my hands off her during the entire visit, always needing to be touching her. To show who she belonged to. At least, she *said* she didn't like it. The way she rode my cock that night said otherwise.

My smile turns into a smirk when I toss back, "Why are you only *just* now out here?"

"Sorry," she says with a sigh. "I forgot how long it takes to put on all these layers."

"You're lucky you're cute in them."

Grabbing the front of her ski jacket with my gloved hand, I tug her closer to give her a quick kiss. It's been two years, and I still can't keep my fucking hands off her.

"Ready to shred some powder?" she asks with a grin.

I fucking snort. "Yeah, you're *really* lucky you're cute."

She looks pretty proud of herself too.

I decide to test her.

"So," I say, lowering my voice to a goading tone, "Lover's Leap?"

Her brows rise at the daring invitation. She considers it for a moment before shrugging. "I'm up for a challenge."

"You always are. Oh, by the way..." I reach into one of the pockets of my jacket and pull out a plastic bag filled with golden, scallop shell-shaped cookies, holding it up in front of her. "I brought a snack."

Her lips part. "Where did you..."

"I asked your mom to make them before we left," I tell her as I return the bag to my pocket.

She stares at me a few moments longer as the corners of her lips slowly lift into a smile. "You're amazing."

"I know. You could show your gratitude on the ride up."

"Logan!"

Laughing, I grab my board, and we start heading through the village toward the lift for the slopes that'll be our quickest route to Blue Sky Basin. There are a few people out already, some of the shops and eateries getting ready to open for the day. The sun is over the mountains now, brightening the sky. Snow crunches beneath our feet as we walk along the path.

We're passing by a coffee shop when the door to the café opens.

At the same time, we hear someone shout from above, "Heads up!"

It happens fast. The man exiting the shop takes a swift step forward, forcing me to take one back to avoid a collision. There's a loud clatter from above, and the next thing I know, the man is catching a bright red snowboard out of midair, right before the end of it can smack me in the head.

I'm frozen, staring at the board in front of my face.

What the fuck just happened?

I don't know, but that would've hurt like hell.

"Sorry!" the voice from above calls out again.

Craning my neck, I peer up to see a young guy leaning over the railing of the balcony with a can of rub-on wax in one hand.

Who the fuck waxes their board on the fucking balcony?

"Um, thanks," I mutter, still in a bit of shock.

When I finally look into the face of my unexpected hero, there's immediate recognition.

"Wait. You..."

The older man flashes a small, knowing smile. The knowing part feels as if he knows a hell of a lot more than I do, but it's not in a patronizing kind of way. Maybe it's just the wisdom that comes with age.

When I finally find the rest of the words I had been searching for, I say, "You were the one who helped me outside the clinic that day."

"I'm glad to see you're doing better."

"Yeah..."

I've thought about that man often. He saved me that day too.

But I'm still staring. There's something else that's nagging at me, and I can't quite put my finger on it.

Elise stands patiently beside me, her gaze moving between me and the stranger. He tucks the snowboard under his arm but doesn't make a move to leave, like he's waiting for me to figure out the mystery on my own.

And then it hits me.

"You used to be my neighbor," I blurt out.

He smiles again and nods. "That was a long time ago."

Even back then when he helped me off that sidewalk, I knew he was familiar.

He was the one who always called the cops when my mother and I would get into it. I hated him for bringing Sheriff Novak around, the inconvenience of dealing with the police when my mother was in a state. But as I grew up and thought about it...

Would I be alive if he hadn't?

"I should get this back to the kid," he says, shifting the snowboard under his arm. "Take care of yourself, Logan."

He turns and walks away, and my gaze follows after him, my jaw a little slack.

Realistically, I shouldn't be surprised he knows my name since we used to live right next to each other. But, for some reason…it knocks the wind out of me.

I have no way of knowing if the chills bringing goosebumps to my arms are from the cold or something else.

"That was your sidewalk angel?"

I blink a few times to refocus and turn to Elise at her question. I told her about what happened that day, but I never called the man that. She could see the impact he had on me and dubbed him that all on her own.

If guardian angels are real, I think I've met mine.

"Yeah," I answer, my voice thick.

Her gaze drifts over to the last place we saw him before he disappeared around the building. She smiles. "I'm glad I got to meet him."

I clear my throat in an attempt to purge all this emotion. "Come on. I've been dying to make out on a ski lift."

Elise laughs, and the sound helps to ground me.

As we continue on our way, the sky appears a little clearer, a little brighter. Maybe it's just because the sun is higher now, or maybe it's because I feel even lighter and warmer than I already have since Elise has been in my life.

If I have sunshine and angels on my side, I think I'll be okay.

ACKNOWLEDGMENTS

First, I have to thank my incredible support system that's surrounded me since my MS diagnosis. While my experience with this illness was very similar to Logan's in the beginning, my circumstances were completely different. My mother has been one of my greatest supports and went to many doctor appointments with me. My partner has been my rock. The rest of my family and friends have shown so much love and encouragement. I don't know if I would've been able to make it through my own storm without any of them.

Next, I'd like to thank my PAs and alpha readers, Amber and Season, who help me more than they could ever know. My beta readers, Amy and Taylor, whose invaluable feedback I always appreciate! And, as always, my amazing street team. Thank you for sticking around.

I'm so grateful to everyone who gave this book a chance. This is something I wanted to write for a long time, and I'm so happy I finally got to share this story. I always write for the reader as much as I do for myself, but this one might've been a little more for me.

Thank you again. To all of you. <3

ABOUT THE AUTHOR

River Hale is a pseudonym, created because her mother once told her that she'll read everything she ever writes. She's a writer with a tea addiction and a love for everything dark, twisted, haunted, and beautiful. She's written and published more appropriate books that her mother is allowed to read under her real name, but she'll always have a special place in her heart for dark romance.

River's Newsletter:
https://riverhale.com/newsletter

Join River's Reader Group:
https://www.facebook.com/groups/riverhaleshellions

- instagram.com/riverhaleauthor
- tiktok.com/@riverhaleauthor
- facebook.com/riverhaleauthor

Made in the USA
Coppell, TX
19 January 2026

68581939R00225